FALLEN MATE

SHADOW CITY: DARK ANGEL

JEN L. GREY

CHAPTER ONE

I DESPISED RUNNING—AT least as much as an angel could dislike things. I preferred to fly, but I couldn't do that easily while following wolf shifters who were following a troubling sensation through the forest.

In general, angels' emotions were one-dimensional, though we sometimes felt a slight increase in sensation that could be described as what I assumed were feelings.

Our large group didn't help when it came to remaining undetected. With ten silver wolf shifters in animal form, plus their alpha, Sterlyn; their acting alpha and her twin brother, Cyrus; their mates, one of whom was the alpha of Shadow City; two Shadow Ridge pack members, including their alpha; the vampire king and queen; and myself—staying silent was impossible. If any supernaturals from Shadow Ridge stumbled upon us this far out and it got back to Azbogah, one of the angel council representatives, I'd be thrown in jail.

Angels weren't allowed past Shadow Ridge's borders.

I was a bit of a rule bender when it came to doing the right thing, and this group was destined to usher in change for the better. I'd felt it when I met Sterlyn, and her actions had never contradicted my reading. Her essence was one of the purest I'd ever sensed, even more so than my mother's.

The breeze had an extra jolt of something today, but I couldn't place it. Maybe this was what Annie had been sensing all along.

"Are you sure this worrying sensation you're experiencing isn't related to your pregnancy?" I asked Annie. "Maybe you're imagining things."

I'd been contemplating how to ask this question for the past few minutes. Other supernatural races and humans tended to prevaricate. If you were too honest, they called you rude, which I still struggled to understand. Although it was tiring, I had to be careful how I worded things when dealing with them.

Sierra's head snapped in my direction, her long, dark blond ponytail whipping in the wind. She was walking between Griffin and me with Sterlyn, Annie, and Cyrus in front of us. She narrowed her gray eyes, and I realized I was somehow still being rude.

What the hell? I'd downplayed what I'd wanted to say. My first instinct had been to ask Annie if she was sure she was feeling something strange and if her disquiet wasn't due to her mourning the death of Eliza, her adoptive mother, who'd been stabbed fatally seconds before getting sucked into a portal to Hell. Not only that, but Annie's biological father—who'd tried to give Annie to a demon and was the reason Eliza had been stabbed and sucked into said portal—had died within minutes of Eliza after months of hunting Annie down and attacking our group. Add on the pregnancy and Annie getting to know her birth mother, and I wouldn't be surprised if her agitation was due to stress...constipation...something other than an *actual* threat. Given the circumstances, I thought I'd worded the question well. "What?"

My mouthy friend threw her hands up as she walked past a large oak tree bearing the orange leaves of November. "What have I told you about being so blunt?"

"I was asking a question, not accusing her of anything." I wished Sierra had shifted instead of staying in human form. She could be honest, but when she did things, it was usually for attention. She cared about us, but she liked being what she considered witty. Her quips were all about shock value, and it grated on me at times.

The ten silver wolves in wolf form tensed. They didn't want us talking.

Cyrus had demanded that most of the silver wolves come as backup because his mate was pregnant. He hovered next to Annie in human form like he expected an enemy to pop out at any second. He'd always been protective of her, but since they'd learned about the baby, he'd been a little over the top.

His dark silver hair, proof he was the child of a silver wolf alpha, reflected the midday sunlight as his eyes turned slate gray. He towered over his mate by more than a foot, his tense body showing bulging muscles, revealing his stress from Annie being out here. He was okay with our checking out the source of her uneasy feeling, but he hadn't wanted her to come. It'd been a point of contention between them. She'd won when she'd said she couldn't tell us how to find it—she had to allow the feeling to pull her there.

Following a weird sensation never resulted in anything good; thus, Sterlyn had backed her brother despite Annie's protest that our core group would've been fine on our own. Due to being of angel descent, silver and demon wolves couldn't bear many children, and we needed to protect Annie.

"It's okay." Annie gave me a strained smile, her honey-brown eyes not sparkling like normal. Her light olive complexion glistened from sweat, and she lifted her brown sugar–colored hair off her neck. "I thought the same thing. A lot happened over the past few weeks, but the sensation is getting stronger, and I don't think it's tied to the baby." She placed a hand on her slightly swollen stomach. "I can't describe it. It's like I *have* to find it. My wolf is going crazy."

"Then we need to check it out," Sterlyn said from beside Annie. Her long silver hair revealed she was fate's chosen alpha of the silver wolves. She glanced over her shoulder at me, her purple iridescent eyes glowing. "We all know what happens when we ignore something unsettling."

Griffin growled. "Yeah. Dick, Matthew, and Azbogah have done wonders." The breeze ruffled his light brown hair, despite the gel that kept the slightly longer portion on top swept to the side. He was easily six and a half feet tall with a little less than half a foot in height on Sterlyn. He was close to the same build as Cyrus, though at the moment, he wasn't as tense.

The three people Griffin had named had caused us numerous problems. But there was a bright side. "At least Dick and Matthew are dead," I offered.

Alex inhaled sharply behind me, and I swallowed my sigh. I was about to get into trouble...again.

"Rosemary!" Sierra protested.

My chest tightened. I kind of felt bad about that one. Matthew had been the vampire king and Alex's older brother. But he'd been corrupt, and Alex hadn't known for a long time. They'd been close for most of Alex's life.

I loved my parents and my friends, and despite being an only child, I could imagine that I'd highly value kinship with a sibling as well. It would bother me if something happened to any of them.

I turned to Alex, ready to apologize. I was certain that was the appropriate thing to do, despite not meaning to cause harm.

Ronnie, his wife, mashed her lips into a line as her emerald eyes darkened. Her copper hair swung over one shoulder as she took her mate's hand. "You don't need to apologize. We know you didn't mean it like that."

I still wanted to. *How odd.*

"She's right," Alex said in his slight, not-quite-British accent. His light blue eyes glistened, making me very uncomfortable. He straightened his shoulders and ran his fingers through his sun-kissed brown hair. Even at three hundred years old, the vampire was still younger than me by about seven hundred years, though I'd never admit it after seeing how often Sierra bothered him about his age. "No need to feel bad," he continued.

I wanted to drop the subject. Just seeing his eyes turn watery made me want to take flight again.

Killian, the Shadow Ridge alpha, murmured behind Alex, "Guys, can we be quiet? If there's a threat, it might be best if we at least *tried* to stay undetected." He arched his brows as his deep chocolate-brown eyes focused on me. His dark brown hair was a little longer than usual. He was slightly smaller than Cyrus and Griffin, but Killian had an athletic body that I admired from time to time. For a shifter, he was attractive, if you were into that sort of thing.

At one time, I hadn't gotten along with Killian and Griffin. That was pre-Sterlyn, when they'd been immature and self-absorbed, but since she'd come into their lives, they'd changed for the better. The two men I could barely tolerate had become my friends, and Killian had saved my ass more times than I wanted to think about.

Darrell huffed next to me in his animal form, and I didn't need to be a wolf shifter with a pack link to know what that meant. He was supporting Killian and telling us to be quiet.

A few squirrels scurried past me, running faster than I'd thought possible. One even fell in its desperate attempt to escape.

"Guys?" Sierra whispered. "What's going on?"

Before anyone could answer her, something charged

the air around us. The sensation was cold and vile, and it activated my angel magic.

Demons.

My wings exploded from my back, slipping through the slits built into my shirt, and I spread them wide. I shot toward the sky to find the source.

A small lump formed in my throat as I flew between two large trees, their branches scraping my fair skin. The faint pain cleared my head as I rose.

Under normal circumstances, I'd take a moment to enjoy the beautiful sky and the cool breeze. Being outside was freeing. For most of my thousand years, I'd been cooped up in the elusive Shadow City, a place constructed to resemble the Heaven the angels had left behind, which I found ironic. Why leave Heaven only to construct a city in its image? But I knew the real reason. In Heaven, they couldn't be in control, but on Earth, the angels thought they could be kings.

Holding my breath, I scanned for signs that someone was near. At first, I couldn't see much. We were drawing close to Sterlyn's childhood neighborhood, a remote settlement where she'd lived all her life until her pack had been slaughtered. The closer I got, the more the air buzzed with negative energy.

Pure evil radiated negativity, and that was the crux of all the problems in the world. No angel wanted to admit it, but we found something alluring about evil, and that petrified us. I understood how an angel could fall. The temptation to not be a protector of the entire world and instead become a part of it, with no rules or boundaries, had corrupted many. I'd never become that weak because I *chose* to remain a warrior.

Everyone was born with the power of choice.

As I reached the former pack neighborhood, I scanned the standard wolf pack houses. All were simple, one-story structures built from the same blueprint and fashioned to be low maintenance.

Why did everything lead back here?

A shadow form appeared beside me, and I was shocked that a demon had sneaked up on me like that. Then Ronnie's overly sweet floral smell filled my nose. I was still acclimating to her demon abilities improving. "A little warning would've been nice."

"Next time, I'll yell." She rolled her eyes.

She had me there. I followed the energy away from the neighborhood and back into the woods with Ronnie by my side. The negative energy was so thick that my skin felt slimy. That was when my attention landed on ten demons hovering in the woods below.

My stomach knotted. I shouldn't have doubted Annie. She was a demon wolf and the rightful demon wolf alpha, though that pack had been dismantled. Three young demon wolf boys had gone with their mothers to their home packs, eliminating the pack for now. The demon wolves had been created to protect demons like the silver wolves had been created to protect everyone else. Of course Annie would sense demons if they were close by.

Everything in me screamed to fight them, but training kicked in. Confidence in my fighting abilities alone was one thing; arrogance was another. It was smarter to wait until the others arrived before attacking. Each one of them was a good fighter, even Sierra. She'd been working her butt off to catch up with everyone else.

Ronnie gestured for me to follow her back to the neighborhood. I obliged because the demons could look up and see us. Strangely, they were just hanging out down there. They had to be waiting for something or someone. My hands clenched.

Something *tugged* me toward the demons, stealing my breath. I'd never felt anything like it before, but my wings suspended me in place.

Ronnie turned around and murmured, "What's wrong?"

Even though I couldn't make out her expression in her shadow form, I knew what I would've seen: clear confusion.

The same thing that ran through me.

"Angel!" a demon yelled from below.

My eyes closed as my cheeks warmed. I'd never made such a miscalculation before, but my damn body had betrayed me. I'd been reckless and gotten caught before we were ready to fight.

"Damn it, Rosemary," Ronnie said with surprise. "The others are on their way."

Her presence was a blessing. If it'd been only me, I wouldn't have been able to communicate with our group without leading the demons right to them. Ronnie had used her soulmate connection with Alex to alert him to our situation telepathically.

I turned to face the demons again, and part of me was relieved that I wasn't leaving. I wasn't usually blood-thirsty, though I enjoyed kicking ass. But the sensation I felt was unfamiliar, like I was a magnet being pulled toward something.

The demons flew toward us, their red eyes bright in the sunlight. The one in the front chuckled darkly. "If we kill this angel and bring this demon home as a traitor, we might move up the ranks."

This would be fun. I loved proving the cocky ones wrong.

Even though instinct urged me to attack, I needed to keep a clear head and not let my emotions rule me. That was what got people into trouble.

"They're scared," another demon chuckled, thinking he could influence me.

My resolve fractured, and I gritted my teeth. The only thing more infuriating than my confounding actions was that I was letting these *demons* rile me up. I wasn't sure which was worse, being talked down to or letting them anger me.

Pounding paws drew closer, and my resolve snapped. The cavalry was here, so I wouldn't be reckless if I attacked now.

I flew toward them, adjusting my feathers into spikes. The only way to kill demons was to behead them. Once they lost their humanity, their heart didn't sustain them, so injuring the organ didn't kill them.

A loud howl warned the demons that we weren't alone.

They paused like they were reconsidering their attack.

Too bad. There was no saving them.

But as I approached the first one, something inside me *jerked*, and I looked away from my target. A cackle warned me that my strange distraction had cost me, and before I could refocus, something sharp stabbed me.

CHAPTER TWO

PAIN COURSED through me as the metallic scent of my blood hit my nose.

I clenched my hands.

I couldn't believe I'd been distracted. I knew better than that, and I deserved the injury for my inattentiveness. Thank the gods no other angels were around to see my horrible mistake. I never would've heard the end of it, especially since I'd been a trained warrior for over nine hundred years. This was the kind of sloppy blunder young fifty-year-olds made, not someone with my experience.

Though I hadn't seen or been around demons much, apart from our recent encounters, I understood how they operated. They treasured power and looked for anything that gave them a high. The shadowy form in front of me watched my face, waiting for me to show my pain.

I might have had a moment of stupidity, but I hadn't

lost complete sense. I kicked the demon in the stomach, and he came close to hitting the ground.

Taking the momentary reprieve, I yanked the knife out of my side, and a mist of blood wafted into the breeze and fell. I cringed, realizing the wolves' fur would be sprinkled with it. They would be concerned, and that was the last thing I wanted. They worried about everyone enough; I didn't want to burden them.

"Rosemary!" Killian growled as he ran from between a large cypress and a redbud tree, looking up at me.

Thankfully, he knew better than to ask if I was okay. If he had, those demons would've homed in on me, wanting to attack the injured person to get their jollies. You were only as strong as your weakest link.

A sour taste filled my mouth. Right now, that was exactly what I was, and I *did not* like it.

I knew of one easy way to fix that, even though it would impair my magic. I opened my left hand and tapped into my core. My hand glowed white even with the sun shining, and I placed it on my side. The wound wasn't too deep and wouldn't take much energy to heal. Extensive healing impacted my abilities for a while, and to recharge quickly, I needed to be within Shadow City, where the special bright lights amped up my powers.

Warm blood coated my hand, but my skin healed seconds after I'd touched it.

By the time the demon reached me again, the pain and the injury were gone. Only the blood on my hand and side and the gaping hole in my burnt orange shirt hinted that I'd been stabbed. The shirt no longer reminded me of the sunset, infuriating me. The bigger problem was that my magic was somewhat depleted, but not enough to slow me down.

Eight demons attacked the wolves, probably realizing it would be hard for the shifters to remove their heads. Thankfully, each of the wolves in human form carried a knife in case we ran into something unusual, although we hadn't expected to find demons. They'd thought Sterlyn and I were being paranoid when we'd told them to arm themselves, but the angel motto was to prepare for anything.

Sterlyn had been trained to always carry a knife. It was a small hint at her silver wolf–angel heritage.

The ninth demon charged Ronnie. Its red eyes glowed with rage.

I shook my head to clear it. If I didn't focus on my fight, I'd get stabbed again. Even though it might be hard to hurt an angel, it wasn't impossible. Our greatest weapons were our wings, which could even deflect a bullet, but using them in that fashion left our bodies exposed like I had moments ago, and we could die as easily as a mortal.

"Lucky kick," the demon rasped. Demons had lost their wings when they'd fallen, but their shadow-like forms allowed them to fly. Only angel descendants could see them, so Griffin, Killian, and Sierra were at a massive disadvantage on the ground. They stayed close to Annie, protecting her. She could inform them when a demon was close.

"Sure. We can say that." I lifted my right hand, which

held his knife. "Yet you're the one who lost a weapon."

"And you're injur—"

I lifted my shirt, revealing the healed patch of skin. Clearly, angels weren't the only ones who'd forgotten facts about each other. Though we were immortal, our memories tended to fade over centuries about things we didn't find important or with which we didn't come into contact regularly.

He paused, some of his arrogance slipping.

The *tug* inside me increased again, and I tried to push away the sensation. It wasn't easy to ignore. Something strange was going on, but I'd have to determine what it was after we'd taken care of these idiots.

I grinned to enrage him. When your opponent grew too angry, they got sloppy, and I wanted him to hate every moment he had to deal with my butt-kicking abilities. I felt some satisfaction in putting my enemy in their place, though I didn't live for the high, unlike the demons. If I allowed it, the moment could go to my head, and killing or hurting another being was wrong.

"What were you saying?" I moved my mahogany hair behind my shoulder to expose my ear and cupped it. "Either I didn't hear you, or something happened to prevent you from finishing that sentence." I grimaced. That sounded Sierra-like, but I was goading an enemy, not my friend.

"It doesn't matter," he growled. "I'm a demon. I can kick any angel's ass."

"Not very likely, especially with my abilities." There was no point in allowing him to think he was something he was not. He wasn't a prince of Hell and couldn't be too strong, or the angels in Shadow City would've detected his maliciousness.

Again, the demon sped toward me.

I kept my attention on him, even though the urge to look around for the source of that *tug* was nearly over-powering. When the demon was within striking distance, he cupped his hands, making it obvious that he was going to grab my right hand in an attempt to disarm me.

My gut screamed it was a fake out. It was a logical strategy—retrieve the weapon before I could use it against him—but his motions were too transparent. He wanted to make sure I thought that, meaning he would actually strike the opposite side, hoping to throw me off enough to get the weapon.

He wasn't quite the idiot I'd thought he was, which made this fight more worthwhile.

Playing along, I moved my right arm away as I prepared to counter his attack on the left. I couldn't let him know I'd figured out his plan, or he would counter my move and attack my right arm after all. I took slow breaths to stay in control of myself and my body. That was imperative to win a fight. If you lost control, even the weakest opponent could defeat you.

As expected, he jerked his hand toward my right arm, then truly went for my left. Just as his fingers clutched my wrist, I swung the knife down on his arm, and the blade stopped when it hit bone. Ugh, of course it'd be a dull blade. I'd wanted to cut his damn hand off.

That was one of the oddest things about the shadow form. They could fit into small crevices, their form molding to its surroundings, but they were solid. We'd learned that the hard way when Ronnie had been injured in a previous battle.

Blue blood poured from his wound as I gripped the knife handle hard, anticipating his next move. When he jerked his hand away, the blade raked against his hand and cut off skin. If I'd thought he'd been bleeding before, that was nothing compared to now. The flow seemed strong enough to make him to bleed out, but demons' bodies technically didn't need blood since their hearts no longer worked.

He growled, "You're going to pay for that."

"Get on with it." I wanted to check on my friends, but I'd been injured enough for today. I refused to let this arrogant prick leave another mark on my body, even if it would be temporary.

The demon charged me, cradling his left hand against his stomach. Desperate to get the weapon away from me, he went for the knife. I spun, flipping my wings around so they became sharp. His red eyes widened as I sliced through his neck, beheading him.

His blood coated my charcoal wings, and my stomach revolted. Though I might be a war strategist, I'd still rather not get blood on me. Flying with blood-coated feathers was more difficult, and the blood would be dry and crusted in my wings by the time I got home to clean them.

I had to let it go. This had happened every time I'd gone into battle here, which had occurred with alarming regularity since I'd become friends with this bunch. Strangely, I wouldn't change a thing, despite it making me feel quite uncomfortable at times.

Ronnie was holding her own against a demon. Her demon dagger had materialized in her fist, proof that her grandfather was Wrath, one of the princes of Hell. He was renowned for having his battle weapons always at hand.

My attention shifted to the wolves below. The weird *pull* kept growing stronger, drawing me toward the outskirts of the battle. I chose to ignore it.

Sterlyn and Cyrus had split up across the field, helping the silver wolves fight the demons. Two demons lay dead on the ground, while the other six continued to attack.

A demon floated away separately, its attention locked on Annie and my friends. It wafted toward them as the others battled the remaining five.

Now that I was free, I flew after it.

My wings felt icky as the blood dried on my feathers, but I kept my eyes locked on my destination. My wings could be restored, but my friends' lives could not. When I landed in front of Killian, he exhaled. "I'm damn glad you're here. Annie keeps saying another demon is coming, and all I can see is a beautiful day with silver wolves attacking the wind."

The corners of my lips tipped upward at the entertaining visual. That was one thing about mortals—they had a unique way of looking at things, their imaginations plentiful, whereas we angels had seen it all, and most things had lost their luster. Sometimes, I wished I could be like the mortals, but just being around them made me see things differently.

"And blue paint splattering all over them," Sierra added, unable to be outwitted.

When the demon got within ten feet of us, he lifted his knife—and since it wasn't a demon knife, my friends noticed it aiming at them.

"I'm assuming that's a demon," Griffin said as he stepped beside me. "It's freaky as hell seeing a knife hovering all by itself."

"At least we aren't completely blind as long as they use non-demonic weapons," Killian muttered, ready to fight.

The demon continued to hover, perhaps considering his best plan of attack.

In a way, them seeing the knife was potentially worse. They couldn't read the shadows' intent, and the demon could make a calculated move and lure them into a trap.

"Just stay back here with Annie." Ugh, I needed to be careful about how I explained things. If an alpha wolf thought I was impugning their leadership, they would try to prove me wrong. It was asinine to think that six months ago, I would've said what I meant without considering their feelings, and now I almost catered to them. "This could be a trap. I need you to stay back and protect her." Annie was strong, and despite Cyrus nagging her about *her condition*, she'd continued to train. She would be a formidable warrior, her wolf in tune with danger despite having been suppressed for nineteen years and syncing with her human side only a month and a half ago.

"But I—" Killian started.

I flew toward the demon, not bothering to listen to him. It would only wind up with me having to say what I thought, ending in hurt feelings, and Killian was a good guy. I didn't want to make him feel inferior, because he wasn't. He just couldn't see the demons, and I didn't want another liability on my hands.

"You killed my brother!" the demon shouted.

If he thought that would get a reaction out of me, he'd learn differently. "You shouldn't have attacked us."

He scoffed and lifted the knife above his head. "You deserve this fate."

I rolled my eyes, not caring how I made this idiot feel. He was more dramatic than Sierra. Instead of humoring him, I sped at him.

He swung the knife downward. I wasn't sure what he was aiming for—it wasn't like that dull blade would cut me in half. The *clang* of the blades meeting resonated, and he lost his grip on the knife. It dropped from his hand, and I attempted to slice his neck, but my knife stopped when it hit the bone.

This knife was worthless. I chucked it to the ground and flipped my feathers around.

"I'm sorry," the demon rasped, clutching his neck

with his hands as if that would prevent me from finishing the job. "We'll leave and not bother you—"

I killed him before he could finish the sentence. Demons could never be trusted. They had an overly sweet sulfuric stench that covered their lies. They were masters of manipulation, and that was why vampires were also good at it. Demons had created vampires, but at a cost. Their strong bloodlust was required to counteract the magic inside them. This demon had probably planned to return to Hell and come right back out to wreak havoc.

Ugh. I couldn't wait to go home and clean, up then rest in my room in complete silence.

Sterlyn and Cyrus had taken down three more demons, while Ronnie worked on her second kill. One demon remained.

When I locked eyes with the demon, he spun around and headed deeper into the woods.

I hated cowards.

As I flew after him, a man stepped from behind a tree, blocking me. He had half a foot on me, coming in around Griffin's height.

I halted, and something coursed through me, flowing toward him.

The sensation was so strong that it stole my breath. I'd never understood what people meant when they said that until this moment. I blinked, taking in his short espresso-brown hair and the hint of chestnut scruff. His mocha-colored eyes made my stomach flutter.

These strong sensations weren't normal.

Then his sweet peony smell knocked sense into me, giving him away. I'd officially lost my mind.

There was no *way* I could be feeling something like that for a demon.

I needed to kill him.

CHAPTER THREE

EVERYTHING in my body screamed at me to not injure him, pissing me off even more. A witch must have been nearby, casting some spell to toy with me. I'd never *felt* this much, and I wasn't sure how to maintain control.

Determined to prove I could overcome this strange draw, I channeled the odd sensations into something I recognized.

Rage.

I slammed into him and suddenly felt my skin super-heating as if it would burn me alive. The heat didn't hurt in a bad way. In fact, I enjoyed the sensation and didn't want it to end.

He inhaled sharply and stumbled back several steps, confusing me. He should've known I wouldn't just stand there. He was preventing me from following the demon for a reason, and I had to ascertain why.

A silver wolf inched toward me, attempting to help me but still engrossed in his own battle.

Taking advantage of the demon's distraction, I lifted myself higher off the ground. He could switch to his shadow form to catch me, but I'd have a few seconds' lead on him.

Something wrapped around my ankle, pulling me back to earth.

What the—

I flapped my wings harder, the searing heat around my ankle informing me of who had a hold of me. His grip was like an anchor, keeping me from going higher.

That was fine. I could counter that move.

I dropped, catching him off guard. He released his hold before he toppled over, obviously trained to fight. The other demons would've fallen as I'd hoped, but not this one.

My feet touched the ground, and I spun around and kicked him in the stomach. He stumbled back a few feet but caught his balance.

Damn it! He was a good adversary.

As if confirming my suspicion, he charged at me, eyes tightening and nostrils flaring, and threw a punch.

I ducked, but when I didn't hear his fist whistle over my head, I crouched and looked up.

His nose wrinkled as he looked at his offending hand.

My head jerked back. Had he pulled his punch?

Whatever. It wasn't my problem. Besides, this could be an act to make me lower my guard.

I kicked out my leg, aiming for his ankles. An instant before my foot could reach him, he jumped, and I hit air.

He twisted and placed his hands on my shoulders,

using me for balance. Then he flipped over me, his fingers digging into my arms and lifting me.

No, I couldn't land on my back.

Countering his movement, I expanded my wings and flapped them, throwing off his balance. Instead of landing on his feet, he fell on his ass, which propelled him onto his back. But he didn't release his hold.

My body slammed into his, and I wound up on top of him. A powerful sensation of warmth and pressure that I didn't want to understand inflamed my core. I'd been hanging around the shifters too long, because I wanted to rub all over him.

I'd never been sick before, but that *had* to be what was going on. My head and body were messed up.

Despite every cell inside me protesting, I jumped to my feet. He blew out a breath, sounding relieved, and I wondered if it was because I was too heavy. I was all muscle, training daily for an inevitable war that had yet to come. The only time I wasn't training was when I was on missions with my friends—and really, this was training, too, because I always wound up engaged in some kind of battle.

Sterlyn, Cyrus, and the other silver wolves ran toward us. I needed to distract him while they circled. They must have eliminated all the demons except for the one that had gotten away.

"Is that all you've got?" I asked as I stood again. I spread my wings and lifted my fisted hands. The span of an angel's wings matched their height, so my wings were close to six feet wide. I fluffed my feathers, wanting to look as large as possible. He needed to understand what he was up against.

He laughed, and my cheeks burned. I hated that thinking.

I spat, "What's so funny?"

"All this time, I thought my people had lied about your kind." He chuckled, and my heart leaped. The sound was more beautiful than any trumpet I'd ever heard. "They said you all like to extend your wings to prove how big you are. I always thought they were making fun of you, yet here you are. It doesn't make me fear you."

Demons made fun of us?

I shouldn't have been surprised. They were petty and juvenile, but the fact that *this* demon was laughing at me made something hurt in my chest. And I didn't like that.

"It's good to know that even after a thousand years of solitude, you have nothing better to do than talk about us." Angels were important, but since I'd grown close with Sterlyn and the others, I'd learned that most people didn't consider us as significant as we liked to think we were. At times, it was hard to comprehend, but over the centuries, the angels had changed, and we weren't viewed as the saviors we'd been once upon a time.

I blamed Azbogah for that, and sometimes, I wondered how he hadn't truly fallen.

The demon's face turned serious, and he set his feet shoulder-width apart, preparing to fight. "We don't only talk about you." His jaw twitched, making his chiseled features sharper and more angular.

My breath caught at his rugged good looks, and I forced myself to breathe. "Okay." I didn't care whether they talked about angels. It didn't make a difference to me. Nothing they said would change my views of the world. Actions spoke louder than words. That was one reason I'd grown close to my shifter and vampire friends: their decisions and plans reflected their words. Even Griffin and Killian had evolved that way, though a year ago, all they'd been focused on was whose bed they could fall into and who could outdrink the other.

The silver wolves weren't in position yet, so I needed to keep his attention. I punched him fast, but just before I connected, I pulled back a little. I still hit his face, but I didn't break his nose as I'd planned.

He sneered and jabbed at my face in return. I lifted my arm, blocking the blow. Surprisingly, the punch didn't hurt, and I wondered if he was holding back, too.

None of that made sense. We didn't know each other, and we were natural enemies.

Flashes of fur behind the cypresses and redbuds informed me that the shifters were closing in. I was shocked that the demon hadn't picked up on their movement, but I wouldn't alert him.

I pretended that I was going to kick him, and he moved to block his stomach. My fighter instinct took over, and I surged my fist into his jaw to knock him out. Again, milliseconds before my fist connected with him, my body adjusted the blow, making it less powerful.

His head jerked back with a slight crunch of bone. He grunted and rubbed his jaw, but he could move it.

The fact that my punch hadn't shattered the bone had my nails cutting into my palms. *That* was a sensation I recognized and welcomed, not these strange ones that were confusing the hell out of me.

A growl escaped me. This was everything I wasn't supposed to do in battle. I'd been trained to never hold back unless there was a strategic reason, and there was no explanation why I would be pulling punches. I could pretend it was because the wolves were getting into position, but I would be lying to myself. Kicking this demon's ass felt *wrong*. I should have ripped his head from his body by now or had blood oozing from as many surfaces as possible, but here I stood, giving him love taps.

We were essentially engaged in foreplay, not fighting to the death.

"You kick like a girl." He waggled his brows. Somehow, the action made him look even more attractive and not stupid like Griffin, Alex, or Cyrus when they did it to their mates.

"So? I am one. What's *your* excuse?" He acted as if my being a woman was a shortcoming, and it was anything but. It seemed only right to point out his weaknesses. I didn't have to be polite to him like I did to my friends.

He scratched the back of his head, his bicep bulging. I tore my gaze away from his body and watched for a sign that he was about to attack. Demons played dirty. He tugged at the collar of his heather-gray shirt. "I don't have one, unfortunately."

My heart picked up its pace. His admission that he

was holding back too made me feel funny. My stomach fluttered, and my armpits grew sweaty. Maybe I *was* getting a stomach bug. Angels didn't get sick, but much had changed. Who knew what the rules were anymore?

"It doesn't matter now," Sterlyn said as she stepped from behind the tree beside me, making her way to my side. The silver wolves followed their alpha's lead, and it was clear we were surrounded. "But we have some questions that need to be answered."

Though my magic was slightly drained, I used a little more, pushing it out to search for signs of more demons close by. He could've been distracting us while they set up a trap. He had helped the demon I'd been chasing to get away, and it could've gone for reinforcements. But I didn't feel anything out of the ordinary other than the man standing in front of me and the faint hint of the demons that had been here.

Cyrus stepped up beside me, the two silver wolves staring the man down. Sterlyn and Cyrus were twins born only a few minutes apart, but they'd grown up separately and in completely different circumstances. Since Cyrus was the boy, some enemies had assumed he'd be the future alpha of the silver wolves and had forced a witch to spell him to seem dead to his parents so they could kidnap him. The plan had been to raise Cyrus to be loyal to his kidnappers and then kill his father so Cyrus could take over the silver wolf pack and force the silver wolves to submit to the kidnappers' will. There had also been a sick side plan to mate Sterlyn with one of their awful allies and create more silver wolves under their command.

But Sterlyn was the actual alpha heir, and she'd been raised by their parents. The night of her pack's slaughter, destiny had stepped in to steer everyone's fate. Forced to flee, Sterlyn had found her fated mate and her twin brother while forging a new pack that was stronger than ever.

Out of everyone here, Annie would know best if demons were close by because she was the alpha demon wolf and the only one of her kind in the area. I turned so the demon couldn't see me and looked at Sterlyn, then flicked my eyes toward Annie, hoping she got my message. "I'll be right back." This was one of the few times I found it inconvenient that I couldn't communicate telepathically with any of them.

"Why?" The demon's brows furrowed.

"That's none of your business."

Sterlyn nodded. As usual, she understood.

Turning on my heel, I marched toward Annie. I could feel the demon's gaze on my back as I walked away. My feet came dangerously close to dragging and slowing my progress. Healing myself might have taken more out of me than I'd realized.

The demon's feet shuffled behind me, and I heard Cyrus take a step and the sound of shoving. "You better stay still and start talking," Cyrus threatened.

The demon laughed. "I won't *talk* with you."

I wanted to turn around to see if I'd been right and he was coming after me, but that was ridiculous. It shouldn't matter to me either way. He could've been trying to behead me or stab me, and he probably didn't expect my friends to have my back. Supernatural races tended to keep to themselves. My guess was that the demon was banking on them allowing him to kill me.

"Are you okay?" Killian asked as I got close. His dark chocolate eyes scanned me, and he touched my arm.

A low hiss sounded from behind me, and I glanced over my shoulder to see the demon frowning and trying to follow me.

How odd.

Cyrus shoved the demon in the chest again. Silver fur sprouted on his arms as he bellowed, half shifted, "I said, stay *fucking* still."

I felt strange having Killian touching me, which was weird. Unnecessary touches weren't common among angels, but this group was touchy-feely, and I was getting better about it, though not all the way comfortable. Killian and I had a strange relationship I couldn't put my finger on, but I'd never felt like I was doing something wrong by letting him touch me.

It didn't help when Sierra arched an eyebrow like she was taking a mental picture of the misinterpreted moment between Killian and me.

"I'm fine." I stepped away from him, forcing his hand to drop.

Stepping into the center of the circle, I lowered my voice so only Annie, Griffin, Killian, and Sierra could hear. "Do you sense anything else near us?"

"I do, but it's not as strong." Annie bit her bottom lip, her honey-brown eyes appearing golden in the sun.

That didn't help me much. "Meaning?"

She lifted her hands. "I'm not sure. It could be that I sensed the demons and that the one in human form is still standing there, making an impression."

"And why *is* he in human form?" Griffin rubbed his chin, staring at the demon. He hadn't taken his eyes off him since Sterlyn had gotten close.

Excellent question. "I'd like to know the same thing." I wanted to say more, but now wasn't the time or place. We were in an open environment, and that other demon had run off.

"I will say this." Annie leaned forward. "I don't feel an immediate threat like I did when we first got here or when we were outside the demon portal when Eliza—" She cut herself off, but she didn't need to say anything further.

That was enough for me. I marched back to the demon and took my spot between Cyrus and Sterlyn. This abomination needed to start talking. "Why are you here?"

"Because it's a beautiful day, and I felt like stretching my legs." The demon's eyes twinkled as he looked into mine. His scowl had been replaced by arrogant humor.

Yeah, I wasn't amused, and he was playing a game. He was useless. My stomach roiled as I flipped my feathers to make them razor-sharp. "Then we have nothing left to discuss." As I moved to behead him, something sharp pierced my chest near my heart.

His eyes widened. "Wait."

For some reason, I did. "Why should I?"

"I want to make a deal." He lifted his hands in surrender.

Making a deal with a demon was never smart, but something inside me screamed at me to listen. The meaning was clear, and there was only one option—he had to die.

CHAPTER FOUR

AS I PREPARED to sever his head, the pain in my chest became excruciating. My heart squeezed, and my stomach churned. Something was definitely wrong, but I doubted angels were susceptible to heart attacks...unless the entire world was changing.

"You'll want to hear what I have to say," the demon said desperately.

This time, I wouldn't allow myself to hesitate. His head was mine.

"Whoa," Sterlyn said as she snatched my arm, pulling me toward her. "Let's humor him."

I tucked my wings in fast, warning, "Don't touch me like that when I'm about to use my feathers to kill someone. I could have cut off your arm, and that's something even I can't heal." Regenerating appendages was beyond my abilities. "And the *demon* already thinks he's funny. Why would we want to inflate his ego more than it already is? He's an idiot and a liability."

Sierra snorted. "Tell us what you really think, Rosemary."

Sometimes, I didn't understand these people. They told me I shouldn't be blunt, and now I wasn't being blunt enough. I couldn't win with them. "I thought I had." I huffed and spun around, not wanting my back to the enemy. "He won't tell us anything, and he should be eliminated before he can pose additional risk. The only thing he's got going for him is his looks. He's arrogant and thinks he's smarter than he truly—"

Her gray eyes lit up, while Sterlyn released my arm.

Ronnie interjected as she moved close to her sister, "She was being sarcastic, Rosemary. You made it clear the first time what you think of him."

Times like these were when I felt like I didn't fit in. Sometimes, their humor didn't make sense to me. "Then why did she say that?"

"It's just an expression, Rosey," the demon jeered. "It must be hard to acclimate to the outside world after being holed up in Shadow City for all those centuries."

Something burned through my body, and the over-whelming urge to punch his sexy face almost overtook my control. "My name *isn't* Rosey."

He shrugged and shifted his weight on his heels. "Your face is pretty pink. I'd say it's a fitting nickname."

Our names were set. Our families didn't call us anything different. The only exception was our parents, who might use nicknames for us due to our rare bond. "I don't care what you find *fitting*. My name is Rosemary."

"He's goading you," Alex said, shaking his head from

where he stood next to Ronnie and Annie. "The more you feed into it, the worse he'll get. He's apparently a male version of Sierra."

"Hey!" Sierra's mouth dropped. "I'm one of a kind."

Alex murmured, "You're one of something, all right."

"I don't know, Sterlyn." Cyrus tapped his fingers on his jeans. "I'm thinking *Rosemary* should behead him. We have plenty of other things we need to handle, and he's trying to unsettle us."

At least Cyrus and I were on the same page.

Killian strolled over to stand beside Cyrus. He stared the demon down and nodded. "He'd be talking if he knew something we'd find useful. He's stalling, either for backup or to slip away."

"Like a coward." Griffin chuckled as he replaced Killian in the spot next to Annie. "He seems like the cowardly type. I think we miscalculated and should cut our losses."

Why had they stopped me, then? Sometimes, their fickleness drove me up the wall. It was one thing to be empathetic but another to let your heart sway logic. Mortals tended to do the latter. "I agree. Will anyone stop me this time?" Whether I liked it or not, I cared if I injured one of them. They'd made me more than indifferent toward them, which was bittersweet. The sensations I experienced around them were a nice change but could cause problems, like when I ran off to help them even though Mother and Father didn't want me to. My parents were allies to this group, but we had enough internal angel problems that they'd rather I help from afar. If they knew I'd helped them close a demon portal, they'd be furious with me—another reason I'd supported the decision to exclude anyone else from that knowledge.

When no one said anything, I rolled my shoulders.

The demon closed his eyes. "I can't go back to Hell."

"Can't?" Griffin furrowed his brows. "Or won't?"

"It's one and the same." The demon put his hands in his jeans pockets. "If you hide me, I'll share things with you."

He must have thought we were idiots. "It's not one and the same, and we don't have time for your games." I rubbed my chest as it constricted again. This was the strangest thing, and I wasn't sure what it meant. Maybe I needed to see a doctor. There had to be one for supernaturals, surely.

"The princes of Hell have my father, and if I go back, they'll hurt him to get to me. They want the demons who can travel the world undetected to do their bidding." His eyes darkened to a black-coffee tone as his body tensed. "You're the best option I have so my father doesn't die, so I'm willing to provide answers for shelter."

Though the air didn't smell more strongly of sulfur, I wasn't sure I believed him. "You're saying if you go back to Hell, you'll be forced to watch your father suffer unless you agree to work for them?"

"No, that's not what I mean." He stared into my eyes. "Things are tense in Hell right now, and the princes of Hell want more power and the freedom to leave. They're trying to use anyone they can to gain that leverage. If I go back and don't have anything useful for them, my dad will be at risk."

He was being vague while attempting to appear forthcoming. This information wasn't anything we hadn't figured out ourselves. Of course the princes of Hell wanted out of there. They wanted to roam Earth and terrorize everyone to feel even more powerful. But if he wanted to engage in a battle of wills, I was all for that. Chess was my favorite board game. "Torture is what they do best. They'll hurt your father regardless of whether you go back."

His jaw twitched. He didn't like being called out, and it bothered me that I'd upset him. My throat dried. I shouldn't have been worried about him. I'd just met the man—er, demon. Now I was confusing things, like I'd accused Sterlyn and the others of doing. "Tell us what you know," I said, "or we'll have no reason to keep you around."

"And if I tell you what I know, there'll be no reason for you to keep me alive." He lifted a hand. "I don't have much of a choice."

Ugh, I wanted to kill the guy right here and now. "We're going in circles."

"Fine," he muttered, making me feel funny. The noise was one of the most alluring sounds I'd ever heard. "I'll tell you more if you take me somewhere safe."

I blinked. This guy was worse than arrogant. Did he think that would work? I opened my mouth to tell him exactly what would happen.

Sterlyn beat me to the punch. "As soon as you

become a hindrance, we'll kill you. I want to make sure you understand that. Nothing changes from this moment." She straightened her shoulders, standing tall.

His eyes lightened, telling me all I needed to know. "No." I shook my head. "Absolutely not." Usually, Sterlyn was sane, but this was so far beyond sane, it wasn't funny.

I glanced at Griffin and the others to back me, but they remained silent. They'd been telepathically discussing things I couldn't be privy to. *Again.* And this was a horrible decision. "Can we talk for a second?" I demanded. They'd all had their say in the matter, but they hadn't listened to me. Shouldn't I be the one to make the call about this, since we were dealing with demons? And Ronnie and Alex hadn't been consulted, either.

I didn't want to argue in front of the demon; otherwise, he'd see that we were turning against one another. He wasn't stupid, so he could already tell I wasn't happy with the situation, but the more I acted out, the more he'd try to divide us. I couldn't let emotion cloud my judgment.

"Sure." Sterlyn glanced at Cyrus. "One wrong move, and you have my permission to kill him."

Cyrus smirked. "I won't think twice."

Sterlyn and I marched away from the others, back in the direction from which we'd come. Ronnie, Annie, and Alex followed us, wanting to be part of the conversation as well. I was perfectly fine with that because we needed to agree on the strategy.

I stopped fifty yards away and turned to them, then

kept my voice low so those who had stayed behind couldn't hear. "This isn't smart."

"I agree," Alex whispered. "That demon is up to something."

"Of course he's up to something." Sterlyn lifted her hands. "I promise you, I'm aware. However, Annie is feeling things she doesn't understand, and those demons got here somehow. Something is off. Obviously, they're using a portal. Taking the demon back with us may be our best strategy to get answers without risking more of our numbers until we figure out another way."

Ronnie pinched the bridge of her nose. "That demon helped the one Rosemary was chasing escape. He stopped her. I watched it happen. There has to be a reason they came here."

At least she and Alex were on my side. "That's what I'm getting at," I said. "You can't take him back to the pack neighborhood. He could learn too much about us, and if the demons find out that Annie is the girl that a prince of Hell wants and she's pregnant, this could go badly."

"It means a lot that you care so much about me," Annie said, and hugged me.

I tensed, not sure what to do, but I didn't pull away. I'd gotten slightly more comfortable with affection, and I patted her arm, hoping I didn't come off as awkward as I felt.

She chuckled. "But we talked about it back there. Cyrus is concerned for the same reasons, but that negative feeling is still swirling inside me. Not intensely, like when it led us here, but like when something tugged at me a few days ago. I'd hate for us to give up a chance to learn useful information."

Feeling. The word struck a chord with me. It all came back to damn feelings. I couldn't completely discount them, because this group had followed their instincts many times and usually gotten it right. At first, I'd been disgusted by that way of making decisions, but I'd felt a connection with Sterlyn, so I'd pushed through and gone along with them, determined to keep her safe. After all, my mother's biggest regret was not protecting the silver wolves when she'd had the chance over a millennium ago, before I was born, and I couldn't make the same mistake. Over time, I'd had to admit that this group had changed my view about all supernatural creatures being arrogant and worthless. "Is a little information worth the risk?"

"When we have nothing else to go on?" Sterlyn countered, and tilted her head. "What other option do we have? Besides, he's not attacking or threatening us. We can't become cold-blooded killers. If we do that, what will separate us from our enemies?"

"This seems too convenient. I could beat it out of him." My stomach churned again, and my breathing picked up. I bounced, not able to stay still.

Alex's focus landed on me. "Vampires try that method often, and it usually doesn't work unless the victim is weak or beaten for an extended period of time. I'm not saying we shouldn't resort to it eventually, but if we pretend to be amicable, maybe he'll let his guard down and reveal something unintentionally." He paused, then asked, "Are you okay? You're acting out of character."

Wonderful. They'd noticed. I'd thought I was hiding my confusion. My hope that my mind was just playing tricks on me disappeared. Obviously, something was very wrong. "I...I feel out of sorts." I wasn't sure how else to describe it.

"What do you mean?" Annie asked with concern. "Are you sick?"

That was the thing—I wasn't sure.

Sterlyn placed the back of her hand on my forehead. "If you are, you can heal yourself, right?"

"I don't know." I'd never had to heal an illness inside myself before, but in theory, I should be able to. If I could heal a wound, surely I could heal a nauseated stomach. "What are you doing?"

"Checking to see if you feel warm." Sterlyn dropped her hand and pursed her lips. "But I'm not sure what your normal temperature is, so I don't know if you have a fever."

"A fever?" I racked my brain, trying to remember what that was. After a few seconds, the memory resurfaced in my mind. "I've never had one. Do wolves get them?"

"Not often, and normally, only at the end of a shifter's life." Sterlyn smiled sadly. "My grandfather had a fever right before he died. Humans get them more often."

"I've never heard of an angel being sick," Alex said, reentering the conversation, which I appreciated.

Responding to sadness wasn't my strong point, though I was slowly getting better. "Me neither, but I'm fine." I wanted to return our focus to our demon problem. "If we're thinking about taking him back to the pack neighborhood, that isn't a good idea. If we're going to hold him, we need to be wise about it."

Sterlyn lifted her chin, maintaining eye contact with me. "We'll take him to the abandoned silver wolf pack neighborhood where the demon wolves first attacked us. No one should know about that location, because all the wolves who hit us there are dead. He won't see anything we don't want him to see."

I should've known she'd thought this out. She never did anything rash, which was one reason I respected her. "Okay. But how will we keep him contained? He could sneak out in his shadow form."

Patting her chest, Annie beamed. "I'm taking care of that. I already texted Circe, and Aurora and Lux are on their way down to cast a spell. That's why we're going there—so the coven in Shadow City won't feel them when they use magic to trap him in one of the houses."

Those two were the youngest of the witches who'd helped close down the portal. The only demons who knew about them had gotten sucked back into Hell, so their help wouldn't cause any issues. "Fine. But we must stay on top of him, especially until they get here."

"We'll take every precaution," Sterlyn vowed.

They'd already decided—there wasn't much I could do. Since their plan was somewhat smart, I'd go along with it.

For now.

"Let's get moving." Ronnie waved for us to follow her back to the others. "More demons could come, and I don't want to deal with that while we're keeping him prisoner."

A lump formed in my throat. That one demon had run off—why hadn't it brought reinforcements?

When our group rejoined the others, everybody was tense, but the demon relaxed as he saw me. My stupid heart fluttered.

"Uh...guys," Annie grunted as she doubled over. "We have another problem."

Negative energy buzzed in the air. Damn it, the demon *had* gone back for reinforcements. No wonder this man had stopped me. He wanted us to die.

CHAPTER FIVE

MY BREATH CAUGHT. We'd walked straight into a trap.

This was why having a bleeding heart wasn't good. If we'd just killed the demon like I wanted to, we wouldn't be in this situation.

"Annie!" Cyrus exclaimed, his face etched with worry as he ran to her.

"What's wrong?" Killian asked from where he stood between Sierra and Griffin.

"We've hung around here too long, and the demon who ran off gathered backup." Ugh, I was infuriated that I hadn't gone with my gut and slit this demon's throat right then and there.

Killian understood the implication without us having to spell it out for him. The demon didn't need to know that Annie could sense his kind. We needed to keep her off their radar for as long as possible.

The demon's eyes narrowed. "I told you the princes

of Hell want me. We need to get out of here. They can't get me."

"Maybe they wouldn't be coming here if you hadn't let your friend escape!" I exclaimed. "I say we hand you over to them." If we weren't going to kill him, he was better off back with the other demons than with us. My chest tightened again. I would have to get someone to look at me when I returned to Shadow City.

"What?" He jerked his head from side to side. "No. Please. My father."

We'd let this go on way too long. "Your father is a demon just like you. Why should I care if he's tortured? For that matter, why do you?"

"Because I *care* about him," he said. "He's the only reason I haven't completely gone to the evil side."

His sincerity shocked me. Demons were even more one-dimensional than angels. Angels could feel a range of emotions, but our experience was muted compared to mortals'. Vampires, shifters, and witches were much closer to mortals emotionally, having human roots, though vampires could lose their humanity if they drank too much blood from the source. Ronnie had been three-quarters human and one-quarter demon before she'd been turned into a vampire, so she was closely tied to her humanity.

"None of that matters right now." Alex's jaw twitched. "The demons are appearing here, and we can't let them go. We'd be here even if this nuisance weren't in our custody."

"Levi," the demon grumbled. "My name is Levi."

"How is that relevant?" I snapped. "Knowing your name doesn't give us any advantage." I hated how his voice and name *tugged* at something inside me. It was the same damn tug that had gotten me injured earlier. I needed him to stop talking and...die.

He opened his mouth to respond, but I had to focus on the threat. I flapped my wings, rising from the ground. "Restrain him and take him to the pack neighborhood, and I'll meet you there when I'm done."

"You think we're going to leave you alone to fight?" Ronnie pivoted to me, placing her hands on her hips. "I get that you're a big bad angel, but we don't know their numbers."

My chest expanded with warmth at her concern, and I rubbed it to ease the sensation I was still growing accustomed to. I'd learned that was what it felt like to have friends. Their concern sometimes made me feel mildly uncomfortable. "You can't leave him with the wolves who can't see him. If he turns into his shadow form, they can't detain or kill him. We need people who can rival him."

Sierra coughed, but the corners of her eyes crinkled like she was laughing. She was an odd individual, and out of everyone here, I understood her the least. Her brain worked on a different wavelength.

Griffin and Killian frowned, and Alex crossed his arms, staring down at his mate.

"I can see him," Cyrus said. He marched over to Levi and grabbed his arm. "If he so much as looks somewhere I don't want him to, I'll kick his ass."

We didn't have time to argue. The demons were

getting closer, their power affecting mine. Cyrus wouldn't leave Annie's side, and I didn't blame him. Both of them could see the demon, no matter his form, so maybe that was the best call.

"That works." Sterlyn nodded. "Griffin, Killian, Sierra, and Alex, why don't you go with them, and if the demons catch up with you, let us know."

That plan didn't sit well with me, either. Cyrus would do anything to keep Annie and their unborn child safe. Though I knew he meant well and he'd proven his loyalty to everyone here, he'd become irrational if Annie was threatened, even handing Levi—er, the demon—to a prince of Hell if required. "A few silver wolves should go with them, too."

Sterlyn surveyed the area and nodded. "That can happen." Her eyes glowed faintly as she communicated via their pack link. I didn't care who went, but they needed to get moving.

"There's no way I'm leaving without you." Alex's jaw twitched as he stared Ronnie down.

Pulling her hair into a low ponytail, Ronnie sighed. "Honey—"

"You're being an idiot, Alex," I interrupted. Something overcame me, and I didn't understand what was happening. My chest hurt, and my hands clenched. I wanted to stomp my foot. All the turmoil had tested my patience, and I didn't have any self-control to spare, so I defaulted to my blunt nature. "You can't see a demon in shadow form. You'd be more of a liability than an asset. You could get *Ronnie* hurt."

His face twisted. "You enjoy pointing out that we can't see them, don't you? That's like the tenth time."

Why was he upset over facts? "I wish you could." Indeed, I was surprised that vampires couldn't—their human heritage must have interfered with that ability. "It would make things much easier."

Ronnie grimaced and placed a hand on his arm. They were using their soulmate bond to speak. If they were going to stand here and chat, I'd go fight the horde alone.

My legs moved toward Levi of their own accord. A smirk creased his face as he watched me approach, and I wanted to punch and kiss him at the same time.

Nope. I meant punch. I *only* wanted to punch him. Nothing else.

As if I needed to prove that to myself, I stuck my finger in his chest and felt a little *zap*. I ground my teeth, determined to act normal. "If you try *anything*, they won't be able to stop me from unleashing my wrath."

He grinned cockily. "Don't tempt me into misbehaving."

My body warmed, and I sucked in a breath. I needed to get away from this *demon*. "I'm serious." I moved to turn away, but something inside me urged me to stop. The most worrisome part was that my legs *almost* halted their movement like I'd lost control of them.

He must have done something to me, but I had no clue what it could be. The one thing I knew was that I wouldn't let this prick succeed at whatever spell he'd gotten a witch to cast, or whatever he'd managed. I was stronger than that.

I took flight, not wanting to talk to anyone else. I needed to get busy. There was too much at stake to let something as trivial as *him* distract me from what really mattered—protecting Earth and my friends.

I hit the air, but even flying didn't ease my predicament. What was swirling inside me was definitely not normal, especially for an angel. There had to be a plausible explanation, and after I released my frustration, I'd figure out what the hell he'd done to me.

A shadowy form appeared beside me, and if it hadn't been for the overly sweet, sugary smell, I would've beheaded the demon. I growled, "You all figured out a plan, finally?"

Ronnie blinked, and I had a feeling it was best I couldn't see her face, or her expression would have *upset* me.

Oh, my gods. I was turning into a mortal.

"Are you okay?" Ronnie asked hesitantly. "You're acting—"

Fifteen demons appeared above the tree line, their glowing red eyes landing on the two of us.

We were outnumbered, but I'd expected that. They were coming in force to fight us. This was the first time demons had ever done me a favor, and I would consider prolonging the fight if it kept me out of this awkward conversation Ronnie was attempting to have.

Logic eluded me as to what was going on with me, so how was I supposed to explain it to anyone else? I was still banking on sickness or some sort of magical influence. With time, either of those ailments should get better.

If not, I'd eliminate the root of the problem.

"Can we head back down to the others?" I asked. Surely *the demon* and whoever was escorting him would be gone by now, so we could lead the other demons to their slaughter.

Ronnie murmured, "They need a few more minutes. They're about half a mile away."

I pushed my wings harder, and the demon in the lead lifted his hand, which held a long, swordlike shadow object. As suspected, the demon who'd fled had brought back stronger reinforcements. Levi had seemed sincere about wanting to go with us, but it was a big red flag that he'd let that demon escape. If he truly wanted to hide from the princes of Hell, why let anyone get back to inform them about what had happened here? He would've been safer if we'd killed every demon.

He had a reason, and I sure as hell would determine what it was.

A sword reached farther than a dagger, so I decided to take on that demon. Ronnie was still a new demon, and her dagger was a quarter the size.

I flew directly at the demon hovering in the air, and the fourteen other demons behind him stopped, waiting for his signal to attack. They were probably battle-trained and would be harder to fight than the ones we'd killed today.

My magic had had time to recharge since healing myself hadn't taken a lot out of me. Had it been a more serious wound, I wouldn't have been up for the fight just now, so I counted that as a blessing.

As I approached the demon, I spun, wrapping my wings around me. I whirled like a cyclone, prepared to bounce the blade off my wings like I did bullets. I could see out of a small slit I'd made right in front of my eyes.

The demon laughed evilly. "Angels are too damn arrogant." He swung the sword at me, and when it hit my wings, his hands shook from the vibrations rushing back toward him.

His red eyes dimmed from what I could only assume was confusion.

I loosened my wings, dropping slightly, and elbowed him in the stomach. Despite his shadowy state, my funny bone hit something solid, proving these abominations had a physical form.

The demon slammed back into the ones behind him, and they all tumbled down a few feet before taking to the air once more.

Ronnie battled one at the end. I watched for a second to make sure she wasn't getting into trouble. She was an excellent fighter for the amount of time she'd trained, and she'd be on my level within a few decades if she kept it up.

The demon's red eyes glowed brightly as he swung the sword like a bat.

I was almost embarrassed that I'd considered him a worthy opponent. Clearly, he hadn't been trained as much as I'd assumed. His dismissal of angels as arrogant would be the death of him. I'd been born to fight and had received the highest marks for my fighting skills and warriorlike abilities in my age group, scoring several points higher than the top male in my class. Mother had been so proud—she wanted me to be everything she hadn't been at my age. She wanted me to fight for what was just and not bow to anyone, even herself. Lately, that had become a sore subject between us, but she'd done her job of raising me well.

Thankfully, this demon wasn't mouthy. I appreciated a silent and determined fighter. He swung the sword again, and I didn't bother wrapping my wings around me. I could tell exactly where he was aiming—my right wing.

I dropped several feet, and his sword swung over my head. The wind blew my hair into my face.

Eight silver wolves howled below as they ran underneath us, and Sterlyn sprinted with them in human form.

"Get them!" my opponent yelled as he floated toward me.

The thirteen demons raced below.

The silver wolves were outnumbered, and as only Sterlyn had hands at the moment, she couldn't be in eight places at once to behead their attackers. I had to eliminate some demons immediately.

"You can't run away from me!" the demon screeched behind me.

I rolled my eyes. And here I'd thought Sierra was dramatic. I flapped my wings harder, aiming for the demon closest to me. I flipped my feathers, turning them razor-sharp, and spun, beheading the demon before it even noticed I was close.

I still needed to do more. I swung toward another, but this demon had seen me. His eyes narrowed and flicked behind me.

The demons were trying to organize a strike against me from both sides, and they didn't think I'd pick up on that. I could let them underestimate me—I'd seen Sterlyn use the tactic several times—but I'd rather die than act weak, especially in front of underground thugs.

I closed my eyes, opening my senses. The demon behind me breathed heavily, anticipating my next move.

When the demon in front of me jerked, I knew the one behind me planned to strike. I wrapped my wings around me and dropped. The sword made a noise as it chopped air, and I sprouted my wings again and soared toward the two demons. My feathers were still on the sharp side, so I spun and sliced off both of their heads, one with each wing.

This was going well. I had to keep up this pace.

A loud, pain-filled howl filled the air, and my skin turned cold. Somebody was hurt. I hadn't done enough.

CHAPTER SIX

I TURNED in midair and saw a demon on top of a silver wolf. It held a knife at the wolf's throat. Though the blade was smaller than the sword I'd avoided, it was large enough to kill anyone.

Swallowing hard, I darted toward the wolf and realized it was Chad.

Sterlyn was several feet away, fighting a demon of her own. Her gaze flicked to Chad. She could get hurt if the demon realized her attention was split.

No one else was going to get injured. Not on my watch.

Flapping my wings hard, I flew as quickly as possible toward Chad. His throat was bleeding, but he dug his claws into the demon. Blue blood dripped onto his silver fur, mixing with the crimson of his own.

The demon screamed, the sound so loud, my eardrums wanted to shatter. The stupid thing must have thought it was a banshee, and my need to kill it intensified for my sanity.

I swung down and grabbed the weapon. The demon grasped my wrist, its nails cutting into my skin. Ice-cold magic filled me, weakening my essence.

Angels and demons were opposites. The longer his magic poured into me, the weaker I'd become. I jerked my arm, forcing the knife to fall to the ground.

"No!" he yelled, and the sound was somehow worse than the screams. He released his hold, desperate to grab his weapon.

The magic hadn't drained me too much, and other than feeling a little dizzy, I was okay. I spun, killed the demon, and focused on my next target.

Negative energy drew closer, and I glanced around to find three demons coordinating an attack against me. I hated that they were using logic—that would make this battle last longer than I'd hoped.

A vampire-like hiss sounded behind me. Now I understood where vampires had gotten the trait.

The three demons floated quickly toward me. I kept all three in view, but I had a sneaking suspicion they were counting on the fourth to surprise me from behind once I engaged in battle with them.

If I let them know I was on to them, they'd change their plan.

I flew straight to the closest demon, who also carried a blade. He floated toward me, but as we drew closer, his eyes flicked to the side. He waved the blade, and I laughed. The demon thought *that* would scare me? I'd just blocked a sword trying to slice me in half.

My wings were still turned to the razor-sharp feathers. Angels could fly like this, but I usually opted for the soft side because it made gliding easier and was safer around my friends. However, this was war, and I wished the angels had access to their weapons. They'd been taken and put into storage when the city borders had closed. The other supernatural races had demanded it for their own safety. With the uptick in demon attacks, it would be nice to determine where they were kept and find one that could work for me. On the other hand, if the Shadow City guards told Azbogah I'd left the city with an angel sword, it would create more problems than we already had. Angels weren't supposed to venture out into the world, and if we took our weapons with us, he'd become furious and demand to know why we needed them.

I'd recently learned that millennia ago, Azbogah had forged an agreement with Wrath. They had agreed that the angels would stay in Shadow City if the demons stayed in Hell. At the time, a war had been looming that would have been catastrophic for both sides; with mutually assured destruction or peace as the only options, they chose to forge a pact. Angels born after the agreement were more focused on training to fight other supernatural races because once we all were enclosed in the city together, the angels had tried to rule over everyone. The silver wolves had spearheaded an uprising that had prevented the angels from becoming the ultimate rulers, forcing them to create the council to share control among all the supernatural races.

Azbogah's plan had always been to regain control of the city, and he had the angels training for the moment. So far, his plans hadn't come to fruition, thanks mainly to my mother and father.

But the balance of energies was important. If too many angels and their weapons moved outside Shadow City, the princes of Hell would know we weren't keeping to the agreement, just as the angels would be aware if a powerful demon left Hell. The energies couldn't be hidden, and that was why Azbogah was against letting the city gates fully open. He was growing desperate over Sterlyn, Griffin, Ronnie, and Alex's attempts to do just that. If other supernaturals could come and go and the angels were forced to stay—well, it wouldn't sit well with the angels. Other supernaturals having more freedom would create more animosity toward Azbogah among the angels who were already on the fence about him.

That was what happened when you messed with the balance.

The demons on the sides raced toward me as if they expected this demon to injure me. They clearly didn't know how to fight an angel, but I was getting more familiar with fighting them. Several months ago, my mother had risked leaving Shadow City to help Ronnie fight her half-demon father, and though her memory had been rusty, she'd known the basics of how to kill demons. With her, Ronnie, and Eliza fighting in tandem, the son of Wrath had died at the hands of his own daughter.

Something shifted in the demon's eyes, and he moved to the right. I was prepared. I swung to my left, offsetting his retreat. He sliced at me as I spun. The tip of his blade hit my wings and bounced off, and the sword fell from his hands. His eyes widened as I circled him, and then I sliced his neck in two.

As I finished my twirl, the other two demons were on me. The one on my right had a machete, while the one on the left had a hunting knife. They coordinated their efforts, focusing on my wings. It had taken them a while, but they'd learned that my wings were both shield and catastrophic weapon. That was one reason angels were nearly invincible, but we could be taken down, especially if an angel became arrogant.

I'd been injured before for that very reason. Even though I was more than one thousand years old, I'd been around demons only a couple of times, the same as my friends. My injuries had been wakeup calls, reminding me that even though I was immortal, I could die.

I twirled again, hoping to chop off their heads, too. They'd obviously seen that tactic because they jumped back, and my wings missed their necks by mere inches.

Normally, I'd have admired their savviness. A true warrior took notes and changed their combat strategy to defeat their enemy. But I had friends at risk and a demon I needed to watch. They were inconveniencing me, and I didn't like that.

Heart racing, I shook my head and flew upward to face them again. I pushed the weird sensations aside to think rationally. That was an advantage I always had, and I couldn't let it change now.

The demons followed me, seeming more confident since I'd missed the mark. That was fine. I wouldn't make the same mistake twice. Their confidence would be their downfall—I'd make sure of it.

I spun toward them and fluffed my feathers. The sunlight illuminated the razor tips, and I'd positioned myself directly in front of the sun, wanting them to fear me. I could only imagine the number of people they'd petrified before since these demons could roam Earth undetected. It was their turn to see how terror felt.

One paused, affected by my visual. However, the one with the machete hurtled toward me, confirming he would be the first one I eliminated. I smiled, wanting him to know he wasn't frightening me.

Every cell in my body wanted me to wrap my wings around me, but I forced them to stay out. This was the moment in the fight when I had to be stronger than my instincts.

As expected, his eyes locked on his target—my heart. I readied myself, waiting for the right moment to attack.

The lift of his arm was my signal. Instead of twirling like he expected, I rushed to one side. He hit the air where I'd been a moment before, and the tip of my wing sliced through him.

Without pausing, I focused on the second demon. From the corner of my eye, I noted the fourth demon, who was supposed to be the undetected attacker. Their plan hadn't worked out, but that didn't sway the final two from carrying on.

I took a moment to glance below. The wolves were holding their own, with Sterlyn working diligently to kill each demon as the wolves wore them down. Ronnie was fighting another demon. Eight remained, including the two demons focused on me. Ronnie must have killed at least two on her own.

Refocusing, I kept one demon in my sight while tracking the other in my peripheral vision. I tried not to tip them about my knowledge.

"Are you going to attack?" I asked the demon ahead of me, forcing him to react before he wanted. He was trying to buy time so the other demon could get closer.

He fidgeted, and I grew tired of the charade. This ended now. I refused to humor them any longer. They'd done enough, and I wanted to get back to *the* demon who was pretending we could trust him.

The only two demon-related people I'd ever trust were Ronnie and Annie. They had been raised as humans with no evil influences, proving that anyone raised in a nurturing environment *could* choose good. But these demons were from Hell, the worst environment anyone could live in. They hadn't had a chance to choose good, which might be unfair for them, but that wasn't my problem.

The demon lifted his hunting knife, trying to grandstand. He was more scared than I'd realized.

Good.

Their deaths deserved to feel as terrible as those of all

the people they'd tortured. I rushed him, not bothering to use my wings for cover. When he swung the knife at my chest, I caught his wrist and curved my wing, removing his head.

I waited for a second, letting the demon planning to attack me from behind come closer. I didn't want to drag this out. I released the wrist and let the rest of the demon's shadowy form fall to the ground.

Maliciousness slammed into me, informing me that the demon was close. I didn't understand how it thought it could reach me undetected. I spun, flapping once to maintain my placement, and then my wings instinctively slashed at the demon behind me.

I missed his neck by an inch and sliced the top of his chest. Blood poured like a brilliant blue waterfall, and he jerked back as if that would save him from his inevitable fate. I finished the job and didn't bother to watch him tumble.

Four demons were left now. Ronnie fought one, and I watched as Sterlyn killed another, which two wolves had pinned. Chad was lying on the ground, but I could hear his heart beating. His blood loss must have been getting to him. I could heal him, but I needed to help the others before I depleted my magic. His wound would be more difficult to heal than my superficial injury from earlier.

Sterlyn ran toward the demon closest to her, so I decided to help the wolves farther away. The wind blew through my hair and feathers as I sped toward them.

The largest silver wolf, Darrell, had a demon held down as the other two wolves flanked the enemy. The wolf on the right went to rip out the demon's throat, but moments before its teeth could connect, the demon threw Darrell off and swung his dagger into the chest of the other silver wolf, whose name I did not know.

A pain-stricken whimper left the wolf, and I reached them as the wolf stumbled back. The demon chuckled maliciously, and I jerked to the side, killing him way too quickly. He'd deserved to die painfully and slowly.

Blood poured from the silver wolf's mouth as he crumpled. I landed beside him, channeling my magic. That process, normally so simple, was still hindered by my prior exertion, but I pushed through the discomfort.

My hands glowed as the wolf's heart stopped beating.

No! This couldn't happen. I couldn't allow another silver wolf to die. I couldn't fail my mother again.

I yanked the dagger out of his chest and dropped it quickly, the cold flames affecting my magic again. I rolled the wolf over as Darrell and another silver wolf I didn't know ran to his side. I placed my hands on his chest, hoping to the gods I wasn't too late.

My magic flowed into him, but his heart didn't start. I kept pushing, and something warm and wet slid down my cheek. Ignoring the strange occurrence, I focused everything on the wolf I was determined to save.

CHAPTER SEVEN

I FUNNELED MORE magic into the wolf's body, but after a few seconds, I exhaled slowly. Normally, when I healed a supernatural being, I felt their magic mix with mine, but I didn't feel any reciprocation this time. I pushed a little more, thinking he just needed a boost, but nothing happened.

I was too late. His heart was too damaged, and he'd died before I reached him.

I wanted to keep pushing, hoping for a miracle, but I had to keep my head on straight. One benefit of being an angel was sensing when you might become irrational and forcing yourself to calm down.

There was someone I could still help—Chad.

His blood loss was serious, so I needed to hurry. He would die if I continued trying to revive someone beyond saving. This wolf's soul had already left his body; he had no magical essence to which I could connect.

Confirming my suspicion, Darrell threw his head

back and howled. The other wolves followed suit, mourning the loss of their brother.

This wolf's pack link had gone cold.

Footsteps hurried toward me, and when Sterlyn reached my side, she touched my arm and murmured, "He's gone."

"I know." I withdrew my magic as I lifted my hands from the silver wolf's body. I didn't know this pack member, but that didn't matter. He was my family, a descendent of my uncle Ophaniel, the father of the silver wolves—the race I'd sworn to protect in his name.

The discomfort of losing someone swirled inside me, and I took a moment to wipe my cheek. Moisture covered my finger, and I looked skyward, expecting to see rain. However, the sun was still out, and the sky was cloudless.

How peculiar.

It must have been sweat, though I didn't feel particularly overheated.

As I stood, Sterlyn's hand dropped from my shoulder. She followed me to Chad. His heartbeat was faint, and his breathing had slowed. The demon must have cut deeper than I'd realized, and if I didn't heal him soon, we would have two silver wolves to mourn.

"Can you save him?" Her voice cracked with emotion.

Her question was a slap to my ego, but after I'd failed to save their packmate, it was legitimate.

"Yes. The other wolf was dead before I reached him," I explained as I knelt beside Chad. "His heart is still beating."

His eyes fluttered, but he wasn't aware enough to keep them open. I had to move quickly. I tapped into my magic and realized it was over halfway drained. Healing Chad would be difficult, but I should be able to stabilize him enough that he could walk.

My hands glowed as I touched the slash on his neck. His warm blood squished under my fingers, and the metallic scent assaulted my nose. Though I'd rather not touch the wound, it would heal more rapidly and with less magic if I did, and I needed every bit of help I could get.

I closed my eyes and pushed my essence into him.

My magic recognized Chad's, its warmth trickling with his familiar but different essence as his magic recognized mine in return. My warmth fused with his, and they danced in unison. His wolf side surged through and began to heal as well. Something akin to a faint howl echoed in my head.

The skin closed underneath my hands, and dizziness overcame me. Being nearly drained of my power was physically and mentally exhausting. Two things would help recharge me—rest and being under the Heaven-like lights that only the Shadow City dome generated here on Earth. Rest alone could do it, but the lights provided an extra boost.

Determination fueled me, and I forced my eyes open. They wanted to close from my heavy fatigue, but I needed Chad to rouse before I stopped. That was the only way I'd know that I'd done enough for him to stand on his own.

My head grew heavy as I continued to push my rapidly depleting magic into him. The warmth that usually centered me was lukewarm at best.

"Rosemary," Sterlyn said with alarm, "are you okay? It's taking longer than normal."

It was taking longer because I'd tried so hard to heal the first wolf. *I'll be fine once I recharge* was what I wanted to say, but my mouth couldn't form the words. A pack link or telepathic bond would have come in handy.

Chad's breathing strengthened, and he groaned. It sounded like music to my ears because I couldn't have gone on much longer. If his throat had still been cut, the noise wouldn't have been as clear.

My magic stopped flowing of its own accord. The only other time I'd felt this close to depleted was when we'd rescued Annie, Cyrus, Mila, Chad, Theo, and Rudie from the demon pack neighborhood. Two of the younger witches from Eliza's coven had gone with us, and though they were powerful, their magic had drained quickly. We'd figured out that I could *heal* their magic while they used it, letting them siphon my essence from me. Because of that, we'd escaped, but freedom had come at a heavy price. I could barely walk or fly for an entire night, which was close to how I felt now.

At least we were no longer under attack, though more demons could come at any second.

My body listed to the side, and Sterlyn wrapped an arm around me. "Rosemary!" she exclaimed.

"Shh," I hissed. "Demons. Tired." My head lay

against her side, and even though it was awkward, I didn't have the energy to lift it.

She must have figured that out because she sighed. "You're too stubborn for your own good. You didn't have to heal him completely, just enough to get him home."

We already had to carry one wolf away, and it would be excruciating for them all. Having to carry a second wolf would have made it that much harder on all of us, and I wouldn't have been in a much better position than I was in now.

Chad stirred beside me, and I opened my eyes long enough to see him stand on all four legs. His smoky topaz eyes were darker than normal, confirming that I hadn't healed him completely, but his heartbeat was strong, and his breathing was steady. The only visible sign that he'd been injured was the dark crimson blood that coated his fur from his neck down to his chest.

Sterlyn helped me to my feet and laid me on something furry. When my hands brushed a warm, sticky surface and Chad's musky honeysuckle scent filled my nose, I realized the wolf was carrying me.

Under normal circumstances, I'd have refused to be carried like this and the silver wolves were about the same size and strength as a normal wolf, but I wouldn't complain about that now.

My eyes closed, and before I realized what was going on, I'd drifted off to sleep.

STRONG ARMS LIFTED ME, stirring me awake. I smelled Killian's musky sandalwood scent as he pulled me against his chest. I was still way too exhausted to do anything, meaning we couldn't have gone too far from our last fighting spot.

We must have reached the others, but I'd thought they'd be farther by now.

I opened my eyes to find Levi standing in front of Killian and me. A scowl marred his face as he held out his hands and said, "You look like you're struggling. Maybe someone else should carry her."

My heart pounded. He was a demon; I shouldn't want to be anywhere near him. I meant—I *didn't* want to be anywhere near him. Failing to save the silver wolf and then healing Chad had turned me illogical.

"*Hell*, no," Killian spat. "If you're implying you can carry her, that's not happening. You're not getting anywhere near her."

An arrogant chuckle escaped Levi. "I hate to inform you, mutt, but I'm pretty damn close to her as we speak."

"Then you'd better back the *fuck* away," Killian growled, his chest vibrating.

"Oh, my gods," Sierra whispered loudly, only pretending to want to be unheard. "I feel like we're watching a show."

Annie nodded. "It's like a paranormal TV show, but I'm surprised you feel that way since you grew up with all this."

"No!" Sierra groaned and smacked Annie's arm. "It's

like a romantic movie! Two boys fighting over a girl, and figures, it isn't me."

Her shenanigans were tiring me out even more, and I lay my head back on Killian's chest, wanting all this to go away.

"So...you want Killian to fight for your heart?" Ronnie snorted, giving the wolf shifter a taste of her own medicine.

"If it meant that a guy who looks like Levi would also be trying, I *could* be game," Sierra shot back without hesitation.

Heat flushed through my body, and the urge to smack her engulfed me. It was a damn good thing I couldn't stand on my own, or I'd have pummeled the mouthy blonde.

"That's enough," Killian snarled, and his chest muscles tensed, causing my head to become uncomfortable. "Move, *demon*, unless you're buying time so more of your buddies can show up."

"I'm trying to make sure that whoever carries her won't drop her," Levi retorted.

Alex cleared his throat. "We have a dead silver wolf who needs burying, and Killian is right—more demons could arrive at any second. I understand that everyone is concerned for Rosemary, but Killian's carried her before. I'm sure he'll handle the job just fine, and we don't trust you."

Silence descended, and I looked within me and noticed that some of my magic had recharged. I should be able to stand. "Put me down. I can walk." I didn't want any more drama, and I definitely didn't want Sierra to start talking again. Walking was the best way to eliminate all those things.

"I don't think that's wise," Sterlyn said. "You used a lot of your magic, and you're still pale."

"Almost the same shade as a bloodsucker." Concern laced Griffin's voice.

They wouldn't stop mothering me, so the best I could do was suck it up. If I insisted on walking, Killian would drive me crazy every few steps, asking if I was okay. Even though my magic was lukewarm again, my energy was still depleted. Anything could zap the sliver of strength away from me at any second.

Someone sighed loudly, and I wasn't sure who it was until Levi said, "Fine. Let's just go."

Killian began moving again. We all wanted to get out of these woods.

Being with the entire group had me feeling safe, more so than when I was with my own kind. Angels were narcissistic. Yes, we wanted to do things for the greater good...but in a way that benefited us and brought attention to ourselves. This group was nothing like that, and for once, I was surrounded by people who would support and protect me no matter the cost.

Levi's sweet peony smell surrounded me, informing me that he was nearby. That should have bothered me, but his scent was the final thing I needed to let down my guard and drift back to sleep.

I WOKE in a place I didn't recognize. The ceiling was low, and I was lying on a couch with a pillow under my head and a blanket over me. Underneath the cover my wings were wrapped around my body like a cocoon.

I sat up quickly and found Sierra on a loveseat next to me. She chuckled. "It's about time, Sleeping Beauty."

"Sleeping Beauty?" She said the oddest things sometimes.

I scanned the area to find us in a simply built home. The walls were painted a generic beige, and I could see the kitchen from my resting spot. Natural wood cabinetry hung on the walls over complementary gray stone countertops.

We must have been at the silver wolves' previous living quarters. I'd been here only once, when we'd come to save Cyrus and his kidnapped pack members. I'd never been inside the houses.

Sierra arched her brows. "The fairytale about the princess who pricked her finger on a spindle and fell asleep?"

Was she on wolfsbane? Because that clarified nothing for me. "I'm no princess. I'm a warrior, and I didn't prick my finger, so that's impossible."

Sierra hung her head and waved a hand. "You know what, forget it."

"Done." I was more than happy to oblige. "Where is everyone?" I kicked off the blanket and threw my legs over the side of the couch. My magic wasn't fully back to normal, but I was at half power. I could fly and walk.

Sierra crossed her arms and glared at me. "It wouldn't

kill you to be more chill. You wore yourself out again, and you had us all concerned."

This was one of those times I had to be careful about what I said. If I said the wrong thing, I'd hurt her feelings. Though she drove me insane, she was kind, and I didn't want to wound her. Her good energy radiated from within, revealing she was a very genuine person, too—just too flamboyant for my taste. "I didn't mean to worry anyone. I just needed to heal the silver wolves."

"I get that, but girl, sometimes I think *you* think we shifters value ourselves over you. We care just as much about you." Sierra's face softened. "You *are* one of us."

Not sure what to say, I remained silent. Hurt etched into her face.

I couldn't win. "I don't think that, but it's my *duty* to protect the silver wolves, and I want to protect my..." I paused, unsure what to call them. "Friends. If any of your lives are at stake, I will do my very best to save you."

Her face morphed into an expression I didn't understand until her eyes glistened, and I regretted saying what I had. I got super awkward when emotions were involved.

She placed a hand on her chest. "I think that's the nicest thing I've ever heard you—"

The front door opened, and my body relaxed. Sterlyn, Annie, and Ronnie entered the living room, their gazes landing on me.

Sterlyn hurried over and hugged me. "I'm glad you're okay."

"What do you guys need me to do?" I wanted to help

them get settled. "Do I need to guard the demon until the witches get here or help bury the wolf?"

Two more girls entered behind Sterlyn and Ronnie. Aurora smiled as she pushed her long, dark bronze hair over her shoulder. Her chestnut eyes focused on me. "The witches have been here for a little while."

"And we have the demon locked in a house." Lux's arctic blue eyes sparkled, contrasting with her wine-red hair.

They seemed happy to be here. Most of the coven stayed close to home, kept hidden by a cloaking spell, so maybe they were excited to get away. I wondered if they felt trapped, like many people living in Shadow City. "How long did I sleep?"

"Not long." Annie walked to the loveseat and sat next to Sierra. "Three hours at most. It's approaching six now. Aurora and Lux got here about thirty minutes ago, and most of the silver wolves went to the graveyard to bury their packmate."

For the past thousand years, the silver wolves had buried near the former pack neighborhood so they could pay that respect to their fallen member. It was risky, but I understood the need for tradition. It kept us grounded in times of turmoil. "Are they okay?"

"I don't think any of us are. One of our own has died, but the best way to honor the memory of our fallen is to continue on so their sacrifice isn't in vain." Sterlyn paused as her shoulders sagged. She was heartbroken, as any alpha would be. "Some headed back to Shadow Ridge already, but half stayed to keep guard until Aurora and Lux arrived. Now that they're here, we'll just need a handful of wolves close by."

There was no question that I would remain. I had to ensure the demon stayed put. If Azbogah found out about the portal issue and that more demons were getting close to Shadow City, he would have a fit. I had to resolve this issue on my own, and that required me here.

Sterlyn's eyes glowed as she spoke through her pack link. She frowned. Something was wrong.

"Did the demon escape already?" I asked, and hurried to the door.

CHAPTER EIGHT

OF COURSE the demon would find a way to get out of here. He'd wanted to know our location and numbers—that was why he'd played along. Thank the gods we hadn't taken him to Shadow Ridge.

"No, he hasn't escaped," Sterlyn replied as my hand touched the doorknob. Her tone of voice wasn't as confident as usual.

I paused and turned back to the room. I couldn't march over there without knowing the facts. Otherwise, I'd be playing into the demon's hands. "Then what's going on?"

Annie grimaced, informing me that Cyrus was likely talking to both of them through their pack link.

My lips pressed together as I tried to calm myself. If they didn't start talking, I'd take matters into my own hands and find out by other means.

"Are you going to share with the group?" Aurora

shifted her weight to one leg. "Because not all of us have people we can telepathically connect with."

For once, I was glad I wasn't stating the obvious. Apart from Aurora and Lux, every single person in this group could link with others except for me. It didn't bother me until moments like this when everyone but me knew what was going on.

Ronnie grimaced. "Yeah, sorry. It's just...we're not sure if Rosemary is up for it."

I tensed. "Up for what?"

"Levi is refusing to talk to anyone but *you*." Sterlyn sighed and examined me. "We're just not sure if you're—"

I straightened my shoulders. Times like these, when I realized they had no clue how much training I'd received, were humbling. I had limitations—we all did—but I could handle *him*. "I'm fine. Where is he?"

The three of them glanced at each other, and I nearly allowed the urge to find him myself to take over. I forced my body to relax. Today was the most I'd ever struggled with an upheaval in my emotions, but that ended now.

"I'll take you to him," Lux offered, and opened the front door. "We just came from there."

As long as I got to him, I didn't care who took me. "That's fine."

"I'll join you, too." Sterlyn headed toward us.

"Well, I'm exhausted." Annie yawned and stood from the love seat. "I'm going to climb into bed. It'll be nice sleeping here. This was our first home after Cyrus and I completed our bond."

I realized we were in Cyrus and Annie's house in the

second silver wolf neighborhood, the one established by his and Sterlyn's late uncle Bart. We were in the back area of the settlement, near the road where most of the houses were completed. My instinct said Levi would be kept in the middle, where he'd have the most chance of being caught if he tried to escape.

Ronnie placed her feet on the love seat. She laid her head on the armrest, wrinkled her nose, and groaned, "Eww. The cushion is warm from your butt."

"Hey!" Sierra plopped down where I'd been lying minutes ago. "She's pregnant. Be glad it's only warm. She could have left a smell behind, if you know what I mean."

I was clueless, but I knew better than to ask. Information I'd rather not know would be sure to follow because that was how Sierra worked.

Annie's mouth dropped. "I did *not* fart. Besides, we're all supernaturals. Everyone would've heard."

Sierra lifted a hand. "I don't know. Silent but deadly exists even in the supernatural world."

As expected, information I'd rather not know.

Shaking her head, Sterlyn chuckled. She found Sierra endearing, though sometimes, I questioned her judgment. Now was definitely one of those times.

Angels had manners, and we shied away from talking about bodily functions. This group tended to focus on them. "Can we go?" I asked.

If the demon wanted to talk to me, that meant he desired to play some sort of game. The arrogant man thought he was smarter than me, but I'd show him. My legs wanted to propel me forward, shoving past everyone to get to him, and the urge disconcerted me. He caused something inside me to want to lash out. It had to be a reaction to his nature.

"Let's." Lux chuckled and stepped through the door.

Outside, the sunset stole my breath, and not because of the pretty blues, pinks, and purples that filled the sky. The sky reinforced that I'd been out for hours, and it bothered me. I should always be aware of how much magic I exerted.

The neighborhood contained forty-eight houses in various stages of completion, built in eight rows of six. A makeshift road ran down the middle. Towering oak trees shielded much of the neighborhood from view so it wasn't easily visible from the sky. Solar panels adorned each roof, so they didn't need power lines. At the very back of the neighborhood was a large clearing where the shifters trained for battle.

Annie's home was the last house at the end of its row. Once through the front door, we turned right, heading toward the road, but after the second house, we took a left. The three of us surveyed our surroundings, looking for a threat. The demons would come for Levi eventually.

"He hasn't said a word since you passed out in Killian's arms." Sterlyn's jaw was set. "When Griffin told Alex you'd awakened, Levi informed them that if they wanted answers, the angel had to be present."

Some tension left my body as we walked up the steps to a house in the row past Annie's and in the middle of the three on this side of the road. "I take it all the houses surrounding him have someone in them, yes?"

"We have five silver wolves, in addition to our group, staying around him," Sterlyn murmured as she touched my arm, likely wanting to share the information with me while Levi couldn't overhear. "So yes, we have him surrounded."

I expected nothing less from her. "Good. The demons will come for him eventually. During training, we were taught they have an uncanny way of being a pain in the ass." I rarely cursed, only when it was fitting, and this was definitely a situation that required strong language. I looked at Lux. "What about the witches?"

She pouted. "I wish we could stay, but Circe wants Aurora and me back. Even though we're not too close to Shadow City, she's not comfortable. We'll be heading out soon. Aurora wanted to spend a few minutes with Annie and Ronnie before we left. They're the closest connection she has to Eliza now that she's gone."

"That's not true. Circe was Eliza's biological daughter. She's the closest blood kin to Eliza." I understood that Aurora was young, but she should've realized this.

Wrapping an arm around my shoulders, Sterlyn gave me a side hug and explained, "She didn't mean blood relative—she meant the two people who were closest to Eliza right before her death. I think that when she kidnapped my brother to save Aurora, Eliza changed fundamentally, and the coven was only beginning to realize her struggle with that decision. Ronnie and Annie grew up with the person Eliza had become."

Mortals made things more complicated than they

needed to be. "She was likely the same person, just desperate for redemption."

"That's true." Sterlyn dropped her arm and squeezed my hand. "But Annie and Ronnie knew her interests and her life developments from the past nineteen years. Circe wasn't privy to that."

Understanding washed over me. Sterlyn had a way of seeing things that guided me to others' perspectives. I'd never experienced that before, and I was grateful for it. Angels didn't inherently think that way. Twenty years was nothing to us, so we didn't dwell on spending that much time apart. This group had made me aware that mortals followed a sort of logic even when it appeared illogical. Every time I realized I'd judged them too quickly and they showed me the error of my ways, my stomach felt strange, and a lump formed at the back of my throat like it had now. "Things aren't quite the same for angels." I wanted them to understand why I'd said what I had.

"I know. You don't need to explain," she said kindly. "I was just hoping I could make you see things in her light."

I scratched the back of my neck and averted my gaze. "I do."

Lux smiled, making me fidget.

Needing a distraction, I hurried into the house. The tugging sensation that had been troubling me subsided, but that didn't lessen my concern about it.

The living room in this house was the same as the one in Annie and Cyrus's home, even down to the couch and loveseat. As usual, Killian was standing. In tense situations, he rarely sat. Instead, he hovered either in front of a window or close to a wall. Now, he was leaning against the wall beside the couch, near the hallway leading to the bedrooms and a guest bathroom. Blood stained his shirt, and my chest tightened. It had come from carrying me, and it was Chad's blood, not mine.

Levi was sprawled on the loveseat, looking at ease, but he couldn't fool me. His foot bounced by the edge of the couch, and his body had sagged to the point of seeming comical instead of relaxed.

Pushing off the wall, Killian shook his head. "You should be resting."

"Oh, yes, Rosey." Levi chuckled arrogantly. "The *wolf shifter* knows how angels work, and it's clear you can't make decisions for yourself."

My ears pounded, and my chest heaved. Who did this demon think he was?

Alex sat on one end of the couch, rubbing his temples. "Dear gods."

"That's not what I meant," Killian gritted out.

Levi beamed and waved an arm. "Then please, enlighten us."

Taking a deep, cleansing breath, I centered myself. This demon wanted to upset us. It would give him some control over the situation, and I refused to allow his plan to succeed.

A low growl came from Griffin, who sat on the opposite end of the couch from Alex. "You know she can leave as quickly as she came."

They were acting as if I weren't in the room, which was intolerable. "No one makes decisions for me. I'm my own person and capable of knowing what's best. These are my friends, who care, and I know exactly what they mean." My gaze settled on the sexy man. I needed him to hear the sincerity of my next words. "And I didn't come because you *asked*. I'm here because you're our enemy, and we need answers. I may have needed to recharge, but that *is not* a common occurrence, and I can kick your ass right now if you don't cooperate."

Lux wiggled her fingers in front of her face. "Let me know if you need my help to make him sing."

"How about making him walk around like a monkey?" Killian sneered. "It seems more fitting, and we wouldn't have our eardrums shattered."

"Monkeys are very intelligent, which, dare I say, is fitting." Levi winked at me as he buffed his fingernails against his chest. His attention went back to Killian. "I've heard that they occasionally throw their shit at people, and frankly, that sounds appealing right about now." He refocused on me. "Don't worry, love. I won't throw any at you."

That traitorous heat flushed through my body again. It still made no sense, especially given the conversation—er, I meant, given him *being a demon*.

"You're a jackass," Killian snarled as dark fur sprouted on his arms.

Levi grinned.

Sterlyn touched my arm and said, "Killian, can I talk to you outside for a minute?"

"What?" His head snapped in her direction. "Now?"

"It's really important." Her focus landed on Griffin, but she didn't speak out loud.

Griffin stood and smacked his best friend on the back. "Come on, man. Let's get some fresh air. We've been holed up in here for a while."

"And leave Rosemary alone with *him*? Alex can't see him in his ugly-ass shadow form." Killian crossed his arms.

I arched a brow at him, wanting him to feel my wrath. "I'm more than capable of handling myself. I've done it for quite some time."

"How long, exactly?" Levi asked, placing his hands behind his head.

The urge to kill him spiked inside me again. "*That* is none of *your* business."

His mouth formed an *O* as his mocha eyes lightened. "They don't know."

"Wait." Alex steepled his fingers. "Are you older than me?"

Yup, the demon was going to die. Not even slowly, like I'd imagined initially. The only acceptable death would be a quick one but as painful as I could make it.

"Let's go," Sterlyn said with something that sounded eerily like laughter breaking through. "Outside."

I wanted to march out there with them, but that would allow Levi to gloat way too much.

The two guys grumbled as they listened to Sterlyn. Even though she technically wasn't their alpha, she was stronger than them, and they both doted on her.

Strangely enough, Killian doted almost as much on me, and I wasn't sure why.

As the three of them exited, Alex's focus never left me. He grinned. "You *are* older than me, aren't you? Now that I think about it, you looked the same when I was a boy. I just never paid attention because I saw you only a handful of times. And Sierra harasses *me* about being old!"

And this was what I'd wanted to prevent. I glared at the vampire king. "If you say *one word*, I'll tell them what happened during Matthew's coronation."

Alex's already pale face lost more color. "You wouldn't."

"This is better than I imagined." Levi sat up on the loveseat and rubbed his hands together, enjoying the chaos he'd created.

"Oh, I would." Conviction laced my words.

"Fine!" Alex scoffed. "Keep your age a secret. At least I know you're older than me."

I smirked. He didn't want me to tell everyone I'd caught him drunk with his pants down, urinating off the royal vampires' mansion rooftop. I'd been flying over the vampire part of Shadow City to meet Mother at the capitol building, and seeing him was something I could never erase from my memory.

Determined to focus on important things, I glared at Levi. "What's going on in Hell?"

"Torture. Corruption." Levi had lifted two fingers and was adding a third.

That was stuff we already knew. "Fine. I'm leaving." I turned.

"They're scrambling over the spell that closed the portal," Levi hurriedly added, apparently desperate for me to stay.

At least he'd brought up what I wanted to ask about. "And if the portal is closed, how did you escape Hell?"

"Now, *that* is a secret for another day." He smiled, looking way too appealing.

Here was the game. He knew we wanted to know that, so he wouldn't share the information we desired. "Then what are you willing to share?"

"I know something that could intrigue you." His eyes tightened, and he leaned forward, as if he was going to tell me something that would change my world.

CHAPTER NINE

SOMETHING HEAVY SEEMED to land on my chest. He was baiting us. Luckily, Alex was relatively old and wise to political games, so his features remained neutral.

Lux was not.

"What do you mean?" Hope filled her voice, and I knew what she was thinking—maybe Eliza wasn't dead.

I needed her to lock it down. "He's baiting us."

We'd all seen Eliza's injury and the desperate look in her eyes as she'd been sucked into the portal. This was one time where emotions caused problems, and I relished that mine weren't as intense as hers.

"That must be where vampires inherited it from." Alex sat back in the seat and crossed his legs, looking regally powerful in a way only a few could pull off.

"Don't flatter him," I said. "Demons and vampires aren't the only ones to employ those tactics." Angels did as well.

Levi scowled, and some of his ease vanished as he

tensed. "I do know several things you would love to know. You know that, or I wouldn't be here right now."

"Or we're humoring you." A *yank* inside my chest urged me to get closer to him, but I kept my feet firmly planted. I would not allow some strange ailment to influence my decisions. Common sense would keep me centered. I forced the tension from my body, except for my feet. They weren't allowed to relax, or I'd be walking over to the enemy. "Using you as bait."

His jaw twitched. "I think it's a little of both."

In fairness, it was, so I couldn't rebut it. He'd smell the lie wafting from me, and I wouldn't be untruthful. I always strove to tell the truth, and I admired those who spoke it. Being truthful was hard, and only strong, righteous people embodied the truth.

The front door opened, and Sterlyn, Killian, and Griffin rejoined us. Killian's eyes were the color of dark chocolate, a sign that he was either upset or stressed. Given the situation, I'd bet the latter.

"What did we miss?" Griffin asked as he took his place on the couch. He threw an arm over the back and settled in, making it clear he had no plans to leave anytime soon.

Levi closed his eyes for a second as if their presence was *such* an inconvenience. When he opened them again, he glared at Killian. Those two had some sort of hateful relationship, even more so than Levi did with the rest of us. Something was tense between them, and I had no idea what it could be, nor did I care. I wanted answers, and Levi's extra loathing for Killian could help get him to spill his secrets.

Picking up on the vibe, Alex chuckled. "Supposedly, he knows something, but with the way he's been pretending, I doubt he has information we'll find relevant." The hint of a lie was missing since the assumption held merit. As of now, Levi hadn't given us anything to prove he was a worthwhile informant.

"I wouldn't be so confident." Levi crossed his arms and placed his feet back on the floor. "Out of everyone here, I would think you and your demonic mate would be the ones wanting this information."

My breath caught, and I had to make my lungs work. I had a feeling he would play off Alex and Ronnie's connection. Everyone knew how irrational mates could be when it came to their other half.

When Alex didn't react, some of my tension dropped.

Alex rolled his eyes. "Yeah, I'm sure. I think we're wasting our time."

"Maybe we should come back tomorrow." Sterlyn shrugged and yawned. "We have a lot to do, so if we can be more productive elsewhere, we should get on that. Let Levi have some time to himself while Killian and Rosemary do a perimeter check."

Hopefully, some of the silver wolves were already running the perimeter, but it wouldn't hurt to have an extra set of eyes. I could take to the sky and see more than they could on the ground.

"Rosemary would be more valuable out there than in

here," Killian agreed quickly.

If Levi wanted me here, I should eliminate my presence. Besides, he wasn't giving us anything. I should have turned and headed to the door, but my feet were glued to the floor. Even though I hadn't wanted them to move a few minutes ago because I'd almost walked over to Levi, I needed them to move now.

Something was wrong, but I didn't want to tell the others and worry them.

Alex glanced at me curiously. He stood and rolled his shoulders. "I should get moving and check in with my sister." Gwen, the vampire princess, oversaw the vampires' day-to-day needs while Alex and Ronnie worked on solving big-picture issues.

"You and Rosey might want to stay if you want this information," Levi cooed, despite his posture stiffening.

My feet felt like lead. I shuffled a few steps toward the door, hoping no one noticed my struggle. The farther away I got from Levi, the heavier my legs became. If this kept happening, I'd have to resort to flying out the damn door. "I need some fresh air." That had to be the issue. Between my magic depleting and the craziness of the day, I needed to fly and clear my head. Checking the perimeter would be a good opportunity to do just that.

"Me, too." Alex crossed the room.

As Alex approached me, Levi frowned. "Your mate is no longer hidden. Everyone knows about her."

Alex stopped in his tracks, playing right into the demon's hands.

Our pretend lackadaisical attitude would vanish if

the vampire king didn't get a handle on himself. Levi had hit where he knew it would hurt Alex, and there was nothing we could do to head it off.

"Oh, do I have your attention now?" Levi taunted.

I reached for Alex too late. The vampire blurred and hovered over the demon. "What do you mean?" he asked.

I rushed toward them, my feet growing lighter with every step. The *yank*ing in my chest pulled me toward something. Unfortunately, I was pretty sure that it was Levi, and it infuriated me. It had to be our angel sides recognizing each other. Maybe his demon nature was desperate to remember what it was like before he fell.

Alex's blue eyes laced with crimson, and his fangs descended as he transitioned to vampire. The smug grin on Levi's face was breathtakingly handsome, stirring my urge to kill him again.

Somehow, I stopped myself from crawling onto Levi's lap. Wait. Was I actually about to do that? Don't get me wrong, I had sexual urges that I fulfilled from time to time. Angels were good at scratching an itch now and then without getting attached. I was very selective about who I bedded, especially after Ingram. He'd been decent, but his ego was enormous. And worse, his attempt to kidnap Annie on behalf of a former wolf shifter council member, Ezra, as part of a wider conspiracy had reinforced my decision to call off our casual relationship. In a way, I should thanking Ezra for validating that decision.

But I'd almost mounted a demon in front of everyone here. I'd gone through a longer dry spell than normal, and it was affecting me more than I'd realized. When I got back to Shadow City, I'd have to remedy that problem before I did something from which I couldn't recover.

I took a deep breath, and Levi's alluring scent filled my nose. Maybe breathing wasn't smart. I opted to breathe through my mouth, which helped somewhat. "Alex, you're falling for his trick."

"I don't give a *fuck*," he rasped, and placed his hands around Levi's throat. "Tell me what you mean."

Torture was the worst way to get information from a demon. They enjoyed it when a person lost control—it gave them power over the individual. But there was no reasoning with Alex. He knew this, but he wanted to protect Ronnie, no matter the cost.

I sighed deeply. The situation was unsalvageable, and when I glanced at Killian for support, the alpha was grinning, enjoying Levi's precarious situation.

Sterlyn headed over to us as I growled, "We'll take you back to that clearing and hand you over to the demons ourselves if you don't start talking."

Levi's face paled.

Maybe there was something to his story after all. A physical reaction couldn't easily be faked, and his heart rate picked up from fear.

"Fine," he grunted. "If the vampire releases me."

Alex's chest heaved, and Sterlyn stepped up beside him, saying soothingly, "Let him go."

A few more seconds passed, and I was certain Alex had lost it, but he released his hold and warned, "If you don't tell us, we'll make good on Rosemary's threat. I need to know if my *wife* is in danger."

Rubbing his neck, Levi let his attention land on me. "One of the demons you fought a couple of weeks ago before the portal closed informed us of a strange demon who has a weapon with the magical essence of Wrath."

Moments before Ronnie had killed her demon father, we'd learned that her grandfather was Wrath, the strongest prince of Hell. I hadn't expected Wrath to hear about Ronnie so soon. I'd assumed he'd eventually learn of her existence, especially since she was immortal now, but I'd hoped it would be after everything had calmed down. I should've known better, especially where this group was concerned. Ever since I'd met them, one problem had piled up onto another, as if destiny had been waiting for this group to finally take care of things that had been centuries in the making. I'd never seen anything like this in my entire millennium of life.

"That doesn't have to mean anything," Griffin said slowly, conveying more than he realized.

Out of everyone here aside from Lux, he was the most untrained. I wanted to slap him, but he was improving...just not as quickly as I'd have liked.

"But it does." Levi dropped his hands into his lap, his eyes scanning my face. "When the demons realized there was another way out, Wrath sent someone in search of his son. That demon came back and told Wrath that a vampire had come looking for his son, asking for his help in eliminating a girl—a girl whose dagger fit the exact description of Wrath's blade, which had been lost on Earth."

A demon's blade allowed only someone of its maker's

bloodline to touch and activate it. It had to be someone strong enough to handle its magic. Ronnie had gained that strength once Alex had turned her.

"I...I don't understand," Lux stammered from behind me.

"A witch as young as you wouldn't." Levi's color returned. "Wrath realized this *girl* was something to him. He thinks he must have fathered a child he didn't know about, but regardless, he *knows* he has a family member on this plane who has his precious blade. He wants it returned."

At least Levi didn't understand Ronnie's relation to Wrath, but thinking she was Wrath's daughter was probably worse than knowing she was his granddaughter...or maybe not. Who knew how Wrath would feel if he learned she was a vampire-demon hybrid?

The possibility of Wrath knowing about Ronnie hadn't seriously crossed my mind, and that bothered me. Of course the demons could feel demonic energies on this plane. The dagger would've hit their radar. I could feel other angels' magical signatures, and that was why, when I'd met Sterlyn and Ronnie, they'd caught my eye. Granted, I hadn't felt as strong of a connection to Ronnie as I had to Sterlyn.

Alex was so tense, I wondered if he was breathing. Since he hadn't passed out, the answer was clear. Vampires needed oxygen because they weren't truly dead. They had a heartbeat, the same as anyone else. They just never aged physically after about twenty, similar to angels and demons. If someone was turned, their aging process stopped unless they were under twenty, and then their biology progressed similar to a born vampire's, thank the gods. We didn't need blood-thirsty small people running around.

"Maybe you aren't *completely* worthless," Killian grumbled.

"Thanks!" Levi said, ignoring the jab. "I aim to please in all ways."

My traitorous body warmed, making me squirm. I *did not* like feeling out of control, and this arrogant scoundrel was challenging me in ways I didn't want to be challenged. Nonetheless, I'd rise above.

I *always* did.

A snarl escaped Killian, and with the combination of my traitorous body, Levi's attention, and Killian's displeasure, I got myself to move. I headed to the door before anything else made me struggle again.

"Hey! Where are you going?" Levi called out. "I just shared information."

"Which means you won't share anything else today." I breezed past Lux and opened the door. "My presence is no longer required."

As I stepped through the doorway, my wings exploded from my back. I needed time alone before anyone asked questions. "I'm checking the perimeter," I said, and took to the sky, needing the freedom that only flying could bring.

I LANDED in front of Annie and Cyrus's house several minutes later. I'd needed a breather to clear my head and check for any threats, but we needed to discuss what we'd learned from Levi.

I entered the house and found Sterlyn, Killian, Griffin, Alex, and Lux already there. Annie and Cyrus were ensconced on the loveseat, and Ronnie and Aurora were sitting on the couch.

Cyrus had twigs in his hair, likely from running the perimeter while we'd talked to Levi.

"Everything okay out there?" Sterlyn asked.

"Nothing is amiss, and I flew a few miles past the silver wolves' perimeter." I folded my wings into my back, giving us more space in the already packed room. I hovered near the door, needing an easy escape. I didn't trust Levi, and I expected an attack at any moment. He might have come here just to see if Ronnie was the girl Wrath was after, and after seeing her fight with the dagger and Alex's reaction, he had all the confirmation he needed.

Ronnie scooted to the center of the couch and patted the end for Alex. "They just told us that Wrath knows about me."

I nodded. There was nothing else to add.

"He won't get near you," Alex vowed.

I wanted to inform him he couldn't promise that, but that was the irrational piece that came into play with them. I'd learned better than to correct them, or I'd come off as rude.

"Why does the sexy demon only want to talk to

Rosey, though?" Sierra pouted. "I would actually flirt back with him, and I'm unmated, too."

I despised that nickname, but I swallowed my complaint. That would only encourage her and Levi.

"Sierra, he's a pompous prick trying to get a reaction. It's bad enough that he's focused on her—he doesn't need to add you to the list." Killian ran a hand down his face. "I swear, if he doesn't let up, I'll kill him whether he has more information or not."

A knot formed in my chest, but I ignored it. "He wants to rile you up, and you're allowing it. And he's harassing me because he hates angels. We can't play into his hands."

Killian grimaced, but he didn't deny it. He'd become reliable like that.

"That's enough for tonight." Sterlyn headed toward the kitchen. "I say it's dinnertime."

Aurora hugged Ronnie and Annie. "Call us if you need anything."

Once the two witches left, the rest of the group acted like things were normal. I envied them because Levi's presence nagged at me. I'd do anything to forget he existed.

———

LATER THAT NIGHT, I tossed and turned in the unfamiliar master bedroom. I wished the bed was why I was struggling to sleep, but it wasn't. It had everything to do with the demon next door.

The *tug* in my chest increased in pressure, and before I comprehended what I was doing, I'd tossed off the covers and sat on the edge of the bed.

I hadn't stayed with the others at Annie and Cyrus's, wanting to be closer to the demon in case he tried anything. From this room, I had a view of the house where he was being held.

A breeze floated through the open window, carrying the cool, crisp scent of the fall night air. I walked to the window and leaned out, scanning the area to see if anyone was nearby. As expected, no one was out, and with the moon descending in the sky, I estimated it was close to two in the morning.

I slipped out the window, unable to stop myself. The urge to get closer to Levi overpowered me. I'd never experienced a loss of control like this before, and my blood ran cold.

Nothing had ever prepared me for this.

It had to be the urge to ensure the demon wasn't up to something. He couldn't be trusted. I was being prudent, that was all.

I moved slowly, not wanting to wake anyone. Shifters had excellent hearing, so even a slight misstep could alert someone. I'd rather they not be aware I was out here, although it wasn't as if I was doing anything wrong.

I tiptoed to the front door. Something within me urged me to open the door and go inside.

My hand was reaching for the doorknob when Levi's deep voice called out, "Rosey? I knew you'd come."

CHAPTER TEN

MY HAND PAUSED mere inches from the handle as alarm broke through my brain fog. How had he known I was here? I held my breath, preventing even my lungs from making noise.

"I know you're there, Rosey." Levi sighed, and something soft hit the other side of the door. It was likely his forehead or forearms.

I closed my eyes and centered myself. He was calling me that nickname to get a reaction from me, and sneaking over here in the middle of the night had informed him that he was on my mind. I wanted to pretend that I'd come for a safety check, but we both knew it went beyond that. For whatever reason, he had my hormones running wild, but I refused to fornicate with someone like *him*. I'd go find Ingram before I succumbed to his temptation.

I grimaced.

Okay, that was clearly untrue, but the fact remained that this...*thing* was off-limits.

My chest *yank*ed toward the door again, as if something inside me were trying to prove a point.

No.

This was *not* happening. I didn't act on impulse. I'd been that way for one thousand years, and I wouldn't let some sexy bottom-dweller change that. It had to be his sinful nature tempting me.

I would rise above. Like always.

I lifted my chin, despite no one being around. I needed to make a point to myself.

An alluring chuckle informed me he knew that I was out here, struggling. There was an edge behind his laugh, probably because he was trapped. Then he said, "I feel it, too. Whatever is brewing between us is strong, but we both know better."

He was right—I *knew* better, and it was stupid for me to be out here, drawn by this strange attraction. I needed to go back into the house and remember what was at stake.

I turned on my heel, making sure I remained quiet. I didn't want to confirm I'd ever been there.

With each step I took, the *tug* grew stronger, but I'd already let the strange sensation influence me more than it ever should have. This charade ended now.

"Good night, Rosey," Levi rasped, an odd tone in his voice. It reminded me of when someone was in pain. "I hope you sleep well."

I scurried back in through the window and jumped into bed as if someone might catch me. Even if they had, it wouldn't be a big deal. I was a grown angel, after all.

Pulling the covers over my body, I flopped onto my side and forced my eyes closed. But my thoughts continued to circle around the man next door, no matter what I did.

Two DAYS LATER, around midnight, I winged my way back from my second flight watch. I'd had to fly again because the urge to see Levi was becoming unbearable. My restlessness was getting worse, and I'd barely slept, no matter how hard I tried. Even though I'd broken down and stayed in one of Annie and Cyrus's extra beds, the pull had grown stronger. In some ways, putting more distance between Levi and me had made things worse, yet being close caused other problems. His presence taunted me and set me on edge.

I'd been flying more each day, forcing myself to stay away from him. I wasn't in the mood to deal with his games. When I'd seen him the next day after we arrived, he'd played more games instead of telling us anything worthwhile, so I'd cut my losses. He needed to learn that giving us answers was the only thing that would make me show up. I wouldn't succumb to whatever was brewing between us.

Ever.

That didn't keep him from my mind, though, and the only reprieve I had was the sky. As soon as my feet touched the ground, the strange urge to see him would overwhelm me. Sterlyn and the others were already commenting on how much I was gone.

Normally, I wasn't one to ignore issues. I addressed them head-on, but the only idea I had for getting more answers was to go back to Shadow City and talk to my mother. If I did that, I might have to tell her we'd closed the portal. She was already in a precarious situation in Shadow City, so the more I could shield her from, the better.

Azbogah had been rallying angels to support him and oppose her, hoping to eliminate her from the council. He was gaining momentum, but Mother was an archangel. It would take more than his measly supporters to take her down. However, the man was relentless, and he'd continue down this course until he was removed or he'd eliminated her. I was banking on his true colors finally being revealed and the council not being able to ignore the truth. I believed in karma, and he'd done enough terrible things that his reckoning was approaching.

Approaching the pack housing, I tried to slow my racing mind. The crushed tea leaf smell of fall filled my lungs, the scent crisper this close to the clouds.

However, not even that could ease my soul, especially with Sierra's constant teasing about how Killian and Levi acted around me and how often I'd been escaping. Each time, I brushed off the comments, saying I needed to keep an eye out since not everyone could see the demons, but the truth was I left more than necessary. I'd admit it if forced, but I was hoping it wouldn't come to that.

I scanned the two silver wolves running the perimeter below. Chad and Theo had guard duty tonight. A raccoon scurried by them several yards away, unfazed since they were in their animal form, while an owl flew underneath me, searching for food.

These were the moments that eased my ancient heart —nature in full effect, animals hunting and foraging as they were intended to do. Their lack of alarm was one sign I searched for when doing a flyover. When animals acted calm and in tune with nature, it signaled that all was safe in the area. Animals inherently felt when something wasn't right, like when there were wars or natural disasters. When they sensed impending danger, they scattered or fled the scene, leaving food and shelter behind. What good was all that if you weren't alive to use it?

I flew a little longer just to make sure all was well. I saw nothing alarming, but something felt off. My wings flapped harder, my body eager to get back to Levi. Even though I hadn't seen him in a day, it felt like weeks.

If these weird sensations heightened any more, I would be forced to do something. I'd either have to send him back to Hell with some sort of threat or message or kill him. I couldn't become like Sierra or the others, distracted by emotions. Then I wouldn't be as valuable to them.

The pack housing came into view, and a strange shiver tingled at the base of my neck. Something *wasn't* right, and the momentary peace I'd found disappeared as I spun around, searching for the source.

At first, my eyes didn't find anything. I flew higher so I could see farther away.

Under usual circumstances, when I had a feeling like this, something bad was about to happen, but with how unbalanced I'd become, it could be my magic sensing I was getting closer to Levi. Nothing was off the table.

A flock of birds scattered toward the sky about ten miles to the northeast, making a racket.

My attention was focused there when a faint malicious aura wafted toward me.

I wasn't close enough to see creatures on the ground near where the birds had fled. I'd have to fly out there, but I didn't want to leave this area yet. If demons were coming, I didn't need to foolishly run off alone and get attacked.

Maybe Annie was feeling something that would confirm my suspicions.

"Rosemary!" Sterlyn's worry-filled voice carried from the pack location. "We need you."

Something was definitely going down. I blinked, and in the dim starlight, I made out a few shadowy figures floating over the trees over twenty miles away, close to Sterlyn's pack home.

Their egress from Hell had to be close to that neighborhood. At least three times now, they'd come from that direction: the other day with the initial attack, then when their backup had come to save Levi, and now this. We had to figure out how they were escaping.

I flew toward Sterlyn, eager to discuss logistics.

I landed in the pack settlement, and everyone, including Annie, was standing in front of the house Levi was trapped in. All the silver wolves except Sterlyn and Cyrus were in wolf form. Annie, Killian, Sierra, and Griffin were in human form, too. Our group would want to talk the strategy through.

Cyrus had his arm wrapped around Annie, and Ronnie stood protectively on her foster sister's other side.

"Did you see anything?" Annie asked, her olive complexion paler than normal. "I'm assuming that's why you were flying."

Addressing her assumption would highlight that when I'd left, I hadn't felt anything off. "Yes, there are demons heading this way. I don't know the numbers because I came here to alert you. I'll get back up there and learn more."

Sierra bounced on her feet at the edge of the group next to Killian. "But they don't know about this location. They could be going somewhere else."

"That's not good. They could be planning an attack on anything—Shadow Ridge, Shadow City, or unsuspecting humans."

Sierra's fighting had improved, but she still grew nervous when a battle was impending and didn't strategize well. She'd been training with Killian's guards for the past few months. Protective of the women with whom he'd grown close, Killian had been against it at first, but when she'd kept putting herself into dangerous situations with the rest of us, he'd relented. She needed to be able to protect herself if she was going to wind up in peril anyway.

"Their appearance seems too convenient." Sterlyn nibbled on her bottom lip. "Maybe we missed a demon and it followed us here. We were preoccupied with Marven's death, Chad's injury"—she glanced at me —"your exhaustion, *and* Levi. We could have overlooked something."

My limbs stiffened. If this kept up, I'd become more muscular with the effort it took to breathe when I wasn't near Levi.

Sterlyn was right. A demon could have followed us without anyone noticing.

Killian's brows furrowed. "Rosemary, what's wrong?"

"Levi keeps bickering with us," I said. "It could be a distraction."

Griffin's teeth clenched. "Son of a bitch."

"We don't *know* that." Alex sighed and rubbed his temples. "It doesn't matter now. What's done is done. All we can do is prepare to fight."

Dwelling on past mistakes would only hinder us from our current objective: killing demons and hoping I could capture another to replace Levi. The scoundrel had me struggling too much. His death would make things easier on me.

"What's the plan?" Ronnie asked, her body flickering in and out as she transformed into a shadow.

"The rest of the silver wolves are on their way here," Cyrus answered, his eyes glowing in the darkness.

"That's another ten wolves. Maybe the demons won't expect that."

That was a good plan. "Have them park a mile or so away so we can surprise the demons when they come."

Sterlyn smirked. "Any surprise we can have on our side will be beneficial."

"Anything else?" Annie asked.

"Make sure they don't get Levi," Killian growled.

I was no longer needed, so I spread my wings. "I'll see if I can glean their numbers." Not waiting for a response, I rocketed into the air.

The wind blew through my hair as I raced more than a mile into the sky. What I saw stole my breath away. Ten demons were closing in, but their attention wasn't on the neighborhood—it was on the two silver wolves racing toward us.

There was no way the wolves could reach us before the demons caught them, so I hurtled toward them. Maybe they weren't coming for Levi but to take us out. We'd been so focused on making sure we didn't lose the demon who'd been taunting us with nebulous information that we hadn't considered the fallen coming to torture us.

That was their very nature.

I flew over Chad and Theo and landed in front of them just as the demons appeared. I wanted to make it clear that the wolves were under my protection—not that the demons would care.

One of the demons laughed maniacally, but I

couldn't make out which one; their mouths were all just shadows. I expanded my wings, wanting to intimidate.

The wolves had stopped retreating now that I was here. They wouldn't leave me behind to fight the demons alone, even if I told them to go. The silver wolves were born protectors and wouldn't leave someone who was clearly outnumbered. They'd be communicating with Sterlyn, though, and I was sure my friends were on their way.

"Have angels grown so foolishly confident?" The one in the center floated toward me, her head tilting as she removed a sword from her side. "They think one girl angel can take down ten demons."

I didn't respond, knowing my silence would irritate her more. Sometimes, even Sterlyn underestimated the power of silence. Being mouthy might anger them, but not bothering to waste oxygen on them spoke volumes, too.

The demon's red eyes glowed brighter as she charged at me.

Good. I preferred action over conversation, anyway.

The nine demons lined up in formation. They weren't here to play around but to kill.

I flipped my wings to the razor-sharp side and soared toward them, and only one of the demons paused. He was the weak link, so he'd be the first one I eliminated.

The one in front swung her sword at me, and I turned my body so the blade hit my wing. I slipped between two more demons and shot toward the one who had stayed behind.

His eyes widened, and he fumbled for his dagger. As he tried to draw it, I spun my body and sliced one wing clear through his neck.

The silver wolves' snarls informed me they had sprung into action. I moved to help them, but three demons jumped into my path. The one with the sword lifted it overhead and swung it downward, aiming for my skull.

I flipped over, placing my wings where my head had been a millisecond ago. The sword crashed into them, and my body slammed to the ground. My stomach, legs, and arms hit the earth, where fallen branches dug into my skin. The scrapes burned, but I'd take that pain over being sliced in half any day.

Someone fisted my hair and yanked my head upright while someone else straddled me from behind. The demon on my back stepped on my wings as she grabbed the section that connected to my back. The sulfuric cotton candy scent of the demon with the sword made me gag. My steel stomach churned. She twisted my head as the demon behind me yanked on my wings. Pain like I'd never felt before racked my body. I swallowed, refusing to show weakness. My hands were numb, and I couldn't move them from the force of impact.

I'd never been so vulnerable in my life, but I couldn't get her off my back.

She placed the sword at my throat and chuckled. "First, we're going to rip the wings from your body. Then I'm going to behead you like you did our brother there." She watched my face for a reaction.

My eyes blurred and burned. It had to be from the pain coursing through my body. Yet another new sensation built in my chest, and it began to quiver. I wouldn't give the *demon* what she searched for—the satisfaction of me begging for my life.

I stared into her eyes and waited for what came next. There was no one here to save me.

CHAPTER ELEVEN

MY STOMACH CLENCHED as I waited for pain and, ultimately, death. I prayed it would be quick despite the demon's desire to dominate me. If the wolves hadn't been close by, they would have slowly tortured me. However, they didn't have the luxury of time on their hands.

The blade bit into my skin, and something dripped from my eyes and rolled down my face.

Tears?

I didn't know I could cry, and I hated that *demons* had made me realize it was possible.

They weren't *worthy* of teaching me anything.

I supposed it was fitting for death. If I were going to feel emotions, it should be during the last moments of my life.

The demon's glowing red eyes squinted as she smiled, and a sour taste filled my mouth. She was enjoying this.

"Ah. Angel tears. I'd almost forgotten what they smelled like." She inhaled deeply.

Adrenaline pumped through my body, quelling some of the pain, and my hands stopped trembling. Determination to remove her smugness coursed through me. I decided to use one of Sterlyn's tactics. I didn't immediately strike but instead let the demon gloat.

Snarls sounded a few feet away as the silver wolves attacked. They were alive, and the only blood that filled the air was mine.

I flexed my wings, making the sharp spikes stand more erect.

"Damn it, Uglan. Speed this up. Her feathers are cutting through the soles of my shoes, and the other wolves are getting close," the demon on my back complained as her feet slackened slightly on my wings.

Uglan groaned as the red in her irises flared. "How sad that we have to cut this short." Her hands twisted my hair further. "The silver in her twilight-shaded eyes tells me I'm finally killing a fate-blessed warrior who's protecting my betrayers."

Coldness hit my stomach. A fate-blessed warrior was of angel descent, which meant she was accusing my people of causing them to fall. But I'd been told that the demons had fallen on their own.

The sword tip dug into my neck. I was running out of time, and I needed to concentrate on getting out of this alive. If I didn't act, I'd be dead in seconds.

It was literally now or never.

Striking out, I grabbed Uglan's hand and pulled the sword away. The sharp edge of the blade cut into my palm, but I pushed through the discomfort. The demon standing on my back lurched from the unexpected movement, but she used the base of my wings to support her weight, stretching the muscles in my back apart.

At least that could heal—a slit throat could not.

Paws pounded as the wolves raced toward us. Reinforcements were arriving.

"No!" Uglan growled, and jabbed the blade at my neck again. She yanked my hair, straining my neck even more. "Rip them out!"

The demon on my back yanked, and my muscles separated further. Bile inched up my throat from the immense pain.

I wasn't getting out of this.

They'd caught me when I was vulnerable and greatly outnumbered. There wasn't a damn thing I could do.

Something blurred at me, and the weight on my back vanished. Uglan's eyes narrowed as she shoved the sword against my neck, desperate for the kill.

I flapped my wings, grimacing as a sharp pain coursed through me. I managed to lift my torso enough to ease the tension on my head and punch Uglan in the stomach with one hand while pushing the sword away from my body with the other. She jerked to the side, ripping out some of my hair.

With my neck finally free, the pain was worth it.

My gaze flicked to the demon who had been on my back. Ronnie had beheaded her with her dagger, and she hovered over the body in shadow form.

She'd saved my life. If she hadn't arrived when she had, I would've been eliminated. I'd never been that close to death before, and I hoped never to experience it again.

Uglan hissed, and her irises brightened. She barreled toward me, swinging her sword.

I wrapped my wings around me, ignoring the searing pain in my back. They moved more slowly than usual, but just when I thought they couldn't get into position in time to save me, they somehow did.

Her sword bounced off, and my body vibrated from the impact. Normally, my feathers absorbed the energy, but not while my wings were damaged. I couldn't hold enough tension in them.

Between the agony and my shaking body, vomit forced its way into my mouth. I'd never thrown up before, but there was no denying I was about to. Acid burned the back of my throat, and I forced myself to swallow it. I didn't want the demon to know how her attack was affecting me.

Needing distance, I spread my dark charcoal feathers apart enough to look through them. Uglan raised her sword, ready to strike.

I wasn't sure how much longer I could hold out. My wing muscles lagged, and I needed to heal myself. I was in a dire situation.

People counted on me to save them. This was the complete opposite, and I didn't like the role reversal. I was a *freaking warrior*, for gods' sake.

Unwrapping my wings, I almost cried out in pain. My blood pumped harder.

As she swung at my head, I ducked, reduced to the mortal way of fighting. I'd been trained in combat on the ground and in the air. It was easier to fight with my wings since they were a part of me, but the pain of using them was unbearable.

The sword swooshed over my head, and I stood up straight and punched the hovering demon in the face. The blow sent her sailing into a large oak tree ten yards away, giving me a moment to regroup.

Three silver wolves charged into the clearing. They sprang into action as Sterlyn and Griffin ran in human form behind them. Until the other eleven silver wolves reached us, this was everyone who could see the demons in shadow form, apart from Annie.

I had a feeling that Annie had stayed at the house to keep an eye on Levi, probably with Killian and Sierra. The two of them were a liability since they couldn't see the demons in this form.

Alex blurred into the area and scanned for Ronnie. Though he couldn't see the demons, he could feel his mate. When his attention landed on me, his body stiffened. "Rosemary, are you okay?"

From his reaction, I assumed I looked as rough as I felt. My mahogany hair blew into my eyes, and I pushed it behind my shoulders. "I'll be fine." I didn't want anyone to worry about me.

Griffin growled, "How can we help?" He had a knife in each hand, ready to fight, but he stood there watching, not sure where to attack.

I understood that he and Alex hadn't wanted to be

left behind and needed to be close to their mates, but they couldn't help us if they couldn't see the enemy. "Could I have one of those knives?"

The demon floated toward me again, her gaze locked on me. Ronnie had killed two of the demons, while I had eliminated one. The five silver wolves and Ronnie were each fighting a demon, and Sterlyn stood by with her knife, ready to remove heads when the time came.

None of us could be attacked from behind without someone knowing.

Good.

"Yeah," Griffin replied, but it was too late for him to hand it to me.

Uglan swung her sword down like an ax, and I twirled to the side. The blade sailed past me and hit the ground, throwing grass and dirt into the air. I kicked her in the back, and she slammed into the earth.

I jumped onto her back and dug my heels into her. It was her turn to see how it felt. I would love to fist her hair or strangle her, but I knew better. She'd use the sword on me, and I was injured enough for one day.

She bucked underneath me, but I was prepared for that. She swung her arm so the sword would reach me, but it missed me by a foot. Soon, she'd try to smoke away. Shadows could do that when needed, so I had to finish her quickly.

I kicked her in the head, forcing her face into the ground, and yelled, "I need that knife!"

"On it!" Sterlyn yelled, and ran toward me. She was

closer to me than anyone else. Her eyes glowed as she communicated with Griffin.

"Alex, come on, man," Griffin said, and pointed toward the closest silver wolves. "They need our help."

They could help when the wolves needed them to chop off the demons' heads.

Sterlyn ran to me right as my foot hit the ground. Uglan had turned into a smoke-like shadow with no head or feet. She was just a large blob rising in front of me. The one good thing was that she couldn't attack us, but the bad part was that we didn't know where her head was to remove it.

Sterlyn appeared beside me, her chest heaving as she stared at the mass. "That still freaks me out when I see them do that."

It unsettled me too, especially since I'd only seen Ronnie do it once before. When we'd learned that demons had come to Shadow Ridge and Shadow Terrace to find Ronnie, we'd started training again on how to fight them. "Yeah, I'd rather they stay in shadow form."

"Aw." Sterlyn smirked. "She's scared and trying desperately not to die, since we can't see her head as easily. I don't blame her—"

"Foolish mutt!" Uglan growled, morphing back into her shadow form. "I'm not scared of anything."

Sterlyn had goaded her, and she'd fallen for it. I was surprised by how effective that strategy proved to be time after time. It highlighted how inflated egos got in the way of success, and I strove to remain grounded in my abilities. Tonight had alerted me that I'd become overconfident. There was nothing like almost having your wings ripped out and your throat slit to put that into perspective.

Even warriors had weaknesses, and it was humbling.

Uglan surged toward us, her target Sterlyn.

Sterlyn lifted her trusty knife and spread her feet shoulder-width apart. She'd expected the demon to attack her.

Then it dawned on me—she had made herself bait to protect me.

Something strange shifted in my chest, a warmth I'd never experienced before. Sterlyn would protect anyone, but this was the first time she'd actively protected *me*. The angels I trained with would have my back, but they wouldn't purposely make themselves a target.

No wonder we were so close. We'd all done this for one another.

I tensed, ready to use my wings, the pain of my injured muscles stinging hot. We needed to end this and get back to Levi and the others. This could be the first wave with a second one following close behind.

The others must have been safe, or some of the silver wolves would have been rushing back to Annie and Cyrus. I didn't feel any additional maliciousness. The demons here were the only negative energies I felt.

As the demon used her sword to strike Sterlyn, I twisted, using my wings. My back felt like it was being ripped in half, but I powered through. I dodged Sterlyn's head and sliced the demon's throat. I had to push the feathers through the bone, which wasn't normal. Usually, they cut through easily, but I was too injured.

My wing went halfway through before I couldn't push it any longer. In pain, the demon dropped her sword. She grabbed my feathers, despite them cutting into her hands, and shoved me away.

Agony speared me from neck to waist. Though I didn't want to, I'd have to use energy to heal myself, or I would be useless.

Sterlyn appeared beside the demon and finished the job. Uglan's head fell and rolled a few feet away. As blue blood poured down her body, it dropped to the ground.

"Heal yourself. I'll help the others," Sterlyn said, and ran off.

That proved how similarly we thought. Half the demons were dead. Alex and Griffin slashed the shadows the wolves were fighting. They weren't beheading them, but they were attacking where the wolves were focused, injuring the demons.

A silver wolf ripped the throat out of the demon Griffin and Alex were attacking together. Griffin focused on the wound and sliced right through its neck. He must have been able to see the blood pouring from the injury.

I tapped into my healing magic, hoping I wouldn't need to drain myself completely. I reached over my shoulder and touched the joint where my wings connected to my back. Once both hands were where the pain was the worst, I *pushed*.

The area around me lit up as warmth pooled inside me. After a few seconds, the pain ebbed to a tolerable level. I took slow, controlled breaths, needing to pace myself. I didn't want to overdo it and wear myself down.

My magic heated as it thrummed through my body. I watched as the rest of the demons were killed, and some of the tension within me released.

Once I felt only a slight discomfort, I pulled my magic back inside me. My energy was down to half its strength, and I needed to keep it for whatever lay ahead.

The silver wolves stood by as Ronnie materialized into her human form. Alex rushed over and took her in his arms. "I *hate* when you do that. I can't see if you're in trouble."

"You'd feel it if I were," she assured him, and kissed his lips quickly.

Sterlyn glanced at me, concern etched onto her face. "Are you okay?"

"I'm a lot better." I fluttered my wings, flipping my feathers to the smooth side. "But we need to get back. More demons will come. Are the other silver wolves here?"

"They're a mile out." Sterlyn surveyed our group for injuries. "They'll meet us at the pack hou—"

A loud *crash* sounded from the direction of the housing. Her eyes glowed as Killian, Cyrus, or both linked with her.

"Shit!" Griffin growled. "Killian said Levi escaped."

My stomach dropped. While we'd been distracted, a demon must have sneaked by us to free Levi.

There was no way that bastard was fleeing.

The *yank* in my chest was stronger than ever before,

leading me back toward the settlement. For the first time, I welcomed the feeling.

"I'll meet you there." I took off into the sky, barreling toward Levi. I had to track him down before he got too far.

CHAPTER TWELVE

MY HEART POUNDED in my ears, and my stomach fluttered. It had to be the result of my near-death experience and the demons having clearly outsmarted us.

The thought sat hard on my tummy.

I should've realized this attack was a distraction, but what could we have done—left Chad and Theo to die? That wouldn't have been acceptable, either. If faced with a choice between Levi breaking free or the silver wolves dying, I would choose to protect them.

They were family.

Ronnie's scent hit my nose as she reached my side.

With my head start, she shouldn't have been able to catch up. My hands clenched, and my rage added a little speed. Even the cool breeze didn't calm my blazing skin. I hadn't realized how affected I was about him being gone until now. "I don't see anything," I told her.

If Levi and the rescue demon were heading back to wherever they'd come from, then logic stated they would have to pass us. The disturbing fact was that these recent demons had been better trained for battle. Had they sneaked by us undetected...again?

The pack housing came into view, and I saw Cyrus and Annie running toward the tree line. My gaze followed, but I didn't see a thing. They must have been chasing Levi and the rescue demon, and the escapees were getting away. Although they'd lost their wings, demons could move quickly through the air.

Despite her demon wolf currently being stronger than the siler wolves due to the phase of the moon, Annie was struggling to keep up with her mate, I assumed it was due to her pregnancy. Though she still kept pace with the others.

Ronnie floated down to them ahead of me, and I didn't have pregnancy as an excuse. I'd allowed myself to be injured, and I had to face the consequences of not defeating my opponent.

"Babe, are you okay?" Cyrus stopped and examined his mate. His brows furrowed like he was unsure whether to keep moving to hopefully catch the enemy or slow down so his pregnant mate didn't exert herself too much.

Those pesky feelings were getting involved in his decision-making. This was why I was very thankful I could stay level-headed.

"I'm fine," she sighed.

Ronnie floated to them. "Rosemary and I will take it from here. Just stay with her and protect her and that baby."

Cyrus's body sagged as he exhaled. "Thank the gods. A demon went that way."

The statement was obvious, but I didn't bother to retort. That would either come off as rude, or catty like Sierra, and I definitely didn't want to chance the latter and draw comparisons to her.

"I'd sure hope so," Ronnie chuckled.

Not wanting to be left behind again, I blew past Ronnie, needing every second of a head start I could get. I flew higher into the sky. It was easier to fly over the trees instead of weaving through them.

As I reached the top of the cypresses, I scanned the skyline for the demon. He had to be blending in with the darkness, using his smoke-like shadow form.

"I see him," Ronnie murmured. Her eyes flicked to the right.

Up in the sky, hovering close to a low-hanging cloud, was the demon. As I'd suspected, he was in his smoke form, blending in. He already had time to his advantage, but he was close enough to distinguish. Even as he pretended to be a cloud, he quickened his pace. He was desperate to get away. Despite Ronnie's speed, she couldn't catch up to him.

I tried not to stare and alert him that we'd found him. He appeared to be alone, but I wasn't sure if it was Levi or whoever'd broken him out. Either way, they'd split up and created another distraction.

Something twinged inside me, and the urge to go back to the house where Levi was staying almost stole my breath. Maybe I could find a clue there. "I'm heading back to the pack housing unless you want me to stay," I told Ronnie. I didn't want to abandon her, but if she decided to follow the demon and try to find out where he was going—perhaps the portal—I couldn't keep up with her.

She nodded but gracefully didn't confirm the thoughts I'd had. "Good idea. Something isn't right." She raised her voice. "I'll keep looking around."

"Okay," I said at normal volume, then whispered, "Don't do anything stupid."

"I won't." Ronnie shrugged. "Let's hope I get something useful."

I scanned my surroundings. There was nothing else out here, and the animals were returning to their normal nighttime activities. The threat had passed, and it would be interesting to see if the demon headed back in the same direction he'd come from. "Fine, but let Alex know if you need me. Or just yell." I could hear her if she shouted loudly enough, but if she needed to be discreet, her mate bond was the way to go.

"Will do." She hovered, watching the demon.

The *yank* toward the house was more intense than ever. Even if I hadn't planned to go back, I couldn't have fought this sensation much longer.

Not wasting another second, I turned and flew toward the housing.

Like rubbing salt in a wound, Alex was already with Annie and Cyrus when I reached them again, with Sterlyn and the others breaking through the tree line into the clearing. I should've been back at the house before they reached this point.

"Where are you going?" Sterlyn asked as I flew past them.

"To the house Levi was staying in to look for clues." Unable to slow down, I pushed past them. Every cell in my body *tugged* me toward that house, and I had to understand why.

As I approached, I saw Killian and Sierra at the edge of the clearing, waiting for the silver wolves to come. But my attention homed in on the house Levi had escaped. At a glance, it appeared to be intact. The front door was open, likely from someone running inside to see if Levi was still there. However, the windows on one side were shattered.

The glass breaking was what we'd heard. The demon had knocked down the perimeter spell holding Levi within it. But how could they have possibly known there was a spell and how to undo it? Just another thing I didn't understand. I growled under my breath. I liked black and white with no gray, and lately, gray was everywhere I turned.

I landed near a broken window and glanced inside.

My chest throbbed, and I rubbed it to ease the discomfort. It figured these strange feelings would come at a time like this. Pushing the discomfort away, I slipped in through the window. Glass crunched under my shoes. The demon had broken it from the outside in.

Levi's sweet peony smell assaulted me, and my eyes burned. It was as if he were still here.

This entire situation was strange. Our connection and the way my mind always settled back on him was exhausting, so maybe his escape was a blessing, despite the fact we hadn't gotten as much information from him as I'd hoped.

I exhaled, allowing myself a moment to get things together.

"Aw, Rosey, don't worry." Levi chuckled from the doorway. "I didn't leave."

The pain in my chest ebbed as I yelped and spun toward him. "What are you *doing* here?" I fisted my hands, ready to fight. This had to be a trap, but all the silver wolves were here, and it would be harder for him to escape now.

That could be the point, but it didn't add up.

He leaned against the door frame and smirked sexily. "I told you. If I go back to Hell, they'll torture my father."

Every time he said that, I expected the stench of a lie to break through, but it never did. "I still don't understand why you care if they do. Don't you get off on torture?"

His jaw twitched as his demeanor slipped. He wrinkled his nose. "Not all demons like torture."

I laughed. What he'd said was preposterous. "That's the first time I've understood a joke."

I usually didn't pick up on jokes. I found them stupid and pointless, making all those rom-coms Sierra demanded we watch even more atrocious. I still didn't understand why mortals found bodily functions and sex so amusing. It was part of nature, and there was nothing funny about that.

Laughing felt foreign to me. My stomach shook, but not in a hurtful way, and I smiled involuntarily. Normally, angels plastered polite smiles on our faces when society dictated it as necessary so we didn't come off as aloof or out of touch with the world, but this felt comfortable.

"It's *not* a joke." Levi crossed his arms and scowled. "Not all demons are torture seekers, and some actually care about others."

My chest shook harder, and a strange sound bubbled from my throat. I covered my mouth with my hands.

Footsteps sounded outside the window, and Sierra asked with concern, "Rosemary? Are you okay?"

Lovely. I must have been louder than I realized. That was enough to end my laughter, and I turned just as she reached the window.

She said, "Are you chok—" Her mouth dropped when she saw Levi. "Wait! You're supposed to be gone."

"I'm having doubts about whether I *should* have stayed," he said, his tone oddly flat.

Sierra lifted her hands in front of her. "I don't understand what's going on here. Rosemary sounded as if she was *laughing*, which I'm pretty sure is impossible, and you're *here*. How is any of this happening?"

Of course, Killian appeared behind her. His irises darkened to that rich, dark chocolate color. "I thought you checked the house and he wasn't here."

"I did!" Sierra turned to him and dropped her hands. "He must have been in shadow form."

For once, I was on the same page as her. This moment was surreal, and my chest felt light, which wasn't rational.

"I was definitely *not* in shadow form." Levi arched a brow as his arrogant demeanor slipped back into place.

This was the Levi I'd come to understand in the limited time we'd spent together.

Sierra placed her hands on her hips. "Then how come I didn't see you?"

"Because I was in the bathroom." Levi drooped his hands back to his sides.

She mashed her lips together and tapped her lip. "Yeah, okay. I didn't check there."

"Why wouldn't you?" I had to remind myself she was still learning. She was *a lot* better than she used to be, but I still wanted to treat her like an angel. When an angel messed up, we were punished. Killian didn't work that way with his bleeding heart and all.

"It's a room I always refused to check at home." She grimaced. "I've seen things that can't be unseen when it comes to my brothers."

I had no clue what she meant, and I didn't want to ask. It probably came back to bodily functions.

I heard Sterlyn and the others approaching from outside.

"Well, surprise, I'm here." Levi wiggled his fingers.

Which brought up a good point. "*Why* are you here?" I demanded.

The front door opened, and the group filed inside. Alex and Ronnie appeared first, with Sterlyn, Griffin, Cyrus, and Annie behind them. They all stood in the entry hall.

Chad and Theo must have been meeting with the other silver wolves outside.

Pushing off the door frame, Levi placed his back to a wall where he could see everyone. Anyone would do that when surrounded by the enemy. I noted it and continued observing his actions.

"I thought you'd be happy that I'm still here." Levi shoved his hands into his jeans pockets. "I'm upset that you're complaining."

"I'm with Rosemary. It makes no sense." Killian narrowed his eyes at the demon.

Levi shrugged. "I told her why, but she doesn't believe me."

"Your father?" I had to give him credit for sticking to his story. "Please. You probably would enjoy inflicting pain on him yourself."

He blew out a breath. "There's no point in continuing this conversation. I *don't* want my father hurt, and I'm *sorry* if that contradicts your view of *all* demons."

My stomach roiled, and I wasn't sure why. The strange feelings had marginally improved over the last day, but now they were getting worse again. They magnified around *him*, and I didn't like it one bit.

"Though I agree with Rosemary, we have a more pressing matter at hand." Sterlyn sighed. "Our location has been compromised. We need to move before more demons come back for retaliation."

She was right, but I hated that he hadn't given us more information. He was hiding something. We could continue down this road, but we wouldn't get far. "Why did the demon leave without you?"

"He gave me an opportunity to escape because they want me back in Hell, but I chose not to take it. I'm invested in staying with you." He smiled sweetly.

"You stayed when you could have run and hidden anywhere else in the world?" Griffin tilted his head. "That's convenient."

"Your group has the princes of Hell and other powerful demons concerned. You've caused them significant problems and are worthy adversaries, more so than anyone else on Earth." Levi lifted his chin. "Of course I want to be close to you."

Alex waved a hand. "I agree. This is pointless. We need to determine our next steps."

"Maybe you should take me back to your pack," Levi suggested.

Killian became a statue, and Cyrus said, "Nice try, but not happening."

He'd suggested that on purpose. He knew we wouldn't take him there. So...why?

"Where else will we go?" Annie pursed her lips. "Those demons were close to the old pack neighborhood. Ronnie told me that's where the other one disappeared to."

"That's simple," Ronnie said, and took Alex's hand.

"You guys head over to Shadow Terrace. The southern houses by the woods, where Joshua and his friends used to live, are vacant. We can set you up there."

Joshua was one of Ronnie and Alex's trusted men. He'd helped Ronnie shortly after she'd transitioned into a vampire, and he'd been there the first time she'd changed into her demon form. Upset that Josh had helped her, rogue vampires who'd wanted Ronnie dead had set Josh's home on fire.

"Won't that cause problems?" Sierra asked.

For the longest time, vampires hadn't allowed other supernatural races into Shadow Terrace.

"No, because we've made it clear our allegiances lie with our family and friends." Alex waved his hand at this group.

"Then that settles it." Sterlyn nodded. "We'll just need to furnish the houses and get the witches to spell whichever house Levi is in."

I wasn't sure if this was the best plan, but without a better alternative, I kept my mouth shut.

"The houses are already furnished, but they haven't been occupied in forever. Let me call and get them cleaned up. It might take an hour, but we should be okay." Alex pulled out his phone and blurred away.

"We'll go pack, then," Annie said, and hesitated. "But I can stay here on watch."

"No, you all go." I crossed my arms and glared at the demon. "I'll stay here." After tonight, I wouldn't be leaving the scoundrel's side.

"Me, too!" Sierra raised her hand. "I'll even check the pot if necessary this time."

"The pot?" Levi's brows furrowed. For once, I wasn't alone in my confusion, although Alex occasionally joined me, too.

"Yeah, the bathroom." Sierra rolled her eyes. "And I thought Rosemary was bad."

"Whatever. We need to get moving." Killian stared at me. "Are you okay with that?"

He wanted to make sure I'd watch both Sierra and Levi. Great, I was turning into a warden. If I said no, I'd never hear the end of it from Sierra. "It's fine, as long as Sierra keeps her mouth shut."

Her jaw dropped. "Rude! That was rude."

"Sometimes, the truth hurts." Ronnie chuckled. "Don't hate her for stating the obvious."

Sierra followed them, complaining, but I was focused on the demon, tired of his confounding attitude.

"Oh, Rosey. You're trying to get me alone." He placed a hand over his heart and batted his eyelashes. "I knew it was only a matter of time before you confessed your love to me."

My chest warmed, and not from anger. No, this ended here, once and for all. I was done playing his game.

CHAPTER THIRTEEN

I SCOWLED AT LEVI, channeling every negative sensation I'd ever felt into my eyes. Though the emotions were muted, they were still there, and I needed to use every ounce of them since I often lost reason when I was near him. "That would *never* happen."

He winked as he leaned back against the door frame. Ogling me, he said, "I love the thrill of the chase."

This man—*no*, demon—was incorrigible, and worse, I didn't find it revolting. That realization had my blood pumping harder. He was attempting to distract me, and I wouldn't fall for it. I'd always prided myself on never losing focus, and I wouldn't let *him* change that. "I'm curious how the demon knew he needed to shatter the window to allow you to escape."

"Straight to the point, love. I enjoy a woman who knows what she wants." He bit his bottom lip.

My heart skipped a beat, and a grin spread across his face. He'd heard my physical reaction. I had to tamp it down, but I wasn't sure how, other than by controlling my breathing. That did calm my physical reactions, but it wouldn't eliminate them completely, especially if the other person was watching for them.

And this *demon* was.

I straightened my back, standing as tall as possible. "I don't care what you *enjoy*. I want you to stop deflecting and give us answers."

He rolled his eyes. "You're no fun, but at least you're gorgeous to look at."

"See. Deflecting." I inhaled sharply to keep my mind clear. "You said if we kept you around, you'd give us information. You've been here three days now, and you've only told us that the demons know about Ronnie. I'd say you aren't holding up your end of the deal."

He pushed off the door frame and strolled toward me. Glass crunched under his shoes until he stood directly in front of me. His irises darkened as they landed on my lips.

I licked them, wondering if he tasted sweet, like his scent.

"There are witches," he murmured.

My brain fogged over, and I struggled to understand what he was saying. "I know there are witches. We brought two here to spell you inside the house."

"I meant in Hell." He chuckled as he leaned closer, his scent making me dizzy. "We have the ones whose souls were tainted."

The swift change in conversation had my brain spinning. I took a step back, needing space, and my ass hit the window frame. I spread my wings to catch my balance just as Levi placed his hands on my waist, keeping me upright.

I'd never been clumsy. This proved how much he was messing with my head.

Letting him affect me this way was *unacceptable*. I was a trained warrior and shouldn't be coming unglued because the most annoying but sexiest man I'd ever seen before was paying me attention. He had to be aware of his effect on me and was using it to manipulate me.

That was what *demons* did.

"Whoa, there," Levi said, his attention flicking to my lips again. "Are you okay?"

My skin tingled where we touched, even through my cotton shirt. I'd never felt anything like it, and the sensation was all too appealing. I wondered what it would feel like if he touched my actual skin, but it was best I didn't find out. Allowing him to do this was bad enough. "I'm fine." I cleared my throat and stepped to the side, forcing his hands to drop.

Something inside me pulsed, urging me to step toward him.

No. That would *not* be happening.

"What's going on in here?" Sierra asked.

I tensed, and my face flushed hot. I hadn't heard her come back—that was how fixated I'd been on *him*. I was officially losing my mind, and Sierra would be the one to witness it. She already teased me about Levi and Killian, and this would only add to her arsenal.

I would salvage the situation the best way I knew

how. I lifted my chin. "Levi was telling me that there are demons in Hell."

"Demons?" Her gray eyes lightened almost to silver. "And this surprises you?"

Oh, shit. I wanted to hide my face. I couldn't believe he had me so flustered that I'd misspoken. This would result in her teasing me continuously. At this point, I *wanted* to tell her my true age so she'd focus on ridiculing me for that instead of this.

Levi smirked and mouthed, *I got you.*

He didn't need to *get* me. He'd been getting me enough. I needed him gone.

Turning to face Sierra, he grinned charismatically, and something burned in my chest.

How *dare* he look at her like that.

I rubbed my temples and tried to calm my breathing. For the first time ever, I understood what it felt like when two sides of myself fought each other. I'd never understood that expression before and thought mortals were just being melodramatic. But it was actually something that occurred, and I didn't like it.

Even with my emotions muted, they still overwhelmed *me.* And they were getting *stronger.* How was that possible?

This *demon* must have broken me.

And I refused to be broken.

"I was about to explain the hierarchy of Hell," Levi explained. "That not all demons are the same."

Yeah, right. He either believed his lies or had been spelled to hide them before he got here.

My heart sank. I hadn't considered that possibility until now. Of *course* there would be witches in Hell. Witches who practiced the magic of the damned would wind up there. Magic never vanished, so they must have figured out a way to channel it in that dimension.

Could everything he'd told me be a lie?

A shrill ring interrupted us, and it took me a second to realize it was my phone. My stomach sank. A call this late was never good.

My father's name flashed across the caller ID. It was almost two in the morning, and my parents were usually fast asleep.

Without hesitation, I answered. "What's wrong?"

"It's...your mother," Pahaliah said, voice cracking. "Something's happened."

"Is she hurt?" My chest constricted. I'd never heard my father sound like this before.

Levi stared at me, his brows furrowing. He took a small step toward me, but I countered his movement with a raised palm. If he touched me, I was afraid I'd crumble.

"She's fine now. We can explain everything once you get here." He sighed. "But we need you right away."

I shouldn't leave...but my mother needed me. She'd always been there for me, and I would never refuse to return the honor. "I'll be there shortly."

I'd moved to hang up the phone when father said loudly, "And Rosemary, be careful. It's not safe for us."

My body tingled with warning. The fact that he sounded different was alarming enough, but he'd never said anything like that before. Shadow City wasn't a *safe* place, per se. There was a lot of turmoil and underhand-edness every day; it was corrupt. But my family had always been safe because Mother was an archangel. Archangels were stronger than other angels, so no one dared fight us. My mother was one of the few archangels remaining on Earth, even though only a few people knew, and most of the ones who did were angels.

I stared at my phone as Sierra stepped fully into the room, her face lined with worry. "What can I do?"

These were the moments that made Sierra endearing. She truly cared, and times like these made her mouthi-ness more tolerable. "I need to talk to Sterlyn."

Even though I desperately wanted to leave, I couldn't. Not like this. If Levi morphed into his shadow form, Sierra wouldn't be able to see him, and the spell was down. He *could* leave.

"She's on her way," Sierra said as she placed a hand on my arm. "I linked with Killian as soon as I heard your dad say something happened to your mom."

Hearing my parents referred to as *mom* and *dad* sounded strange. Angels were formal when it came to names and relationships; I always thought of them as my mother and father or by their names. However, I didn't correct her. She was a shifter, and that was how they spoke about their families. "Thanks."

"Should I go with you?" Levi suggested, his body tensing slightly.

"I might be upset, but that doesn't mean I'm stupid." The mere suggestion was absurd, and if I flew into the city with him, it would cause panic.

Demons weren't allowed in Shadow City or the surrounding areas, just as angels weren't supposed to leave. There was only one exception that I was aware of, and that was when Alex's brother, Matthew—the former vampire king—had brought Ronnie's father to Shadow Terrace to kill her.

He shrugged. "What can I say? You look exhausted. I'd hate for you to go anywhere alone while you're upset."

"I'm fine." There was no way I'd take him there. His staying at the edge of Shadow Terrace was bad enough.

The front door opened, and Sterlyn strolled in with Griffin right behind. Her eyes met mine, and she said, "Go on. I'm here now."

That was all I needed. "Call me if you need me."

I flew out the window as fast as I could with my magic depleted. Part of me was desperate to get to Shadow City and find out what had happened to my mother, but another part didn't want to leave. That strange warring sensation came over me again, though I had no choice.

I always came through for those in my heart.

As I FLEW over Shadow Ridge toward Shadow City, I noted the surroundings. The whimsical town had a two-lane road that ran through its center, lined with brick shops and restaurants that flowed for several miles. Over the years, Killian's ancestors had adopted the role of protectors on this side of the river and had built up the town to make it blend with the rest of the modern world. These bordering towns had to work with humans and other outsiders to bring food and other essentials into Shadow City.

Despite shifters operating the town, humans visited regularly. Fall was the most popular tourist season and accounted for over fifty percent of the annual intake— something I knew from all the Shadow City council meetings I'd sat in on.

At this late hour, only a few people were on the streets. Most were college students out to party with their friends. I flew high enough in the sky that they likely wouldn't notice me, and if they did, they'd think I was a large bird.

Supernaturals were required to keep our existence secret. Though we were stronger than humans, they had sheer numbers on us, and even angels couldn't survive a nuclear blast.

As the large bridge that connected Shadow Ridge to Shadow City came into view, I began to fly closer to the ground. Once I reached the beginning of the bridge, humans would no longer be able to see me. The witches of Shadow City had created a cloaking spell to prevent any humans from seeing the bridge or the large, domed city in the middle of the river. They'd even created an illusion that the Tennessee River wasn't nearly as wide as it was, and a spell prevented boats from getting too close to the city, making any humans that approached not want to get anywhere near the towns or island to keep the illusion of size.

The bridge was gigantic. Sterlyn likened it to a famous bridge in California, with its immense towers that jutted high into the sky. Even I appreciated the graceful design.

The massive city walls came into view, standing well over one hundred stories high. The city's emblem, which my mother had created, was carved on the outer wall over and over again. It was a picture of the city's skyline with a huge paw print hovering between the two tallest skyscrapers. Mother had insisted on the paw print in honor of her brother, who had died, and the silver wolves who had escaped that brutal fate.

I flew lower toward the sturdy gate that opened into the city. The moment the guard wolves saw me, they turned the crank slowly, lifting the heavy wooden entry. The guards knew me, but even if they hadn't, all angels lived inside the city, so there was no question of whether I should be admitted—it was rather who should be let out. Though Sterlyn and Griffin were fighting to fully open the doors to Shadow City, so far, only a handful of people were approved to come and go—those with direct connections to the council, and students attending nearby Shadow Ridge University to learn about the modern world. Every angel who left knew they weren't allowed to go farther than Shadow Ridge and were expected to return to Shadow City every night.

When the gate was open high enough, I slipped inside. There was no point in making them raise it all the way like they had to when people arrived in cars. As I stepped into the city, the beautiful colors of the air swirled around me. Mother had informed me that this was how Heaven looked, and that the angels had brought a piece of home with them when they'd come to Earth.

My magic had already begun to replenish itself, something that the sparkling colors, as part of the magical heavenly atmosphere, made happen much more quickly.

A few night owls were out and about here, too. However, most bars and restaurants were closing up and sending everyone home, except for the vampire establishments.

It was hard to imagine that this city was over one thousand years old. The buildings looked modern and fresh. In the center of the skyline was one of my favorite structures, a large stucco-coated building with a huge dome of purple glass. The only thing that would've made me like the building more was if the purple had been burnt orange, but purple meant royal, which was what the angels aspired to be.

Able to move more quickly as my magic surged within me, I pushed ahead toward the back side of the city. Once past the section where the vampire and shifter parts met, I breezed over the sizable forest area that we maintained for the shifters, which separated the angels' section of the city from everyone else's. Soon, the large glass-covered condominiums that the angels called home came into view.

The construction was similar to Griffin and Sterlyn's condo building in the city. But while the wolves had been inspired by the angels' homes, our buildings were made of glass, even inside, to feel as close to the sky and Heaven as possible. Though the floors and ceilings were solid, the bedrooms and bathrooms boasted glass walls that frosted for privacy.

When I reached the residence I shared with my parents, a group of twenty angels was standing outside on the lawn. In the center, my mother and father were facing down Azbogah.

He glared down at my parents from his towering seven-foot height. He purposely spiked his caramel hair high and wore all black to make himself more intimidating. His midnight wings were fluffed out to appear as big as possible, and his soulless winter-gray eyes stared daggers at my mother.

As usual, my mother looked regal, despite displaying a weariness I'd never seen before. The blood-red lipstick on her full lips wasn't even smudged. Her amber hair was pulled back into a neat bun, and her forest green eyes, surrounded by long black eyelashes, gleamed with life. Her soul glowed with pure goodness, sticking out starkly among the others; that was how good she was. She didn't bother fluffing her dark feathers, not needing to give the illusion of control—she had it.

Father stood close to her, and he contrasted starkly with Azbogah. His white feathers looked radiant even in the darkness, and his butterscotch-blond hair could almost pass for white at times. His piercing sky blue eyes focused on me, and his shoulders relaxed.

What was most troubling was that lines had been clearly drawn. Eight angels stood behind my parents, while nine stood behind Azbogah.

The closest angel behind Azbogah turned to me, his familiar moss green eyes widening. His ivory skin was almost the same shade as Father's wings, and his usual self-absorbed aura was firmly in place.

Ingram. The angel who'd tried to kidnap Annie.

The female angel behind him was Eleanor. Her long, dark golden hair hit her lower back, and her dark blue eyes filled with hate as they locked with mine. She placed a hand on Ingram's shoulder almost possessively. She despised me, mainly because Mother had raised her. That was, until Mother had become pregnant with me, and then she'd found another family to take Eleanor in.

"She's finally here, Azbogah," Ingram said smugly. "I wonder where she's been."

"And this will further prove my point." Azbogah addressed the angels standing behind my parents. He turned to me and asked, "Where, precisely, have you been?"

I wanted to turn and fly away, since I was unsure of what had happened or what I should avoid saying. He had me exactly where he wanted me, and Father hadn't prepared me at all. I didn't know what to say, but I had to say *something*.

I took a deep breath, hoping I didn't make things worse.

CHAPTER FOURTEEN

GOING WITH MY GUT, I defaulted to what I thought everyone should do: tell the truth. Even when it was hard, I believed everyone should be accountable for their actions—including me.

"I was with my friends." Even though I was telling the truth, I didn't have to have loose lips. If they were to ask, say, "Are you harboring a demon?" then I would be honest. I just hoped they didn't ask.

"Friends," Ingram sneered, and fluttered his tawny brown feathers.

Azbogah turned and glared at the angel. "I'm the one leading the questioning, not you."

"Questioning?" Mother asked while remaining aloof. "I didn't realize I was on trial. If so, you're handling this inappropriately. If this is an inquisition at which a judgment will be formed, either all the angels or the Shadow City Council should be in attendance. We aren't a dictatorship anymore, don't you remember?"

I mashed my lips together to hide the smile that threatened to slip through. Azbogah thought he was above everything, and every angel feared putting him in his place—except my mother. Rumor had it that at one time, even she had been hesitant, but after Ophaniel's death, everything changed. In Heaven, Azbogah had been the angel of judgment, but when the sector of angels had come to Earth, we'd left our heavenly roles behind.

But change wasn't easy for anyone, especially angels who had lived for longer than humans could comprehend. When mortals said they were stuck in their ways, it always gave angels pause. Humans were clueless about what being truly inflexible was. Case in point, this situation.

A vein in Azbogah's neck bulged. "Are you saying you *should* be tried, Yelahiah?"

Father *tsk*ed. "That wasn't what she was saying."

I was unsure of what had occurred to cause this confrontation, especially in the middle of the night. The one constant was that Azbogah used every opportunity to make my parents look bad, especially my mother. She'd ended their relationship over a millennium ago after Ophaniel had died, having had enough of his rigid ways, and from what I'd been told, intense negative feelings had immediately replaced whatever positive emotions he might have had toward her. Azbogah had an ego, and being discarded clearly hadn't sat well with him.

Much like Ingram.

I cringed, still ashamed I'd had a casual relationship with him. It had meant more to him than me, but that was because he wanted to be affiliated in any capacity with an archangel. Angels didn't feel love in the same way other races did, so I knew he wasn't suffering from a broken heart but rather hurt pride. "If we're questioning motives," I said, "I find it very interesting that the angel who left Shadow City for the very first time to kidnap a demon wolf at the behest of a now-convicted former council member is the one supporting you the most."

Ingram scowled. "I was let off for that mistake and learned the error of my ways."

"She does have an *excellent* point." Mother's irises lightened. "Here you are, casting judgment on me for not wanting to persecute a misguided wolf shifter when you did the same thing with Ezra and Ingram. And Ezra's new home is prison."

A misguided wolf shifter. My mind raced at the possibilities. Something had happened that involved a wolf shifter, and Azbogah had probably orchestrated it to make Sterlyn and Griffin appear deficient as leaders *and* make Mother look like she protected the shifters more than her own people.

I was disappointed that I hadn't assumed that from the start. Azbogah was always doing something to discredit the wolf shifter council members and my mother. With Ezra's seat vacant, he was taking his attacks on their reputations up a notch, not wanting Griffin and Sterlyn to influence who took the open shifter seat.

Sterlyn had been talking to Cyrus, stating that the silver wolves were rejoining society and that he should take the spot, but he was focused on his pregnant mate and didn't want to make her more of a target. He was also focused on integrating the silver wolf pack into supernatural society.

My choice was Killian. That was a suggestion I would broach with them soon. To me, it made sense that the alpha of the pack that had protected the city for centuries had a say in matters.

Azbogah jerked his head in my direction. He scowled, likely regretting my arrival. "It would be better for you, little one, to stay out of this matter."

Little one.

Eleanor bared her teeth as if she were jealous. She shouldn't be.

Azbogah called me that on rare occasions, and I despised it. There had been times, especially when I was younger, that I'd noticed him watching me. *Not* in a sexually charged way, thank the gods, but with a strange, marked interest.

When young angels graduated from warrior training, we held a ceremony that every angel attended. There were only a handful of graduates every century, so the ceremony was a huge deal. After mine, Azbogah had made it a point to find me. He'd congratulated me and told me that he was proud.

It was the strangest moment of my life, and I had no idea why he'd done so. He was the man who had killed my uncle and taken every opportunity to make Mother look unfit to lead.

When I'd informed him that his kind words were not necessary and that he should say them to someone like

Ingram, who relished praise, he'd seemed unhappy. However, I'd made it clear that I neither needed nor wanted his validation.

I didn't want him to notice me *at all*. The fact that he hadn't fallen meant he *truly* thought he was doing something noble, but I wasn't sure what.

Realizing he'd pulled me aside, Mother had hurried over, but I'd already handled it. She'd raised me to not need anyone to save me, and she'd been an excellent teacher.

"This is my *home*, and you're accusing my mother of something, though I'm not sure what," I said. I wouldn't cower to him. Maybe I should. Standing up to him had made us targets. However, I was *tired* of hiding. Maybe Sterlyn, Annie, and Ronnie had rubbed off on me more than I'd realized. I didn't want to appease him, but rather, I wanted to stand strong. "Besides, you supported my presence."

His head jerked back, nostrils flaring. Again, I wasn't pulling punches. A few months before my graduation ceremony, he'd started advocating for me to attend council meetings as the next in line to my mother and father, who each had a seat. Azbogah didn't have any children, and when he'd gotten behind me, Mother had feared he was trying to sway me to his side. For better or worse, he was charismatic toward those he wanted as allies. But I knew where my allegiance stood—with the people of Earth.

Angels had been created to protect the souls of the innocent. The ones who did their best despite all the setbacks and their faults went to Heaven, and the angels who had come to Earth were here to guide them along the way, which had included helping the supernatural races build a haven for those in need. That had been the original intent for Shadow City, but Azbogah had single-handedly changed its purpose shortly after the angels' arrival, which had prevented us from following the destiny Fate had intended. He and Mother had been in a relationship for centuries, and despite not being an archangel, he'd been accepted—even by my mother—as the key decision-maker due to his experience with judgment.

Under his guidance, Shadow City became a city for the strong instead of the intended haven with angels as the rulers. Then Ophaniel had created the silver wolves with their pure, unbiased purpose, and they had helped the supernatural races rally together and stand up to Azbogah and the angels. That had resulted in Azbogah's revenge killing of Ophaniel for fathering the race that had taken down the angels' reign on Earth.

"That was before I realized your mother had turned soft and that you would follow right in her wings." The dark angel's jaw twitched. "You're as much of a liability as your parents are."

I lifted my chin. "For trying to do what's right?"

"When did your 'right' become what is best for *them*," he spat, gesturing to the shifter and vampire sides of the city, "and not for *us*? Yes, Ingram made a mistake and worked with Ezra, but he didn't understand what was at stake, and he's learned what happens when you work with a *wolf*."

"First of all, the silver wolves are part *angel*," Mother snapped, trying to divert his attention to her. She'd always shielded me from him, and for the longest time, I'd let her, but something was different inside me. I couldn't remain the silent ally I'd always been.

An angel behind Azbogah chuckled and murmured, "Abominations."

I scanned the group, and my gaze landed on Cael, one of the more attractive angels in Shadow City. His gunmetal-blue irises contrasted with his dark brown skin. He and Azbogah were best friends, so although I'd considered approaching him for a casual sexual encounter in the past, his alignment with the man who viewed my family as the enemy had stopped me.

Unlike the dark angel, Cael dressed down by angel standards, similar to me. He wore dark slacks and a gray polo shirt. Out of everyone here, my style was the most casual, which included jeans and T-shirts, a recent change I'd made when I began attending Shadow Ridge University. Part of what they taught us was how to blend in with the average human, and wardrobing was one of the tactics.

"What you *think* of them is irrelevant." Mother scoffed and rocked back on her heels, appearing at ease, but something was off with her. There was an undertone to her words, one I picked up on whenever she was concerned. She lifted a hand. "An archangel created the silver wolves, and they are tied to us. I don't understand why you harbor so much hate toward my brother's children. He didn't *mean* to create them. Fate intervened, and we *know* better than to go against her wishes when they are outlined by the Divine."

"Just because something *was* created doesn't mean it should have been," Azbogah countered. "And this proves I'm right to be concerned about your leadership on the council. You put the welfare of your brother's children before your own people." He puffed out his chest proudly.

If Annie were here, she'd say he was peacocking, a term I'd never understood until she'd shown me a video of a peacock fluffing its feathers. It was fitting, and though it hurt to admit, angels tended to do that.

Even me at times.

"That's not true, Azbogah, and you know it." Father ran a hand down his face.

Father was a truly kind man. Out of all the angels I'd ever met, he was the most human of us. He felt more emotions, understood them, and had more empathy. Still not at mortal levels, but more than the rest of us, and he *hated* controversy. I often wondered why he'd ever started dating Mother after she'd ended things with Azbogah. Azbogah was notorious for striking down his enemies, and by becoming her lover, Pahaliah had essentially challenged him. Then he'd gone a step further by accepting a seat on the council. He was the only other archangel in Shadow City, but he didn't rule with an iron fist. Rather, he truly believed we could live in peace with justice and love for all. His role in Heaven had been that of peacemaker, putting him at natural odds with Azbogah.

The only other archangels in existence were a handful who had stayed behind in Heaven, while the remaining five had fallen and lived in Hell.

"I *know* it?" Azbogah laughed maliciously. "She thwarts everything I attempt to accomplish for the betterment of angels! How can *you* stand beside her?"

Since angels weren't overly emotional, it was rare for one to choose a life partner as my mother and father had. Most angels didn't understand their relationship— including me—but unlike the others, I *respected* their choice. There was something appealing about having the same person to go home to, time and time again.

"Because she truly does what's right for everyone, and not only for us. Maybe that's something we should all start doing." Father took Mother's hand and literally stood beside her.

My chest warmed, and my throat dried.

What the *hell* was wrong with me? I blinked to clear my eyes, and I focused on the matter before me. "What happened?" Someone needed to fill me in, especially if I was going to be part of whatever came of this.

Ingram smirked and crossed his arms. "You'd know if you hadn't been too busy hanging out with others outside your own people."

He took every opportunity to make a snide comment. He and Azbogah were two of a kind. "Just because my friends and I kicked your feathery butt doesn't mean you should be jealous."

His face fell, and a few angels chuckled.

"I couldn't sleep tonight, so I went for a flight and decided to stop by the capitol building to do some work," Mother explained before Azbogah could jump in and tell his version of the story. "When I left to head back home, a group of wolf shifters attacked me."

That was eerily similar to what had happened when the council had forced Ronnie, still human at the time, to stay in Shadow City. We'd learned that Ezra had secretly organized an attack on Matthew, Azbogah, and Griffin outside the capitol building one day. In the aftermath of that fight, three vampires had attacked Ronnie, leading to Ezra storming into Griffin and Sterlyn's condo later that night to take her into custody and detain her in the name of keeping her "safe" at the city's artifact building, a location managed by non-wolf shifters.

"And *Ezra* is in jail." Azbogah glanced at each angel standing behind Mother and Father, then turned to his supporters. "Which proves that Ezra wasn't the only reason for the wolf shifters acting out and that the *silver wolf* and Griffin do not have control over the wolves, let alone all the shifters."

I wanted to roll my eyes. Sterlyn and Griffin should have been here. Azbogah was taking advantage of their absence. But what would they do? Annie, Cyrus, and their packs needed them, too, and if Hell was going crazy, that was more of a priority. It was what Sierra would call a "damned if you do, damned if you don't" situation.

It bothered me that I was beginning to understand

her sayings. My entire existence had stopped making any sense.

"This *isn't* the council." Mother gritted her teeth. "But we do need to leave now to meet with them."

My phone buzzed, and I pulled it from my pocket, irritated by the interruption.

When I saw the words, the world went dim.

CHAPTER FIFTEEN

NO. This couldn't be happening.

I'd known better than to leave and come here, but what else could I have done? Father had said they needed me, and clearly, they did. Had I not shown up, Azbogah would've leveraged that against Mother, since he'd found out I wasn't in the city.

I read Sterlyn's text, hoping the words were a mistake.

Darrell just linked with us. Levi escaped.

My heart hammered as everything around me faded into the background. My chest hurt, the pressure almost undoing me.

Before I could type out a response, my phone buzzed again.

The wolves are looking for him, but Ronnie, Alex, Griffin, and I are heading to

Shadow City for an emergency council meeting about the attack on your mother.

That was how distracted I'd become. I hadn't even processed that those four would be on their way here. Levi had probably used their exit as an opportunity to escape, but why hadn't he left earlier when the demon had shattered the spell's perimeter? Why wait until now?

Unfortunately, we couldn't do anything about it. Our hands were tied.

Levi had seemed adamant that he didn't want to go back to Hell, but maybe he didn't have anything else to share with us and had cut his losses. Either way, he was gone, and my chest panged with a ridiculous sort of pain. I should have been more pragmatic—that was my specialty.

Or rather, it had been before I met *him*.

We'd learned two important pieces of information from him: Wrath knew about Ronnie, and there were witches living in Hell, helping demons. That last fact wasn't surprising, but none of us had been to Hell, so we weren't sure how it worked. I'd never been to Heaven to understand it, either.

My parents had told me stories about the souls that lived there. Like Hell, Heaven was another dimension and resembled Earth. No one aged, and each person lived in their own personal version of Heaven. The climate and environment were whatever the person viewed as ideal, along with the house they lived in.

Angels could see the variations, and they also saw Heaven as it truly was: always daylight, with air made of colors like those here within the city's walls. The buildings were large and modern, almost identical to the ones in Shadow City, and all the souls lived in harmony.

"*Rosemary*," Mother said loudly, bringing my focus back to the present.

I scanned the area and realized the other angels were flying off. Only my parents and I remained behind.

"Yes," I replied automatically. I had to get my shit together. It was a *good* thing Levi was gone. Even if he went back to Hell, we hadn't shared anything with him that they didn't already know, other than Annie being pregnant. But he didn't know she was a *demon* wolf. She hadn't shifted since she'd become pregnant, not wanting to change forms while carrying a child. Pregnant shifters usually stayed in human form for the duration so they wouldn't stress their fetus.

Father tilted his head. "Are you okay?"

My breath caught. He'd never asked me that before. Whichever way I answered could be misconstrued as a lie, and I wouldn't allow the *demon* to force me to lie to my parents. So I changed the subject. "I'd be better if I knew what was going on," I murmured, low enough to be certain that only the two of them could hear me.

"Then let's fly together," Mother responded as she flapped her wings and rose from the ground. "We need to not dawdle."

The three of us took to the sky and headed toward the capitol building, Father on my left and Mother on my right. Azbogah flew ahead alone, rushing toward the building like an angel on a mission, likely to talk with

Erin and his other council allies. Their numbers were diminishing, which was why he wanted to choose who took over the empty shifter seat.

Though we were in a rush, we had the truth on our side, and the truth had a way of coming out—eventually.

The wind blew through my hair, and the flickers of colorful light in the night sky had me almost fully recharged. "What happened?"

Mother rubbed her hands together. "As I explained, I was coming out of the council building when a group of shifters attacked me. It was very odd—they apologized to me before beginning the assault."

"Apologized?" Things around here got stranger every day. I'd never heard of an apology before an attack. Had they been forced to attack my mother?

Father chuckled. "That's what I said."

"They said the attack was in retribution for the stolen artifacts." Mother pinched the bridge of her nose. This was the most worried I'd ever seen her.

My stomach soured. "What stolen artifacts?" I hadn't heard about that. The artifact building was heavily spelled, and the police force monitored it at *all* times. Ronnie had gotten her demon blade from the artifact building, but that was because her heritage had connected her to the blade. She hadn't meant to take it with her—it had magically appeared in her hand, and it continued to appear whenever she was under threat. "When did that happen? And why would they attack you?"

"No one has been alerted to it." Father's lips mashed into a line. "The shifters said they were walking past the building when they saw someone fly away. The back lock to the storage garage was broken, and one of *Yelahiah's* feathers was left next to it. They said they didn't trust the police force to handle it, since the majority of them are shifters and report through the ranks to Griffin and Sterlyn. They know Kira, who is in charge of the police force, is close with those two. Between that and how close Griffin and Sterlyn are to Rosemary, they didn't trust things would be handled impartially, so they took matters into their own hands."

My limbs grew heavy. "Whoever coordinated the attacks wants the police force to take inventory of the artifacts in the building." This day kept getting worse and worse. If the attack coordinator wanted the building to be searched, that meant something was missing. Azbogah must have weaseled Erin, the head of Shadow City's witch coven, into helping him remove some items. The coven was responsible for setting the spells to prevent thievery. I laughed bitterly, the sound rubbing my throat raw. "They'll find something missing. Then the police will inform the council."

"My thoughts precisely." Mother sighed as we flew over the oak trees of the lush makeshift forest below. "There's no telling what's been taken, or if anything even has been."

"Dear, you know *something* is missing." Pahaliah bit his bottom lip. "Otherwise, the attack on you wouldn't have happened. The break in and attack were rigged to get someone to look into the inventory with evidence planted that it was you."

Rigged. That described the situation perfectly. Azbogah had something up his sleeve, and he was setting the stage for his next move.

As we flew over downtown Shadow City, I saw the Shadow Ridge side of the gate opening. My friends were arriving, and Levi could be anywhere.

Somehow, I felt even more weighed down. I wasn't sure what state I'd be in once the council meeting was over. Every meeting left me feeling drained. With the members trying to outmaneuver one another, it was a constant game of chess.

The gigantic capitol building came into view. Its rectangular shape covered the entire block, and it had an imposing, cathedral-like dome on top. The only public parking in the entire city sat beside it in case any council members were coming in from one of the bordering towns, as Sterlyn, Griffin, Alex, and Ronnie often did.

As we approached the building, the three of us remained silent. We had to be careful of listening ears, especially with supernatural races that could hear things from miles away.

We landed, and Father opened the tall, sturdy hunter green door and led the way inside. I followed Mother into the building, stepping onto the marble floor. The entryway was huge and mostly empty but for a small coffee stand in one corner, which was closed since the time was approaching three in the morning. Too bad. I would have appreciated several shots of caffeine right now.

The yellow-stained walls were in desperate need of repainting. They'd been white once, but time had not been kind to them. Azbogah was under the impression that the aging coloration set the right tone for the council: devoted even over time.

No one chose to fight him on that. A battle over giving the place a makeover wasn't worth having, especially when there were so many more important things to challenge him on.

We strode to the hunter green doorway on the far side of the hall. When we stepped into the council meeting room, I wasn't surprised to find Erin, Breena, and Diana already there with Azbogah.

Gwen, the vampire princess, was there as well, but she was sitting at the very end of the table on the left side. Her crossed legs had caused the skirt of her black minidress to inch up her thighs, and her long, shapely limbs were further emphasized by her black stilettos. Her shoulder-length ivory hair was styled in messy waves like normal, and her cranberry lips were perfectly done. Brown eyeliner around her chestnut eyes completed her fiercely fabulous look.

The witches and Azbogah stood against the far wall behind the U-shaped table at the center of the room, the opening of the U facing the doorway.

Erin trailed one long black fingernail down Azbogah's chest, which looked comical given her almost two-foot shorter frame. She leaned toward him, her scarlet-streaked black hair falling over her shoulders and accentuating her large bosom. She was always angling for the dark angel's attention, and he obliged her to keep her favor.

"Desperation isn't a good look on anyone," I said. If she'd been a friend, I would've tried to word it more delicately, but none of my friends would ever act this pathetic. Maybe Erin needed to hear how everyone perceived her, because for a woman who was supposed to be strong, she sure drooled over an angel who didn't care about her a lot.

Diana's jaw dropped, and she gasped. "How *dare* you talk to our priestess like that?" She flipped her long maroon hair over her shoulder as her ebony eyes glared. The evilness of her soul almost rivaled Erin's.

I should've expected that reaction. Witches were mortal, after all, and even the ones who radiated evil didn't like hearing the truth. "I was trying to be helpful."

From beside Diana, Breena scoffed softly. Her coffee-shaded eyes darkened as the edges of her black-stained lips tipped upward. She had her waist-length, deep forest-brown hair pulled into a messy bun with pieces falling around her face. "They don't appreciate that."

Diana wrinkled her nose and rasped, "I don't understand how you're even my sister at times."

That was two of us. Breena radiated pureness, unlike Erin and Diana. Erin had raised the two girls after her sister, the coven's former priestess, had died many years ago. Her sister had wanted to change things, and following her untimely death—which had never been looked into—Erin had claimed the girls as her own. Breena had managed to keep her mother's pure soul, whereas Erin's baseness had tainted Diana. Now Diana and Erin tried to squash Breena's goodness.

Dropping her hand, Erin straightened her shoulders. "We still have time to fix her."

Fix her?

Something was seriously wrong with these people. However, according to council rules, we weren't to get involved with other supernaturals' affairs unless it threatened every race. In my mind, people with Erin's essence shouldn't be allowed to lead. Azbogah wasn't purely good, but he also wasn't as tainted as Erin—a fact I was still trying to wrap my head around.

"That sure sounds like something my late brother would say." Gwen smiled sweetly, revealing her sharp teeth. "We saw how things ended for him."

Erin's gaze settled on her as she ground out, "Are you threatening me?"

What was it with people getting upset every time they heard something they didn't like? It had been like that for centuries, but just because people didn't like facts didn't mean they shouldn't be said. This ridiculous attitude was why I had a hard time connecting with most mortals.

"If you feel like I was, maybe you need to do some soul searching." Gwen's irises lightened as if she'd told a joke.

Again, I felt like I was missing something, which wasn't all that unusual. If Erin did try to search for her soul, that could lead to other discussions I didn't want to be privy to.

The back door opened, and Sterlyn, Griffin, Ronnie, and Alex entered. We'd been waiting on them, but seeing them put me more on edge. Their faces were grim, likely because Levi had vanished. I wanted to ask questions, but now wasn't the time.

Sterlyn glanced at me, the purple irises of her eyes darker than normal. Usually, she was like Mother, composed in the face of an adversary, but something had her on edge, too, and I feared it was more than just Levi.

"Ahh...so the shifter representatives and their vampire groupies decided to join us," Azbogah said as he took the third seat from the left in the middle of the U.

"If by *groupies*, you mean vampire *king* and *queen*, you'd be correct," Alex said regally as he patted his sister on the shoulder and made his way to sit beside Azbogah. "Remember that if you want to be disrespectful, we can answer in return; however, all sides will be able to name-call."

"Why are we here, Azbogah?" Sterlyn asked as she marched to the other seat beside him. "It's the middle of the night."

"Oh, I'm *sorry*." Azbogah placed a hand over his heart and leaned toward her. "Is a shifter riot not important enough for an emergency council meeting to be called?"

Erin chuckled. "Maybe that's the problem. The leaders who are supposed to be controlling the shifters don't find their defiance all that important. Or *maybe* they coordinated the efforts."

"You two have to stop," Griffin said, standing beside me. "We would never condone something like that, and Yelahiah is someone we respect and admire."

Diana inhaled sharply. "Oh, so if it was one of the witches here or Azbogah being blamed for a potential security attack, that would be a different story."

"Don't blame us for your shortcomings," Ronnie murmured to me.

I glared at her, but she'd said it low enough that no one else had heard. If Azbogah had, he'd be addressing it.

She winked at me, but her eyes were still tight.

"That's not what I meant." Sterlyn spread her arms out. "We should be searching for the attackers, not coming here to talk about searching for them."

"I agree with that." Father headed toward his seat on the right arm of the table. When he reached the third chair, he pulled his wings inside his body and sat. "Every minute we're here makes it harder to find the culprits."

Azbogah lifted his chin. "Which is why Sterlyn and Griffin not living here permanently is an even *bigger* burden. Ezra may have been misguided, but he was here when it counted. They had to travel from outside the city with no backup representative inside, causing this delay."

Yet another "reason" Azbogah should have influence over the shifter replacement. This was more about grandstanding and wasting time than anything else.

"That's not fair." Sterlyn turned her face toward him.

"Kira is a shifter on the police force whom we trust as we trust the guards."

"You mean the *fox* shifter you *appointed* as head of the police force and leader of the fox shifter pack when that position should have gone to a male?" Azbogah smirked. "And if the artifact building was broken into—which seems likely—it happened under *her* watch."

Oh, dear gods. Of course he'd have arranged the break-in for that reason alone. This was more than just having a say in the new shifter appointee. This was about making every one of his opponents look incompetent. Maybe he was angling to replace all the people who weren't aligned with him.

Gwen's brows furrowed. "What does the artifact building have to do with anything?"

Clearly, not everyone had heard. Mother quickly retold the story, beating Azbogah to the chase again.

"Then we need to check the artifact building and ensure it has been broken into instead of wasting time here," Ronnie said.

"Kira's on her way there now," Griffin answered. "We called her en route."

Erin sashayed to her seat next to Sterlyn and placed her hands on the back of the chair. "I hope the building wasn't broken into and she had no idea that it happened."

"Well, during my time there, I saw the spells you put in place in the building." Ronnie smiled sweetly. "So if someone did get through, that would be a reflection on you as well."

That was true. I knew the coven spelled the warehouse-like building for security, but I'd never been beyond the lobby. Only the police force was allowed in, plus the witches when a spell needed to be recast.

"If that's true, then we'll find the culprit and deal with them immediately." Her gaze landed on Diana and Breena. "No matter who it is."

Her words hung in the air.

A *yank* in my chest nearly stole my breath away.

Levi. He was *here*.

My stomach turned cold. If Azbogah figured out that the demon was near, there was no telling what would happen.

"Rosemary, what's wrong?" Mother asked, her irises lightening.

All eyes turned to me.

I needed to leave, but I wasn't sure how to do it. However, with each second I hesitated, someone could find Levi—and Azbogah would finally get that control he so desperately craved.

CHAPTER SIXTEEN

I TOOK A SLOW, steadying breath. Just because I felt the *yank* didn't mean it was Levi. I'd been feeling strange for days, so it could be anything.

My heart picked up its pace, not listening to logic. Something inside me *knew* it was Levi. He had escaped, and he was still messing with my head.

Azbogah's face lined with concern. I grimaced. He was incapable of feeling anything for someone other than himself. I saw right through the façade he put on so others would think he cared.

I knew the real angel behind the mask.

"Rosemary?" Father echoed.

All eyes remained on me, and the council waited for my response.

"I'm feeling odd." That was the safest thing I could muster. I didn't want to lie, but I also didn't think Levi was *actually* here. There was no way he could be—the entire city was spelled and watched at all times. If anything unauthorized tried to get through, we'd all be alerted. I didn't need to create a problem where there wasn't one.

"What does that mean?" Erin asked. She leaned back in her seat and glanced at Azbogah. "I thought angels couldn't get sick."

His jaw twitched. "We can't."

I hadn't thought through what I was going to say. This demon kept causing problems for me even when he wasn't around. Anger burned in my chest.

"The only time angels feel off is when..." Mother trailed off.

I gasped. "I'm *not* pregnant!" I'd had a dry spell for the past six months, mainly due to my newfound friends. They kept me busy, and my sex life had taken a hit. However, that was for the best because my options were not of high caliber, anyway.

Father chuckled. "I'm not sure if I should be relieved or upset. You're almost one—"

"I get it," I cut him off. I'd never been this rude to my parents before, but I did *not* want any of my friends to learn my age.

Ronnie's emerald irises sparkled with interest. "How old are you?"

"I didn't—" Alex started, but I glared at him.

Most angels didn't care about sharing their age. The older we were, the more knowledgeable we became, in theory. However, most angels didn't have mortal friends who liked to nag a person to death. I'd rather remain mysterious than reveal my years to them. "If you will excuse me, I need to check on something."

Sterlyn tilted her head but said nothing. She knew something was off, and I couldn't communicate to her exactly what.

"Do you need someone to go with you?" Ronnie stood, ready to make her way to me.

I already felt crazy. The last thing I needed was someone else watching me devolve. My two sides were at war once more, and I couldn't ignore the urge to follow the *tug*. "No, I'm good." My feet moved toward the door of their own accord.

I was truly at the sensation's mercy. I needed to make sure Levi wasn't in Shadow City.

That would be disastrous.

Not waiting for anyone else to chime in, I hurried out the door, leaving bewildered faces behind. That might be for the best. The council was all about control and making sure things ran without a hitch, and I'd just blown that up.

I wasn't sure if I should be proud or ashamed, but it didn't matter. I had a mission to accomplish.

I was outside the capitol building within seconds, taking to the air and following the tug. Best case, I'd have a flight around the city without finding anything, but I knew that wouldn't be the outcome.

How was it possible for me to know that? Levi couldn't be in here; I had to be chasing a figment of my imagination. Apparently, I had to prove that to myself, or the sensation might never go away.

The moon had descended halfway to the horizon, informing me that it was close to four in the morning. The sun would rise in a couple of hours. Nocturnal supernaturals were still on the streets, but the city was at its most calm.

Sometimes, I got up before dawn to fly inside this city where I felt alone. Growing up in a place surrounded by walls made you feel trapped. That was why, when a few angels were offered the opportunity to attend Shadow Ridge University outside of the city, I'd been eager to go.

Most of my race didn't want to leave these walls, happy with being confined to a place that reminded them of home, but not me. Maybe if I'd lived in Heaven before, I'd feel different, but part of me had always been desperate to get out. And since I was a future council member, I'd had the first option to attend the school. Azbogah allowed only a handful of us to leave. I'd always suspected he kept the number so small due to the agreement the demons and angels had made more than a millennium ago, and that had been confirmed recently when Ronnie's demon dagger had made an appearance. The demon blade had been in the most secret compartment of the artifact building, away from the masses in the garage. I wondered what else was in there. If there was one dagger, could there be more?

Living in an enclosed city made for chaotic life, especially when you had nocturnal shifters like nighthawks, nightjars, hedgehogs, and panthers, as well as witches who enjoyed the benefits of the moon, plus half the vampire population, which preferred moonlight to the bright sky. It was rare that the city wasn't at constant odds.

Unsurprisingly, I found myself pulled toward the artifact building. After all the drama, maybe that was what had been tugging at me and not some imaginary connection with a *demon*.

I flew over the large skyscrapers, heading toward an area of the city that wasn't as heavily trafficked. The council had built the building close to the city wall so it could be approached from only three sides, not four. If anyone came this way, the police force grew wary and kept an eye on them.

About five hundred years ago, before the building was spelled, Azbogah's former comrade, the angel Jegudiel, had tried to break in. The guards had gotten wind of the plan and thwarted it, and Azbogah had made an example out of Jegudiel for betraying the angels and trying to steal artifacts that hadn't been his to take. He'd sentenced Jegudiel to solitude indefinitely, a harsh punishment for an immortal.

Noises came from not too far away, and I flapped my wings harder. I darted through the sky and soon came upon a group of shifters.

Kira's poppy-red hair shone like a beacon through the crowd of shifter men surrounding her. As I rushed toward her, the *pulling* sensation in my chest yanked harder. When a shifter suddenly got thrown about five feet away, my breathing halted, and my wings faltered. Quickly, I threw them out to slow my descent.

Kira wasn't strong enough to do that.

"Run for cover," a familiar, sexy voice commanded in his human form.

No, that wasn't right. He shouldn't have been here!

I could no longer deny that I'd felt Levi's presence and been drawn to him. I hadn't noticed before, but nothing malicious wafted off him, confusing me further. It *had* to be a spell.

Another shifter flew across the roadway and landed next to the first, who was getting to his feet. The unique, mesmerizing lime green eyes of the rising shifter informed me he was a black panther. I wondered if this could be the same panther who'd been part of the attack on Azbogah, Matthew, and Griffin at the capitol building months ago. He'd gotten away, and we'd never caught him.

I'd never seen Levi fight before, not even when my friends and I had attacked his allies—he'd stayed back. He was a force of nature. His moves were efficient and strong, and he had the other two shifters down before they could defend themselves.

These shifters weren't fighters. Assuming this was the same group that had attacked my mother, their apology to her and their lack of skills here strengthened my conviction that they were doing this against their will. Someone was holding something over them.

I landed next to Levi, but the four shifters had already taken off, running in opposite directions. I wanted to go after them and determine their identities, but Levi's presence in the city was the bigger issue.

More disturbing was that standing next to Levi felt *right*—like I was destined to be there—and that was equivalent of a cold shower. Being with a demon was never right, and I had to quit feeling this attraction to him.

My gaze settled on him as I rasped, "What the *hell* are you doing here?"

Kira called out, her voice shaky, "You know him?"

That was a loaded question. I spun to face her and found her normal golden complexion pale and her eyes a darker green than her emerald. She'd always been petite by shifter standards, despite foxes being smaller, on average, than many other shifter races, but right now, she looked downright tiny.

"Rosey and I go way back." Levi winked at me, but his body was tense, taking away some of his arrogance.

I wanted to correct him, but that would amuse him too much. I knew he wanted me to object, and that unsettled me. I shouldn't know him that well. "Are you okay?" I asked the fox shifter. The best tactic here was to deflect, and it wasn't hard, given how shaken up she was.

"Thanks to *him*," Kira said, glancing adoringly at Levi.

My hands clenched so hard that blood pooled under my nails. I didn't like the way she was looking at him, and I stepped slightly in front of him, blocking her view.

Levi chuckled, and my body warmed.

I had to tamp this down. Despite him being the

sexiest man I'd ever seen, admitting any kind of attraction to him would be disastrous, even if he could make me scream.

Somehow, I *knew* he could make me do way more than scream.

He touched my arm, and an electrifying buzz sprang between us. I nearly moaned, but I swallowed the noise down. He leaned into me, speaking low for only me to hear. "Love, you don't need to worry. I have eyes for only one woman here."

My breath caught, and black spots danced across my vision.

My reaction to him was *not* normal. I'd never experienced anything like it in my very long life, and I didn't understand what it meant.

Encouraged by my reaction, he placed his other hand on my lower back and murmured so close, his breath brushed my ear, "And that one woman is you."

Stomach fluttering, I forced myself to step from his grasp, though part of me screamed in protest. I didn't have time to get all feely around him. I shouldn't have been able to get feely in general, but that was *exactly* what was happening.

Kira took a few steps toward me. "Hey, are you okay?"

She'd just gotten attacked, and she was asking me if I was okay? My life had officially been altered, and it was all because of this man beside me.

I should've killed him before he had the chance to speak to us that day. Now I was becoming a silly, mortal-like person, and the symptoms were worsening the more I was around him.

"I should be asking you that." I needed to contact Sterlyn. "But we have a bigger issue." I pulled out my phone and typed a message to the silver wolf, telling her about the attack on Kira and Levi's presence here, and hit *Send*. She'd let Griffin know, too.

"Bigger than a woman being chased down by four men three times her size?" Levi stepped up beside me. He stood too close, our arms brushing.

The worst part was that I didn't have it in me to step away from him again. "They were probably the same shifters who attacked my mother this morning."

Levi's head snapped in my direction. "How is your mother?"

I wasn't sure how to process his concern. He had to be an excellent actor, even better than Azbogah, because had I not known his true nature, I would've believed him. "She's fine." I didn't want to tell him more than that. "How did you get in here?"

Kira scratched her head. "Isn't he an angel?"

"No, he's not. And he shouldn't be here." I glanced around at the empty roads. We had to get moving before someone saw him.

"Then what is he?" Kira squinted, and then her eyes widened.

She was a smart girl. I didn't want to say it out loud in case someone was close by, listening. The shifters who'd attacked her could have circled back.

A cell phone rang, and Kira pulled hers out of her pocket. "Hello?"

I could hear Sterlyn on the other end of the phone. "Are you okay?"

"Yes! Rosemary's *friend* saved me from four shifters who jumped me." Kira glanced around and waved for us to follow her. "It was so weird. They apologized as they attacked, but I didn't have time to pull out my gun."

"Did you recognize any of them?" Sterlyn's tone was tense.

Kira grimaced. "Yeah. It's some guys I went to school with. That's why I didn't even think they would attack me. We were friends."

"We'll address that when we meet up with you, but right now, can you tell me a good location to pick up Rosemary and her friend?"

Picking up her pace, Kira headed toward the city wall. "Behind the artifact building. I've got to get in there and check things out. I was heading that way when the attack happened."

"That sounds good. When you're done, can you meet Griffin and me at the condo?" Sterlyn asked.

I wasn't surprised by the request. Those two would need to stay in the city, especially as Kira knew the shifters involved. With this turmoil and the council down one shifter member, they didn't have another option.

"Yeah, see ya." Kira hung up and placed her phone back into her pocket. She glanced at me and shook her head. "You guys sure know how to attract trouble."

That was a fair assessment. "I won't disagree. My life

has grown more intense since I befriended Sterlyn and her crew."

"But what can you do when it's family, right?" Kira frowned, and I wondered if the stress of her new role was taking a toll.

"The wolf shifter is your *family*?" Levi ran a hand through his hair, his bicep bulging.

The fact I noticed anything of his bulging was a problem, but my eyes had a mind of their own and glanced at his crotch. It was easy to see what he was working with, which would bode well for him in the bedroom.

His gaze flicked to mine, and he snickered. "Like what you see?"

Not bothering to respond, I focused forward, remaining close to him in case he tried to escape again. He didn't need to know that I had, in fact, enjoyed the view, or that Sterlyn was a very distant relative. It was, frankly, none of his business.

The artifact building came into view. The structure was similar to any warehouse one would find outside these walls. There was an office in the lobby in front, but anything beyond the front area was spelled, and only a handful of authorized people were allowed inside.

"What's kept in this artifact building?" Levi placed his hands in his pockets, attempting to come off as lackadaisical.

He wouldn't get the answers he was looking for. No demon needed to know more than he already did. I snapped, "None of your business."

"Fine. Maybe Red will help me," Levi said, hurrying to catch up to Kira. "We were off to a good start."

The way he rushed to catch up to her and had given her a nickname made my blood boil, but I had no right to be upset. He was nothing to me, so I took deep breaths to keep my head on straight.

We reached the entrance, and Kira pointed at the back of the building. "I appreciate you saving me, but I can't take you in with me. This isn't a place for people to know about, especially anyone from outside our city. If you go around the back, there's a parking lot where you can wait undetected while I check things out."

"Thank you." I'd learned that mortals wanted to be told that you appreciated them. They couldn't just know it; they had to be *verbally* told.

Kira chuckled as she took off toward the front door. "Rosemary, you're full of surprises."

I wasn't sure if that was a compliment or an insult, but it didn't matter. Lately, I was even surprising myself.

As the two of us headed toward the back, I stayed close to Levi, refusing to let him escape again. He should never have gotten into the city, and I had so many questions, but I couldn't ask them, not here, not now. I didn't trust someone not to be listening. He hadn't used his shadow form, so maybe no one would realize he was a demon. He didn't have negative energy wafting off him, so maybe he could stay undetected like Ronnie.

"Hey, is your mother okay?" he asked again.

No. He didn't get to flirt with Kira and then act

concerned about my family. I wouldn't be manipulated. Not anymore.

I faced him, ready to end this game. He must have anticipated the move because he placed one hand on my hip and pulled me against him.

My head spun, and I *almost* fell for his act. However, this was part of his game. I'd have to beat him in his own war.

CHAPTER SEVENTEEN

EVERYTHING inside me screamed to stay in place. My hip buzzed where his hand touched it, flames of desire coursing through me. The sensation was painfully delicious.

The strong emotions both terrified me and made me feel...alive.

If this was a fraction of what Sterlyn, Ronnie, and Annie felt for their mates, no wonder they were always touching and never wanted to be apart. I felt bad about being so hard on Griffin whenever he complained about Sterlyn always being in danger.

Unable to stop myself, I licked my lips, and Levi's eyes homed in on my mouth as he inhaled sharply.

I wondered what it'd feel like if he kissed me. Would he taste the same as he smelled?

His head lowered toward mine, his breath fanning my face.

Spearmint filled my nose.

That was what he'd taste like, and the combination of peony and spearmint made my mouth water.

At least the attraction wasn't one-sided. If we just slept together, would we get past the sexual tension pulsing between us?

No. He was a demon, and I could never live with myself if I gave in to this temptation. A fling would be unacceptable, even if he *was* fetching.

His lips came within inches of mine. A gentle buzz wafted between us as he breathed, "Rosemary." The word *yank*ed hard, and I took a small step toward him, our chests now touching.

I almost moaned, but I caught it in time.

Somehow, I kept enough of my wits about me to not close the distance, but I was at the mercy of his touch. I'd never experienced something so mind-blowing before, and that included rough sex with all my past partners. My heart beat faster, and I placed my hand on his chest, but I couldn't bring myself to shove him away.

Instead, I clutched his shirt, desperately wanting more but terrified to take it.

When I didn't close the distance, he pulled back hesitantly. His eyes darkened with desire. "You're so damn gorgeous, Rosey," he rasped.

Rosey.

Red.

That was enough to snap me out of the moment and break through the haze. "Well, I'm sure *Red* is more your speed. Maybe you two could take advantage of each other instead?"

Was something wrong with me? Why did the thought of him with Kira make me sick to my stomach? I was *not* enjoying this feeling.

"How did you even get—oh, the nickname." He gave me his familiar cocky smirk. "Did that upset you?"

"What?" My voice went high-pitched, and I couldn't believe what was happening. I *was* acting like a jealous mortal. What had become of me?

I stepped back, releasing my hold on his shirt. His hands dropped to his sides. His eyes lightened like he found something funny, angering me more.

He enjoyed making me feel crazy. Worse, I was allowing him to do it.

I lifted my chin and controlled my breathing. I'd given him control of the situation, and that was unacceptable. The best thing I could do was pretend none of this had happened.

Desperate to change the subject, I racked my brain for an acceptable conversation to have out in public, behind a highly guarded building. Nothing surfaced, so instead of regaining control, I stood there with my mouth hanging partly open.

The urge to deny what he'd said strengthened, but I refused to succumb. I didn't need to become flustered and start lying; I had to keep my integrity intact, even in this situation.

He stepped toward me again, and I countered his advance, but that didn't dissuade him. He took another step, capturing my hand. "Seriously, it's a habit. I didn't mean to upset you." He waggled his brows, and he managed to look even sexier. "However, I kind of like your reaction, so regardless, I'd say it was a success."

My skin tingled where he touched my hand. The pleasant sensation made my stomach flutter.

There *had* to be something wrong with me. Could witches perform love spells? Not that I *loved* him, but maybe a spell had me feeling discombobulated around him. "Good to know you were manipulating me." I cringed. I'd just admitted that it bothered me, but he already *knew*. I wasn't telling him any new information, and the nice sensation ebbed as annoyance coursed through me. "Oh, wait. That's right. It's your *nature*." I couldn't say *demon*, but he'd get the message loud and clear.

"Oh, yes." His eyes tightened, and he released my hand. He no longer seemed calm and collected. "I'm so glad you keep telling me that. I *might* forget what I am and what you *think* of me."

That stumped me. My anger deflated, and my chest constricted. He was upset with me, but I didn't know why. Everything I'd said was true, so why was he acting like I'd insulted him? "It's not just me. *Everyone* knows that."

He laughed humorlessly, and his face was lined with an emotion that resembled pain. He growled, "Because you've taken the time to get to know me. It's not like you're prejudiced or anything."

I blinked, at a loss for words. "How can someone be prejudiced when they *know* the truth?"

Closing his eyes, he pinched the bridge of his nose. "You've clearly got all the answers."

"Thank you." That was the nicest thing he'd said to me that I actually believed. I valued finding the truth and answers, and it was gratifying when people noticed.

His eyes flicked to me, and his brows furrowed. "I wasn't being serious." He tilted his head, examining me. "I just wish you'd try to get to *know* me before lumping me in with your stereotype. Have you ever been to Hell?"

I didn't understand his point. "I don't have to go there to know—"

"You know what? Forget it." He sighed. "I can't force you to see me."

"Gladly." I'd love to forget more than this conversation. I'd like to forget *him*.

My heart panged, calling me a liar and infuriating me more. *Fine*. I wished I'd never met him.

The pang turned into a sharp, piercing sensation.

I needed to move on from this internal conversation because it was providing me with great discomfort. And not the discomfort of pain I enjoyed—this was more earth-shattering, and unfortunately, I wasn't theatrical like Sierra. Instead, I did the safest thing I could do: I changed the subject. "They should be here any second." I wanted to turn away from him, but I couldn't. Not here, and not like this. He could slip away, and I couldn't be foolish.

He'd sneaked inside Shadow City, and I wasn't sure why. If I'd had a guess, then I could determine a way to thwart his efforts, but I was clueless about his intent.

The fact that he'd learned about the artifact building worried me even more. We kept knowledge about the building low-key, even within the city, and the contents were definitely on a need-to-know basis. Supernaturals were power-hungry, which was how the city had become what it was today. Anyone with high aspirations for power and control could seek out these artifacts to gain leverage. We'd learned what happened when the angels had tried to take over long ago, and we wanted to ensure that never happened again.

People like Azbogah posed the biggest risk. Since the police force employed a mix of supernatural races, they were in charge of protecting the building. The council oversaw the security detail, and the witches performed security spells. All of this was meant to be a balance of power...in theory. That worked well until collusion occurred.

Levi lifted his hands, emphasizing he wasn't touching me, and stepped away. "I get the hint. I'll back off." His expression crumpled, and he exhaled. "I was being a jackass earlier, so I guess you have a right to be upset. It was kind of manipulative. But seriously, you're the only girl who has ever caught my eye."

His accountability made me feel as if the ground were shifting under my feet. My frustration ebbed, and I tried to cling to it. I couldn't fall for this next calculated move. Did he think I was a silly mortal girl who would believe he'd only ever had eyes for me? "I get that you aren't used to being around angels, but I know better than to fall for a player like you. I'm sure you've used that line a hundred times before." When you lived indefinitely, you had a way of saying the same thing again and again.

"You'd know if I were lying." He stepped toward me, closing the distance again. He grimaced like he hadn't meant to, but we were drawn together by a force beyond our control.

The *tug* in my chest almost had me taking another step to rub against him.

Almost.

I squelched the need enough to keep my feet planted firmly on the ground. "Not if you were spelled."

"I wish that were the case." His hand inched toward my cheek. "It'd make things much easier—for both of us."

I wouldn't argue against that. I wanted to lie, but that wouldn't change anything. My feelings would remain the same, and I wouldn't let a demon make me go against everything ingrained in me. Against who I wanted to be— a person who stood strong and never wavered, even when looking an adversary in the face. Lying would be wavering, and beyond that, he knew the effect he had on me.

There were certain sounds and smells no one could hide, and my attraction was obvious. Besides, he was a *very* handsome man—muscular but not overly so, and with half a foot on me. He was my exact type. Fate must have laughed when she'd known we'd cross paths.

A familiar engine rumbled closer. The vehicle was heading our way, meaning my friends were coming to pick us up.

Levi dropped his hands a whisper from my skin, and a lump formed in my throat.

I wanted him to touch me. His touch was like nothing I'd experienced before, but every time he touched me made things more difficult between us. The best thing I could do was forget the scent of his breath and the feel of his rough fingers.

Even with all my internal prep, the *yank* inside me didn't allow me to move away, and I knew that if he touched me again, I wouldn't stop it from happening. My resolve was weakening, and my body wasn't listening to my mind anymore—a huge problem for a trained warrior. I had to rely on myself because I was the only one I could always count on.

Being alone with him wasn't smart. Whether this attraction was the result of a magical spell or strong chemistry, we couldn't let it control us. Even if I wanted to be with him, it would never work.

We were from different worlds. Different dimensions —literally. Places where the other wasn't welcome.

We needed distance from each other before we did something we couldn't come back from.

This dilemma could be one-sided, I mused, especially if there was a spell involved. I had to consider he could be stringing me along to obtain whatever the demons desired.

When I'd thought he'd left, my feelings had grown substantially stronger. My weakness could have been a result of me not expecting to see him again. I wouldn't *allow* those feelings to be more than that. I'd get control over the strangeness roiling through me. I always rose to a challenge, and this was no different.

Finding that resolve gave me some inner peace, and my chest loosened despite the pain coursing through my heart.

Alex's slate-gray Mercedes SUV prowled up to us. Ronnie rolled down her tinted window and waved us in. "Let's go."

I'd expected Sterlyn and Griffin to be with them, but with the shifter attacks, they were probably being watched more closely than were the vampire royals. Azbogah still had an in with the shifters, meaning either that Ezra had had an accomplice or that the angel was working with someone else, possibly Kira's power-hungry cousin, Grady. "Where are Sterlyn and Griffin?" I asked.

"At the condo." Ronnie lifted her brows. "They have an inkling of what's going on." She tilted her head toward the artifact building.

She had to mean Kira, telling me I was right about my suspicions. My stomach soured.

Grady.

We'd have to prove it.

Kira's father had wanted his nephew to take over as leader of the foxes, despite Kira being the heir apparent. She was female, and they'd wanted a male in charge. Kira had sought out Griffin and Sterlyn for support and helped them determine who'd been involved in the attacks on Sterlyn and their allies on the shifter side of things several weeks ago, which ultimately had incriminated Ezra. In exchange, Sterlyn and Griffin had backed her as leader of the foxes and had gone a step further by putting her in charge of the Shadow City police force. Perhaps this was Azbogah's way of striking back at Kira and the shifter council members in one fell swoop.

I waited for Levi to move, but he stayed firmly beside me.

"After you," he said sweetly, gesturing to the back car door.

No way in hell was that happening. If I turned my back on him, he could change into his shadow form and float away.

"It's best if she flies," Alex said loudly enough for us to hear outside. "Rosemary riding with us in the city would seem strange."

We needed to keep up appearances. In fact, I should probably stay with my parents tonight, but I couldn't risk Levi escaping again. If I tailed them, I could keep an eye on things. "True. I rarely ride in vehicles."

Levi shrugged and brushed his fingers down my arm as he walked by. My skin felt as if it had caught fire. He said suggestively, "I guess my dream of making out with you in the back seat of a vehicle will have to be put on hold until a later date."

"What?" Ronnie choked as her gaze landed on me.

The scoundrel.

I glared at him, knowing he was alluding to our almost-kiss. "That will *not* happen." I was certain of that. Even with the tug, Ronnie and Alex's presence would keep me rational.

He winked at me. "*Not* is not *never*. I'll take it."

He climbed into the SUV as Ronnie's forehead wrinkled with concern. I could practically feel the questions running through her mind.

When we got back to Shadow Terrace, she'd seek me out to have one of those conversations girls tended to have about feelings and emotions. I'd always avoided those, but Levi's presence was changing things.

And the one thing I knew was that I didn't like it.

"I'll follow you." Normally, I'd fly ahead, but not with Levi in the back seat. I wanted to keep him in front of me. If he tried anything funny, I could end it before it began.

"Okay. What are we going to do when they ask about him?" said Ronnie, glancing over her shoulder.

"It won't come to that." Alex put the SUV back into drive. "They'll see us and open the doors without question. Levi better just stay hidden. We can't risk him smoking and alerting the angels to his presence."

"Well, that might be hard—" Levi started.

I cut him off. "I'm sure you can manage it, since you must have arrived here in a similar manner."

He grinned at me as he grabbed the door handle. "You've got me there, Rosey. I kind of like it." He shut the door, letting his words linger.

My blood pumped faster, but I kept my face neutral, not wanting him to see that he'd gotten a reaction.

Ronnie glanced at me again and mouthed, *We need to talk*, before rolling up her window.

Gods. There was no getting out of it. She'd tell the others, and they'd hunt me down.

Not bothering to respond, I took to the sky as Alex pulled away.

He navigated the city toward the vampire section, heading to Shadow Terrace. Some of the tension in my body eased.

I flew close, not wanting to give Levi the option to even consider escape. I wanted him to feel as if I were breathing down his neck.

As we made our way to the vampire area, the buildings grew wider, turning into condominiums and apartments instead of businesses. When we reached the four-story Renaissance Revival–style building that was the royal vampire mansion, the sun rose over the horizon, and city lights swirled in the new light of day.

Thankfully, I'd been in the city long enough to recharge. I might need that energy once we got outside the gates.

At the exit, I hovered over the SUV.

When the gate didn't lift within a few seconds, I realized something was wrong.

A vampire appeared from the guard station beside the gate. His yellow eyes locked on me as he walked by.

If I didn't do something, he'd find Levi.

CHAPTER EIGHTEEN

WE WERE SO close to getting Levi out undetected. I inhaled and flew toward the vampire, and we reached Alex's door at the same time.

"Is there a problem?" I asked. I rarely went in or out through the Shadow Terrace gate, so I had no idea who this man was, but I found it odd that they were stopping their king and queen from leaving.

The vampire squinted at me, then turned to Alex.

I straightened my back. This bloodsucker didn't get to *ignore* me. My parents were current council members, and I was their heir. "Answer me."

Alex opened his door and climbed out of the vehicle.

My wings stilled, and I held my breath. I glanced inside the SUV in time to see Levi wave at me.

If he had any clue about the trouble we could be in, he wouldn't be having fun.

But maybe that was why he'd come. He could be trying to get us caught harboring a demon. If they learned about him, Azbogah and Erin could use him against us to replace Alex and Ronnie.

Alex's hair looked messier than normal, and his lips were pursed. My stomach dropped.

"What's going on, Kieran?" Alex shut the door and leaned against it.

My body relaxed marginally. With the door closed and Ronnie in the car, Levi might behave.

Unless, that is, he was waiting for the perfect opportunity to cause a scene.

My lungs quit working.

The guard pulled at the hem of his black shirt. The Shadow City emblem was outlined in gold on his chest, the uniform signifying he was a protector of the wall and the connection to the outside world.

Being a guard was a coveted position. Vampires served on the Shadow Terrace side—the vampire side—whereas wolf shifters served as guards on the Shadow Ridge side because of the pack link they had with Griffin, Shadow City's alpha. The police force consisted mainly of other shifter races, since no one wanted the Shadow City alpha to have the ability to exert his alpha will on both the city guards and the police force. There had to be checks and balances.

"The angel was trailing you..." The guard lifted his black hat, revealing smushed light-brown hair.

I scoffed. "We're *friends*." Though Alex and Ronnie were attempting to change the current rule that no supernaturals other than vampires were allowed inside

Shadow Terrace, my going there was still an unspoken no-no.

"She's right." Alex arched his brow. "You know that anyone who is allowed to leave the city can now come to the Shadow Terrace side. Have you been denying requests?"

Kieran shook his head. "No one, as far as I know, has asked."

"Then the problem is solved. Rosemary has our blessing to accompany us." Alex stood and reached for the door handle.

The guard remained in place. Something else was going on.

Taking a shaky breath, Kieran said, "Her mother was attacked tonight, and Azbogah contacted us—"

Alex spun toward him, blurring. Crimson bled into his light blue eyes. "To whom is your allegiance?"

I had to give him credit. The vampire knew when to be intimidating. I was thankful he was handling it; if I stepped in, I'd make the situation more turbulent.

The council would frown upon me bullying or attacking a member of another supernatural race. Each supernatural race handled their own punishments. In cross-supernatural conflicts or with issues that threatened the entire city, the council became involved. Azbogah often pitted the supernatural races against each other when he wanted influence over something.

The guard's jaw dropped, and he tugged at his shirt collar. "You, my king."

"Good. Now open the damn gate." Alex towered over the guard.

Kieran's head bobbed up and down. "Of course, Your Highness."

When the guard didn't move, Alex hissed. He didn't normally get an attitude with his people, but it had been a long day, and we were all tense.

I could use a good rest, and I required less sleep than my friends did. I could only imagine how worn they all felt.

Alex and I stood there as the guard retreated to the gatehouse, where the controls to lift the gate were located. Finally, Alex opened the car door and slipped back inside.

I scanned the area for anyone who might be watching us. Azbogah was probably monitoring who was coming and going more closely, using the attack on my Mother as his excuse. His true intent, no doubt, was to gain control.

I was sure he would be thrilled to know I was leaving with Alex and the others.

I lifted into the sky and returned to my position at the back of the car. So far, Levi hadn't done anything shady, but we weren't out of the city yet.

Surprisingly, part of me didn't expect the demon to do anything.

My breath caught, and I wanted to slap myself. I couldn't start trusting him. He hadn't earned it, and demons were expert manipulators. I couldn't fall for his tricks. It was beneath me.

Flapping my wings harder than necessary, I tried to expend some of my excess energy. Levi was getting into my head. If we were going to get any more information from him, we had to think objectively and stay a few steps ahead of him.

As the gate opened, the bridge and the town of Shadow Terrace came into view. The bridge was a replica of the one on the Shadow Ridge side, and they'd been built at the same time. However, the two towns felt nothing alike.

Shadow Terrace had a more antiquated feel, with cobblestone roads and old-fashioned gaslights illuminating its sidewalks. The buildings were painted a uniform white and topped with red roofs. The only thing that varied was their size; some structures were one story tall, while the tallest was four stories high. An enormous gray stone cathedral with a dome on top dominated the center of town. It sat across the street from what had once been the most popular vampire bar. The cathedral had been built a hundred years ago, and the bar—Thirsty's—had been strategically located nearby to lure human tourists inside.

Alex and Ronnie had closed down Thirsty's after discovering vampires had been using it as a place to feed directly from humans, which was not allowed. When vampires fed straight from a human, they risked both killing their victim and losing their own humanity. They grew so sensitive to light that even moonlight could make their skin feel as if it were on fire, but worse, they became obsessed with feeding and killing. Such vampires had to be executed for the safety of humans and supernaturals alike.

I flew high again to avoid detection by humans.

My eyes stayed locked on the vehicle as Alex drove through the city, passing several humans heading toward the lone hotel. A couple held hands, and the man scanned their surrounding area cautiously, protecting the woman.

My mouth dried when I realized these humans were leaving the blood bank. They'd "donated" blood to the local hospital, which was a ploy. Their blood would be used to feed the vampires. Feeding via blood bags prevented crazed bloodlust and the loss of humanity, and it satisfied the vampires' hunger. Though I didn't agree with the way they tricked humans into donating, it was a way for vampires and humans to live in the same world safely, so I bit my tongue.

The *tug* in my chest was becoming hard to resist again, and I focused on maintaining control.

On the outskirts of the town, Alex turned right. The houses grew farther apart, reminding me of Killian's neighborhood, down to the backyards abutting the woods. They were still in the same style as the rest of the town, but this section was full of two-story homes. They had no front yards, the entrances opening onto the cobblestone street, but grass strips separated them on the sides. The house at the very end of the road had burned down, its roof caved in.

Alex stopped in front of the house next to the burned one and parked.

I landed beside the car, surveying the area as the front door opened, revealing Annie and Cyrus.

"It's about damn time you all got here," Annie said as she stepped outside and placed a hand on her belly. Her pregnancy wasn't noticeable yet, but whenever she did that, it moved her shirt so one could see the slight bump.

The scolding was unnecessary. "We wanted to get here too," I said. "Believe me." Did she think we wanted to spend time in Shadow City with a *demon*?

Her face fell. "I'm sorry. I didn't mean it like that."

"She knows." Ronnie climbed out of the car, giving me what Sierra referred to as the stink-eye.

"Maybe she should be a little nicer." Cyrus frowned as he wrapped his arm around his wife.

Levi got out and slammed the back door, then stood beside me, glaring at Cyrus.

I had no idea why he was upset, but I was more concerned that his presence beside me put my body at ease. He shouldn't have *any* effect on me, let alone a calming one.

Killian marched out the door, and he glanced at me, then at Levi. A scowl crossed his face as he made a beeline for me.

Levi stepped in front of me, blocking Killian's advance.

"What are you doing, *de—*" Killian growled.

"Levi. His name is *Levi*," I interrupted, and stepped around the annoying demon. Though we might be out of Shadow City, we were still in Shadow Terrace, and while unlikely, people could be in these woods or close enough to overhear our conversation. We couldn't go throwing the D-word around.

"Aw, Rosey." Levi smirked. "I *knew* you cared."

Sierra snorted as she stepped into the doorway of the house. "I kinda like your nickname for her."

"Don't," Levi and I said at the same time.

I jerked back and stared at him as if he had two heads.

"Interesting." Sierra's irises lightened, and she rubbed her hands.

"That's one way of putting it." Ronnie squinted at me.

Oh, dear gods. I didn't have the energy to contend with them. "When will Aurora and Lux get here?" Their herbal smell was missing.

"They aren't coming." Annie's tone was somber.

My blood ran cold. We needed them to recreate the perimeter spell. "Today?"

"Definitely not today." Annie stared down the cobblestone road. "And probably not this week. Circe doesn't want them practicing magic this close to Shadow City. They're trying to convince her otherwise."

I'd planned on staying close to Levi, but this would require me to stay even closer than I'd planned—like, same-room type of close, which wouldn't allow me to keep any distance from him.

My heart rate increased, and my mind screamed *no*. "That changes things."

"We have a plan," Cyrus assured me, and gestured to the house next door. "We'll have two people watching the house at all times. Theo and Chad are out there now, positioned at the sides so they can see around the front and back. We're counting on the ones who can see him to keep an eye on the front. That way, he won't be able to slip out without detection."

Ronnie yawned and covered her mouth to hide the fatigue, but we were all feeling it.

Alex tucked her against his side. "We have the house next door set up as well, so we won't be on top of one another." He gestured to the houses beside the one they'd exited. "We can split up however you see fit."

There was no question where I was staying. "I'll share a room with Levi."

"*What*?" Killian turned to me. "No way. If someone needs to share with him, I'll do it."

"If I can choose—" Levi started.

Killian snarled, "You don't get to *choose*. It'll be me."

Smirking, Sierra made her way to Ronnie. "This is just like—"

"If you say a movie title right now, I may hit you." Ronnie glared. "I'm not in the mood, and I'm so damn tired."

I needed to think like a mortal. "In an ideal situation, Killian, I would agree with you. However, if he shifts, you won't be able to see him." I hoped Killian understood my cryptic message. "I need to be there. If he's discovered, the blame for his presence will fall on me because of what he is."

Killian's shoulders sagged, and his jaw twitched. He reacted like that when he saw reason but didn't like the answer. However, he was a strategist, so he understood that my point was valid.

"Fine," he rasped. "But I'll stay in the house as well."

Now *that* I wouldn't argue with. He'd make sure I didn't do something stupid. "Okay."

He rolled his shoulders.

"We'll stay there, too," Ronnie said quickly. "Annie, Cyrus, and Sierra can split up."

Ronnie didn't want Annie too close to Levi if something happened. She was almost as protective of her foster sister as Cyrus was.

"That works for me." Cyrus appeared happy with the plan. "Sierra, you can have the house to the right all to yourself."

"Hell, no." Sierra shook her head. "I'm not staying solo. I won't be able to see *him* or *his kind* attack. My ass will be with you two."

Cyrus pouted. He'd wanted a house alone with his mate.

"She has us there," Annie said, and looped her arm through his.

"Exactly." Sierra wrapped her arm around Annie and tugged her toward the house on the right. "Let's go. I'm not pregnant, and even I'm exhausted."

Standing rigid, Killian wrinkled his nose at Levi. The alpha wolf didn't trust him, and I didn't blame him.

The feeling was mutual...or it *should* have been.

"We're all on edge. Let's get some rest." Alex headed for the house.

Not wanting to deal with the testosterone swirling

around me, I ordered Levi, "Walk." I needed peace and quiet and rest to get this craziness inside me under control.

"Yes, dear." He winked and followed Ronnie inside. Killian trailed behind me, and all five of us wound up in a sizable living room with beige walls. The floor plan was simple and modern, with canned lights and two tan leather couches that sat perpendicular to each other, positioned across from a television mounted in the center of the opposite wall. In the far-right corner, a wooden door led out back.

As we walked through the living room to a hallway, I noted a staircase to the left and the kitchen right in front of us, with the dining room to the right. Light beige cabinets lined the kitchen wall, and the sink sat beneath a window facing the woods. The stovetop was placed to the right of it, midway between the sink and the end of the counter. The tile backsplash was a darker beige. The entire kitchen complemented the beige walls, which appeared to stay uniform throughout the house. The space included an eat-in area with a circular wooden table surrounded by six matching wooden chairs.

I noted the large window centered behind the table as a potential exit Levi could use.

We took the oak staircase to the top floor. The faint scent of dahlias drifted in from outside, reminding me that fall was here.

At the top, a hallway led to four doors. Three bedrooms were to the left, right, and in front of us, with a hall bathroom catty-corner between the second and third bedrooms.

"Rosemary and Levi should stay in this room." Alex pointed to the one on the right. "The window faces the front, which would make it harder for Levi to access the woods, and there's a couch. Killian, you should stay in the room on the left. It's the smallest and has a twin bed, which would make it difficult for Ronnie and me to... sleep together."

He meant *have sex*, but I didn't care enough to correct him. This was a good plan for me.

"That works." Killian ran a hand through his hair. "Rosemary, if you need me..."

Ronnie's laser vision landed on me again.

"I know." I could take care of myself, but I held those words back. I just wanted to get away from her uncomfortable stare. "I'm going to get some sleep."

I marched into the room, no longer worried about staying behind Levi. Ronnie was here, so if he tried something, she'd stop him.

The room was bigger than I'd expected. The rooms were all the same bland beige color, but there was a queen bed against the right wall and a long cloth-covered couch in front of the window, the perfect place for me to sleep. It even had pillows.

The others said goodnight and split up into their respective rooms.

Levi walked in behind me as I pulled my wings into my back and flopped down on the couch.

"I can sleep there," he offered.

Oh, I was sure he could. "I'm good." I turned on my side to see him, and he stood next to the bed, staring down at me.

The bed had a fluffy forest-brown comforter with four large, poofy pillows. It looked very inviting, and hopefully, that would knock him out for a while so we could get some sleep.

I closed my eyes, desperate for silence even if I couldn't truly rest. I needed to process the events of the day and get my head on straight.

After a few minutes, the bed squeaked. Levi murmured, "Stubborn woman." His sweet scent grew stronger, and suddenly, a blanket was thrown over me.

My heart warmed, and I fidgeted from the sensation. I opened my eyes and was thankful to see he'd already turned away from me and was crawling into bed.

Not wanting him to catch me watching him, I snapped my eyes shut again, and when his breathing leveled, I fell fast asleep.

A PRESENCE HOVERED OVER ME, stirring me from my slumber. I didn't know how long I'd been resting, but one thing was clear.

Levi was going to attack, but this time, he'd picked on someone who was a worthy match.

CHAPTER NINETEEN

I KEPT MY EYES SHUT, focusing on my senses of smell and sound. I wanted him to get close enough that I could strike efficiently.

Something panged in my chest, but I ignored it. Letting my emotions dictate my actions would result in my death.

He hovered over me, and this was the moment I'd been dreading...I meant, waiting for.

I struck, grabbing him by the throat. My eyes popped open, and I watched as his wide eyes changed, flashing with anger. He dropped the edge of the comforter he'd been lifting to suffocate me with.

"You were going to smother me with a *comforter?*" He must not have considered me a threat if he thought that would do me in. Shoving him away, I released my hold.

He swallowed and rubbed his neck. "Yes, that's

exactly what I was doing. Gods, you're so narrow-mind-ed." His bleak tone was one he'd never used before.

The pain in my chest sharpened, which was unac-ceptable. It shouldn't matter if he was upset. He'd tried to hurt me. Granted, it had been in a horribly uncalculated move. "For thinking you want to *kill* me?" I wouldn't let him off the hook that easily.

"Why would I *want* that?" He raised his hands. "I haven't attacked you once. In fact, I *protected* you that day in the woods when I shouldn't have!"

I laughed. For the second time, I truly found a situa-tion funny. "You prevented me from catching up with your demon friend! *You* saved *him*, not me." I would've chopped that demon's head off within seconds if Levi hadn't gotten in my way.

"You have all the answers, don't you?" He dropped his hands as his nostrils flared. "No wonder angels don't get along with others very well. You can't get past your egos to understand that something might be different from what you *perceive* it to be."

"My best friends are shifters and d—vampires." I'd almost said *demonic vampires*, but I'd caught myself. There were certain things he didn't need to know. "That negates your point."

My throat dried because whether I *wanted* to admit it or not, it bothered me that he was angry with me.

"Because they somehow got through to you. And hell, I'm *trying*." He gestured to the cover on the ground. "I wasn't trying to smother you, Rosey. The cover fell off, and you were shivering. I was trying to keep you warm.

You'd been sleeping so peacefully..." He exhaled. "I made a poor decision. Don't worry. I won't do that again."

He'd been trying to cover me? My chest felt uncomfortable again, and my blood heated. He had covered me up when we'd gone to bed. Was he trying to get me to lower my guard? Maybe I should play along, try to beat him at his own game and back him into a corner. "Why would you do that? We're enemies."

"Are we?" he asked as he sat on the edge of his bed.

That was such a stupid question. "Of course. You're—"

"A demon." He rolled his eyes. "Believe me, you've made it clear. But have you considered the possibility that *maybe* not every demon enjoys terrorizing people?"

I shook my head. "Why would I? You lost your humanity when you fell."

"Not all of us chose to lose our humanity. My father didn't have a choice but to leave with the demons, and I'm a born demon." He glanced at his body. "I was born this way."

As I processed his words, I couldn't swallow. I hadn't considered demons having children, but of course they could. They had a reproductive system, and Ronnie was a quarter demon. She was proof they could have offspring. "Still, you are what you are," I said, though my words had lost their *oomph*.

Ronnie was part demon, and she was good, and so was Annie, despite being a demon wolf. But Annie and Ronnie had been raised on Earth by Eliza. Born demon or not, Levi had been raised in Hell. He *couldn't* be good.

Could he?

No. That complicated things. Every demon we'd attacked had been out for blood. He *had* to be playing me. But my heart disagreed. The question of *what if* kept circling my mind. I had to figure out a way to make it stop.

"Wait." His words sat hard on me. "What do you mean your father didn't have a choice? How could he have left Shadow City if he hadn't fallen?"

"The woman he loved, my mother, fell, and he came to Hell to be with her." His answer was robotic and lacking emotion, as if he'd heard the story so often that it had lost its meaning...or he'd rehearsed his answer until it came out matter-of-factly.

An angel fell in love with a demon.

The words were so simple but held so much significance. My fingers tingled as hope spread through my body, like my heart was telling me to go pluck my feathers.

I needed to suspend these weird sensations and get back on track. There was too much at stake to get all mortal-like.

"So you're half angel?" Maybe there was hope for him.

"The princes of Hell stipulated that for my father to be let into Hell, he had to fall. So he *is* a demon. He lost his wings, but he did it in the name of love." His irises lightened from mocha to cappuccino, and the corners of his lips tipped upward. "My parents were happy together."

Were.

I shouldn't want to learn about him, but I couldn't stop myself. My mouth betrayed me as I asked, "What happened?"

"My mother died." The warmth vanished from his eyes, and his expression hardened.

I remained silent, waiting for him to continue, but he said nothing else. All I could tell was that whatever had happened to his mother upset him, and I *truly* didn't want to push him.

I was allowing my emotions to break through.

Silence hung between us, and I wasn't sure what to say or do. I never handled such situations well, and I'd learned that sometimes, silence was the best option, even if I came off as aloof.

However, I wanted him to lose the pained expression etched into his face. I asked the question that had been hounding me since, well...I glanced at the clock, realizing I'd slept for only an hour, so it was still less than ten hours ago. "How did you get inside Shadow City?"

He ran a hand down his face. "I figured that question was coming."

"You keep saying I'm wrong about how I view you, so show me the truth." I was allowing him to prove that my brain was right. I wanted—no, *needed* him to become ornery.

He smiled crookedly, and it was even more alluring.

My head dizzied, and I realized I was holding my breath. I sat upright, hoping that having a solid floor under my feet would keep me grounded.

Something needed to.

"Well played, Rosey." He chuckled. "Maybe you're more charming than I gave you credit for."

I lifted my chin, refusing to feel either flattered or embarrassed. I schooled my expression, hiding my discomfort.

"I'll bite." He stood and walked over.

My heart pounded like a jackhammer. The thought of him biting me had desire pooling in my stomach, and I jerked my hands up to cover my neck. "No, don't." My voice rose, sounding a little raspy and completely contradicting my words.

"What?" His brows furrowed until his focus landed on my hands. He burst into laughter and flopped onto the couch beside me, sitting on top of the comforter. "I didn't mean literally."

Flames licked my face. I'd never felt this weird sensation before, but I wanted to bury my head in my hands, or better yet, under a couch cushion. Somehow, I refrained, but I was certain I was running a fever.

He grinned cockily and leaned toward me. His tantalizing smell wafted into my nose as he whispered, "Unless you want me to. I'd totally be—"

I cleared my throat way too loudly. I had to pull myself together. However, I choked on my saliva. The more I was around him, the dumber I became. I'd always prided myself on my calm demeanor, yet here I was, choking from a sexual innuendo.

When had I become *that* girl? I didn't like it one bit.

My eyes grew bleary again as I swallowed hard to

stop my hacking. Whatever was going on between us had to be killing my brain cells.

"Are you okay?" He placed a hand on my back and patted me.

The action overrode the pleasant buzzing sensation. I'd seen this action only one time in person, and it had been a mother burping her child. "I can expel gas just fine on my own."

"Good to know, but I was trying to help you stop choking." His eyes lightened again. "Not burp you."

I had no clue how patting my back would help me stop choking, but now that he'd said it, I recalled seeing something like that in a few of the stupid movies Sierra had made us watch. I never understood how hitting someone's back could save them from choking. If anything, I'd think it would make them choke harder, but mortals did many counterintuitive things. If I had been eating, the action might make more sense, but we were just sitting here, conversing. However, I didn't want to get distracted by a pointless conversation, so I refocused. "Is this your way of avoiding the topic?"

"No." He sighed and spread his legs so the one next to me touched mine. "I was trying to save your life, but I've gotta say, you're making me work hard for it."

"This *isn't* a game." Maybe it was to him, but it wasn't to me. "I'm not trying to make you work for anything." The buzzing from his hand and leg touching me was making my brain fuzzy, so I stood and strode across the room. I needed distance, and I was already losing my wits around him. I couldn't let him take down every single one of my defenses. "I just want to know how you got into the city."

He placed his hands behind his head and leaned back.

Mother plucker. I'd lost my mind. He'd placed himself at the window and driven me clear across the room.

"You're truly beautiful, especially when you're flustered." He smiled adoringly and openly ogled me.

I couldn't believe my recklessness as I marched back to him, but instead of sitting, I stood in front of him. If he shifted, I could easily grab him. I placed my hands on my hips, wanting him to know I was losing my patience. "I'm waiting."

"Fine." He shrugged and dropped his hands into his lap. "When Sterlyn and her mate were talking about needing to get back to Shadow City, the guard watching the window got distracted. I"—he paused and winced —"took the opportunity to transform into my shadow form, get under the Navigator, and cling to the bottom."

Hearing that he could become a shadow helped me gain control over my heart, and I filled in the rest of the pieces. "And the spells didn't work to keep you out or notify the witches of your presence." I had to give it to him, he was smart. We would need to address this. If he'd thought of it, he wouldn't be the only one, and we needed to secure our border.

Maybe having most people locked inside wasn't a bad thing. Since the majority of Shadow City's residents weren't acclimated into the world, we hadn't been forced to deal with people coming and going...that we'd known of.

In the last few months, we'd become aware that a witch had been leaving Shadow City with no one the wiser until Annie had spotted witch bones in the woods. On top of that, Ronnie had seen similar bones on the roof of Thirsty's. Their locations meant someone was casting a spell to spy on both sides of the river. Eliza hadn't been able to pick up the caster's magical essence because it had been depleted before she'd arrived, but she'd had one guess as to who would know that kind of magic and be willing to use it—Erin and her coven. With trouble popping up left and right, our group hadn't had time to confront Erin or address the issue. Confronting a powerful coven wasn't something we could do without thinking it through. Once we touched the bones, the person who'd carved the runes into them would be alerted.

And now a demon had gotten in by using our own vehicle as a taxi.

Shadow City wasn't as secure as people liked to think.

He lifted a hand. "See, that's why I didn't want to tell you."

At least I could give him credit for his honesty. "Because I'll thwart any other attempts to ensure you can't breach our security?"

He leaned his head back. "That's not why."

"Then please, do share."

"Because of the way you're looking at me." He

flashed to his feet and stood inches from me. He stared into my eyes, and the connection between us intensified. "You look disgusted, and it *hurts*."

"Hurts?" I parroted. His body heat washed over me, and before my brain could interject, I took an involuntary step toward him.

He cupped my cheek and ran his thumb across my skin. "You're becoming *everything* to me. I've never experienced anything close to this before, but the more time I spend with you, the stronger these feelings become. Knowing you don't feel the same way is breaking me."

His words spoke to my soul, and his touch had electricity coursing between us. I didn't understand what was going on, but this was more than just sexual attraction.

Step back, I commanded myself, but my body betrayed me. My feet were glued to the floor, and I couldn't have pushed his hand away if my life had depended on it. His touch *felt* right, like an extension of myself that I hadn't understood I was missing.

"You're not alone," I whispered, the words escaping before I could take them back.

A low groan emanated from him as he placed his forehead against mine. Something inside me pushed forward, weakening my legs.

He rasped, "What do you mean? You care about me, too?"

"I..." I didn't know. I didn't understand what I felt for him. It was infuriatingly illogical, but I couldn't deny it. "I *think* I do, but we're from different worlds. It can't happen. Something like this can't work. All we're doing is setting ourselves up to fall."

"My parents fought for each other. Why can't we?" He tilted my head so I could look at him.

My stomach fluttered. "But your father had to fall."

"Falling isn't what you think." His breath fanned my face. "Not all demons are the way we've been portrayed. Some wish they could leave Hell, just like my father and me. We don't want to be there any longer."

Something he said tickled the back of my mind, but I couldn't place it. His wording felt off, but all I could focus on was the energy charging between us. "Okay," I whispered. I didn't always want to argue with him. That seemed important at this moment.

His gaze landed on my lips, and his head lowered toward mine.

My mind remained silent when I needed it to be strong.

His lips touched mine, and a jolt of energy sprang between us. Something inside me shifted, this one moment of weakness changing everything. I didn't think I could ever *not* kiss him.

My hands wrapped around his neck as his tongue slipped inside my mouth. His spearmint taste washed over me, and my body pressed against his.

The doorknob jiggled, and logic slammed back into me. As the door opened, I tried to stumble back, not wanting to get caught, but Levi wrapped his arms around me, anchoring my body to his.

CHAPTER TWENTY

I WAS TOO STUNNED to fight Levi, especially when my body didn't want to put distance between us, anyway.

As the door opened wider, Killian's musky sandal-wood scent floated into the room. Between the smell and Killian's snarling, I woke enough to move.

When I stepped to the side, Levi dropped one arm, but he kept the other locked around my waist. The buzz from his touch and the possessive action had my stomach doing flips again. Killian's irises darkened to ebony as he took in our precarious situation.

"What the *hell* is going on in here?" he demanded.

I grimaced. If Ronnie and Alex hadn't been awake, they would be now. Even the wolves outside keeping guard had probably heard him.

"None of *your* business." Levi stepped closer to me.

My chest constricted. Had he kissed me, hoping Killian would catch us? Could it have been a ploy for which I'd stupidly fallen?

Killian stepped into the room, his eyes glowing as his wolf surged forward. He was protective of those he loved, and he felt like *I* needed protecting.

The startling realization was that maybe I did. I'd never let emotions sway me before.

I'd never *had* emotions until *him.*

A *demon.*

That was enough for my brain to take control again, and I stepped away from Levi. I needed him to stop touching me, but just as desperately, I wanted him to touch me again. All over. My desires were polar opposites.

I was in a horrible situation. My brain was ashamed of me whenever I let emotion rule, but at the same time, my heart hurt when I fought our connection. There *wasn't* a right solution. If Levi had been another angel I could trust, this would be *so* much easier.

But he wasn't.

Killian clenched his fists, and his chest heaved. "*She* is my business. I can't stand by and watch her…"

I wanted to hang my head in shame since I could guess why he'd stopped speaking. Anything he said would be mean and cause me pain, but maybe I needed to hear it. I glanced at him and nodded. "You can continue. Say what you mean." I was being a nincompoop.

Some of the anger melted from his face, but a scowl remained. "No, Rosemary…"

Fine. If he wouldn't finish it, I would. "Watch her be

stupid? Watch her succumb to demonic influences? Watch her make a complete and utter fool of herself?"

Levi laughed humorlessly. "Wow. Don't hold back."

The sound made the back of my throat hurt. I hadn't meant to upset Levi, but Killian needed to put my head back on straight.

Somebody had to, because I'd officially lost all reason.

Still, I couldn't move past hurting Levi. Even with my brain screaming at me not to care, I *did* care, and that was the whole crux of the problem. His well-being was as important as my own.

"I didn't mean..." I trailed off, my silence betraying me. That was exactly what I'd meant, and lying would only make things worse.

I'd become mortal-like, wanting to fix things by telling a white lie—something at which I'd turned up my nose not even a week ago.

Killian squinted at Levi. "See, that's one thing I *appreciate* about Rosemary. She always tells the truth, even when the other person doesn't want to hear it."

I felt punched in the gut. I rarely got injured, and for words to pain me was brand new. I was over one thousand years old—nothing new should be happening at this juncture of my life. But I realized that if honesty was going to hurt, maybe it should be given with empathy. All those times Sierra had gotten on me about my rudeness sank in. There was a difference between honesty and cruelty—I'd just never understood it before now.

"I'm working hard to get her to *see* me." Levi puffed

out his chest. "I don't need other people's negativity influencing her more than it already has."

My heart dropped, and I wished this rollercoaster inside me would stop. I missed feeling numb, especially with all these conflicting thoughts and emotions flowing through me. However, his words had struck a chord. I'd formed my opinion about all demons before I'd even met one. That stark awareness slammed into me. I hadn't formed that opinion from my own experience, and most of the demons I'd met recently had reinforced everything I'd been told...except for Annie and Ronnie.

So...I couldn't have been completely wrong.

Surely.

I always strove to be a good person—it was one of the most prominent desires inside me—but experiencing all this had taken things to a different level.

"Negativity?" Killian bellowed, his body quivering. "The truth isn't negative."

Ronnie and Alex's door swung open, and the two of them appeared behind Killian.

Eyes flicking back and forth between Levi and Killian, Ronnie mouthed at me, *Do something.*

Do something? I had no clue what to do. I was having a hard enough time dealing with my inner turmoil.

Oh, dear gods. I was turning into Sierra, but not mouthy. Just dramatic.

"You've only seen the demons they *allow* to come to Earth to cause terror." Levi took a menacing step toward Killian. "That would be like me assuming all wolves pee on trees because I've seen several do it."

"That's original." Killian's nose wrinkled. "Make dog jokes."

"What's the problem here?" Alex asked as he slipped into the room. He wore black sweatpants and a white cotton shirt instead of his normal suit and button-down. I had to give him credit—he looked regal even in comfortable clothing.

"There's no problem," Levi bit out, his glare remaining on Killian.

Killian snorted. "Really? Walking in on the two of you kissing was *nothing*?"

My face heated. I hadn't expected him to call me out in front of everyone. He was usually more considerate, but he was also upset.

"Don't take your jealousy out on me," Levi said as he stepped closer to me. He reached for my hand, and something white-hot flashed through me.

He wanted to use me to mess with Killian, and I'd had enough of both of them. "You two, stop it now." I yanked my hand out of Levi's reach and stuck a finger in his face. "You can't blame us for not trusting you. Every full-blooded demon we've come across has been bad, and let's not forget how you stopped me from chasing after one *and* sneaked into Shadow City."

"Shadow City is a point of contention in Hell. Do you blame me for being curious about it?" Levi arched a brow, but he averted his gaze from mine and shrugged as his face turned into a mask of indifference. "If I'd been honest, you wouldn't have taken me there."

My heart squeezed. He was hiding something.

"And I already told you why I stopped you from going after Belphogor." He stepped toward me. "I was protecting you. He was leading you into a trap."

That last part I believed. The emotion behind his words was proof enough. "What trap?"

"Don't humor him by pretending you believe him," Killian scoffed. "He's skirting the truth so he won't lie while trying to get in your pants. Don't let him make you dumb."

I lost it. I spun on my heel, facing one of my closest friends. "Make one more comment like that, and I'll make you wish you'd never spoken." We'd never had words like these, but I was over his disrespect.

The anger on his face morphed to confusion as he furrowed his brows. "What?"

Ronnie sighed, but I chose to ignore her disappointment. I got that I was handling this all wrong, but I couldn't stop myself.

"Make one more comment about him manipulating me to get into my pants. I dare you." Anger swirled inside me.

"Rosemary?" His voice rose. "Are you okay? You're not acting like yourself."

I pressed my lips together. He was right, and it scared me. I didn't recognize myself anymore. All I knew was that I wanted to trust Levi but also knew I couldn't. And having Killian charge in here to grandstand had tipped me over the edge. "I know."

I had to leave, or I'd continue to make an ass of

myself. I exhaled and moved past Killian and Alex, then Ronnie.

"Hey," she said, but I didn't stop. I continued toward the stairs.

Normally, at a time like this, I'd fly, but I refused to leave the area. I didn't want to go far and risk Levi disappearing again.

I didn't trust him, even though I *wanted* to.

Fresh air might do me wonders, so I marched down the stairs toward the front door. My wings itched to explode from my back, but the sun was up, and even though we were near the woods, humans could be hiking nearby. My wings needed to stay put.

Unfortunately, my ears were working just fine.

"Look what you did," Levi snapped. "You upset her."

"Me!" Killian's tone was low. "You're the one messing with her mind."

Even when I wasn't in the room, they were bickering.

Ronnie sighed. "I'll go talk to her. Levi, no funny business. Two silver wolves are watching the house, and Rosemary and I will be right outside."

"I told you, I don't want to leave," he groaned. "You'd *know* if I were lying."

"Not necessarily," Alex interjected. He sounded tired and frustrated, mirroring my own emotions.

I reached the front door, eager to have a moment to myself. Ever since Levi had come into the picture, I'd felt as if someone were watching me. Every time I turned around, someone was giving me a strange expression, and I knew why—Levi affected me.

As I opened the door, Ronnie blurred beside me.

Great. I wouldn't even have a moment alone to collect my thoughts before having to talk to someone else.

The urge to flee almost overwhelmed me. I'd been a loner my whole life, and even though I'd gotten close to this group, I still liked my own company when we weren't under threat. After living for several centuries, I'd begun to relish alone time, especially when I'd befriended a group of individuals who each had more emotions than the entire angel race. My favorite thing to do in the world was to fly high, where the world vanished and I was in my most natural state.

But I couldn't leave because of Levi, and Mother was struggling with keeping Azbogah in line. I should have been there to help her and Father, but my hands were tied, and I didn't want to tell them why. It would give Azbogah more leverage, and we had enough problems.

Normally, I didn't keep anything from my mother. I went to her for counsel because she'd been alive for most of eternity. I couldn't comprehend it, and I was her only child.

Even with my limited emotions, Mother and I were closer than any other angelic parent and child duo I'd encountered, and I relished that. Maybe I was a tad more emotional than the average angel. However, in my current state, I was a train wreck by angelic standards.

Outside, the sun was rising, indicating it was after seven in the morning. The cool air swirled over my skin, chilling some of my anger. I could hear the faint conversations of the nearby humans who had risen early to enjoy the fall day in the quaint town. If only they realized the dangers that surrounded them.

Ronnie came out beside me.

I walked across the cobbled road to where I had a clear view of Levi's and my bedroom. Something inside me instinctively knew Levi was still in there. It helped that I could hear the men murmuring, too.

Not wanting to start the conversation, I remained quiet, staring at the window. If he even thought about floating out of that room, I'd be up there to catch him within seconds.

Ronnie also didn't speak. I had a feeling she was waiting me out, but she hadn't learned that time worked differently for me. Eventually, she'd learn, since she was now immortal, but right now, she was truly young, only in her early twenties.

As the sun climbed higher in the sky, my emotions settled. I was still more *feely* than I was used to, but nothing like what I'd been upstairs. The emotions Levi evoked were both amazing and horrible.

After a while, Ronnie huffed. "Are you going to say anything?"

There it was. "I'm trying not to." I didn't want to have this conversation. She'd want me to explain things I didn't understand myself.

"How long has this been going on?" she asked. "Since you saw him?"

I had to give her credit—she'd caught me off guard. "What are you talking about?"

"I noticed the day of the first demon attack that you

were distracted. You were injured in the attack, and that never happens. I figured there was another imminent threat coming, and that was what had shifted your focus." Ronnie kicked the ground, trying not to come off as confrontational. "Maybe...there was another reason."

I understood the tactic she was employing—she was showing concern to be disarming and not seem overbearing. "You don't have to approach me as if you can't risk being honest."

She smirked. "Well, okay." She inhaled, preparing herself. "I think you and Levi have a unique connection, and it started the moment you got near him."

Maybe I shouldn't have encouraged her to be *that* direct. She hadn't held back at all. I'd hoped she would take the middle ground, but I respected her bluntness. At least she wasn't insulting my intelligence or making accusations. She was fact-finding. "There is something. I wish I could deny it, but you'd know I was lying. But it doesn't make *sense*. We're from different worlds, quite literally. It's like a witch put a love spell on me." As soon as the word *love* had left my lips, I wanted desperately to take it back. I hadn't meant to say it, and I wasn't sure a witch could actually perform one.

Ronnie nodded. "Maybe, but he's feeling it, too. If it were a spell, you'd think he'd have made sure he wasn't influenced as well. Otherwise, he risks not following through on whatever his objective is."

My chest expanded. Part of me wondered if the connection between us might be real, but it squashed that thought. Hope like that could get me hurt, and I had to stay pragmatic. "He could be pretending."

"*Girl*, please." Ronnie chuckled and leaned into me. "He has it worse for you than you do for him. That can't be faked. I've seen the way he watches you when you're not paying attention. If he were pretending, he'd only do that when you were looking."

She had to stop saying stuff like that. It was only making my heart beat too rapidly. "Then why were you giving me the constipated look?"

"The *what?*" Her mouth dropped open.

I wasn't sure how else to explain it. "That face you make when you want to talk with someone."

Ronnie blinked. "Wow. Okay. Apparently, I need to work on *that* face, but it was a look of concern."

"If he feels the same way, why are you worried?" That should put her at ease.

She rolled her eyes. "Because, like you said, you're from vastly different worlds. It'd be hard to make it work —believe me, I speak from experience." She gestured upstairs toward Alex. "And it'll probably be even harder for you. Your people are enemies, and let's not forget, he's still keeping things from us."

"I picked up on that, too." I shouldn't be surprised that she'd noticed. She was a great queen. Even though she hadn't been raised as royalty, she understood how to relate to people and connect with them. And she sincerely *cared*. "I guess we need to beat it out of him."

"You just want to kick his ass." Ronnie's emerald eyes

lightened. "But it's true you catch more flies with honey than vinegar."

A normal sensation of confusion settled over me. This was how I routinely felt when talking with my friends, and the normalcy of the moment was exactly what I needed. "We aren't trying to catch flies."

"It's a saying." She waved a hand, discarding my silly statement. "It means it's easier to find out things or get your way when you do it with kindness and empathy instead of threats and violence."

That was the problem—I *didn't* want to be kind to him. That would lead me back down the road upon which we'd just embarked. If Killian hadn't interrupted us, I had a sneaking suspicion that some loud moaning would've woken them all instead. "There has to be a different way."

"You two are just like Alex and me when we met." She grinned. "He was an arrogant flirt, and I was a hot mess determined not to be with him. We saw how well that turned out."

"But you two are fated mates...soulmates...whatever you want to call it. Either way, it's not the same thing." Angels used to have relationships like that, but when the demons fell, it was like that part of us was erased. There wasn't a way for me to have a mate, which was probably for the best if the attraction I'd have felt in that case were even stronger than what I was feeling for Levi.

She tilted her head, examining me. "Are you sure? Because—"

The front door opened, and Killian stuck his head

out. "I hate to interrupt, but Sterlyn, Kira, and Griffin are on their way, and I was hoping I could talk with Rosemary alone before they get here."

I was still upset with Killian and didn't want to talk to him. I opened my mouth to tell him no, but Ronnie nodded.

"I'll watch Levi and make sure he behaves." Ronnie started to head inside, then paused and met my eyes. "Just think about what we talked about." She walked past Killian and into the house.

"I'm going for a walk." I didn't want to be mean, but I wasn't ready to talk to him yet.

Before I could turn around, Killian gently took my hand. "Just a minute, please. If you still want to go after we've talked, I won't stop you." He smiled sadly, giving me puppy dog eyes.

A week ago, they wouldn't have affected me, but I found myself nodding.

I wasn't sure I liked who I was becoming, and I braced myself to hear what he had to say.

CHAPTER TWENTY-ONE

I WAITED. I wanted him to lead the conversation. If I spoke, it would probably make things worse. Not trusting Levi was one thing, but Killian speaking negatively about me like that in front of Levi had taken my ire to a whole different level.

Killian's face scrunched, and that was when I was over it.

I removed my hand from his and turned on my heel. I felt trapped, and I hated it. I didn't want to go back inside the house, and I didn't want to stay out here with Killian. But I also *refused* to leave. The last time I did, Levi escaped. There were no options, but the least appealing one was remaining outside until Sterlyn and the others arrived.

I walked down the side of the house, closer to where the guards were.

Both silver wolves were staring at the house, pretending not to notice us outside. They were good soldiers, focusing on the risk and not allowing themselves to be distracted. And to think, a few months ago, Chad and Theo had been a liability since they'd been determined to fight Cyrus on any decision he made as pack leader.

The change in their attitudes was startling, much like the emotions running through me.

"Rosemary, *please*, wait." Killian grabbed my hand again, and I tensed.

"When someone doesn't want to be touched, you shouldn't force them." I faced him, arching a brow. I felt like the old Rosemary as some of my emotions calmed.

He dropped my hand. "You're right. I'm sorry."

I nodded, relishing the toned-down feelings. I believed this was what mortals described as numb, but that had always been my norm. It was comforting, refreshing, and part of me craved simplicity.

"Again." He grimaced.

I crossed my arms. "Again? You only said it once."

The corners of his mouth tipped upward. "There she is."

Glancing over my shoulder, I expected to see Sterlyn, but no one was behind me. "There who is? I don't see anyone."

He chuckled. "The Rosemary I recognize."

My heart rate increased. Well, there went my momentary reprieve. "And here I thought you wanted to talk with me. I didn't realize you were coming out here to insult me further."

"I..." His jaw dropped. "I mean..." He growled as he ran a hand through his hair.

Lifting my chin, I stared him down. Though I might feel insane, I was still a strong woman and wouldn't cower to anyone.

He exhaled, and his shoulders sagged. "I'm sorry. I'm being an ass. I just don't understand what's going on."

My anger deflated as he became more like the Killian I knew. "Me neither. I feel insane."

"Yeah?" he asked, his dark chocolate irises lightening. "What do you mean? Did that *demon* do something to you?"

Laughter bubbled out of me, surprising us both. "See? This is an example. I never understood why mortals laughed at the strangest times, and I *just* did it. I don't understand what's going on. I'm just...I *feel* things so much more than I used to."

He tugged at the collar of his hunter green shirt. "Did he do something to cause it, though?"

That was a loaded question, and Killian clearly hadn't wanted to ask it. He was probably afraid I would snap at him again, and to be fair, it was possible. I hadn't known until it was too late that I was becoming emotionally charged.

However, the concerned lines etched into his forehead had my emotions ebbing again. He wasn't trying to be a jerk; he truly was concerned about my well-being. "No, I don't think so." It felt more natural opening up to him than anyone else, and I had no clue why. It'd always been that way. "That day we ran into the demons, I got hurt because I *felt* something inside me." Despite having had a similar conversation with Ronnie, I felt more vulnerable. She'd guessed, whereas with Killian, I was coming clean.

He tilted his head. "What do you mean?"

"I don't know." I tensed, bothered that I didn't know how to explain it. "I was pulled toward Levi even before I saw him. The weird sensations keep growing stronger, and the calmness I normally feel is out of my grasp. Every time I'm close to him, my feelings become more intense."

"Like a mate bond?" He shook his head, his eyes widening. "Can you be bonded to a *demon*? Do angels even have mates?"

A grin sneaked onto my face, an expression that didn't occur naturally for me...or it hadn't until now. Killian sounded more terrified than I felt. "I think there have been a handful of occurrences, but every angel who had a mate perished before I was born. It's been centuries since anything like that has happened, even with all the angels who came to Earth to live in one location. So our assumption is that we don't have fated mates, or what we call 'preordained mates.' Although demons were angels before they changed, so...maybe?" Saying it out loud sounded bizarre, but if Levi wasn't spelled, this was a possibility.

"But you aren't sure?" he asked hopefully.

"I...I don't know. I've never felt this way toward anyone before." I stared at him, trying to understand what I was seeing. Pragmatic Rosemary would've just answered and moved on, but that look on Killian's face unsettled me. "Why?" As soon as I asked the question, I wanted to take it back. I likely didn't want to hear his answer.

He chuckled and scratched the back of his neck. "I'm not sure if I like this more attuned version of you."

That could be taken as either a compliment or an insult. I wasn't sure how he'd intended it. "What do you mean?"

"You've always been able to pick up on things. You're very perceptive, but emotions usually don't register with you." He put his hands into his pockets and avoided my eyes.

Memories of watching stupid movies with Sierra flitted through my mind. Most of the drama could've been prevented if the main characters had been honest instead of hiding their thoughts and feelings. Now I understood why they did it—expressing how you felt made you uncomfortable, especially if you were unsure of the other person, but the old Rosemary was *right*. Not handling things head-on could cause more issues. Though I didn't want to ask, I knew it was best if I didn't drop the conversation. "What are you not telling me?"

The confident alpha disappeared in front of me. Killian crossed his arms and stared at the cobblestone ground. "I...I always thought that if you were going to feel that way about someone, it might be nice if..." He trailed off and cleared his throat uncomfortably.

Despite now feeling things, I apparently still wasn't good at picking up on social cues. Obviously, he was uncomfortable telling me something, but I wasn't following. "Is there a certain angel you saw me with?" As I thought through the male angels, none of them affected me, definitely nothing compared to Levi.

At the thought of his name, my eyes flicked up at the bedroom window.

"Uh...not exactly." He kicked the stone with his heel. "I thought maybe, when we were older, if we hadn't found our mates...that maybe..."

I forced my attention back to Killian, and it was way harder than I wanted to admit. I wanted to be up there with Levi, trying to apologize for the words that had hurt him earlier, but he'd been in the wrong, too, trying to use me to get to Killian. I couldn't be too eager to reconcile things between us. Besides, Killian was very ineloquently trying to tell me something, and he deserved all my attention.

"Maybe what?" I still wasn't sure where he was going, even though my gut told me I should know.

He laughed as his cheeks turned pink. "Wow. I...I always thought I'd be smoother when this moment came."

My heart stopped. No wonder Sierra had commented that it was like one of the movies we watched.

"I've had a crush on you for a while, now," Killian murmured, and glanced at me. "I always thought you'd figure it out, but it's obvious you haven't."

I stared at him. For a moment, I couldn't speak. Killian was very attractive, and he'd become an amazing guy. Women threw themselves at him at every opportunity. Maybe if I'd been a mortal, I'd have felt something other than friendship for him...or I might have before meeting Levi. But my affection for him was one of friendly kinship. I'd had no *idea*...

"You're a wolf. I'm an angel." I grimaced. That sounded horrible, but it was more than that.

Killian huffed as if I'd punched him. "I know that, and I'm being foolish."

Ugh, I didn't know how to fix this. "Plus, you always said you wanted to find your fated mate, and you're one of my closest friends. I would *never* want that to change."

He nodded, but his gaze flicked to the woods. "You don't have to explain. It's fine. You don't feel the same way. Got it." He walked back toward the front of the house.

This was going poorly. No wonder people avoided such conversations. But leading him on wasn't right, either. In fairness, I hadn't realized he was interested in me. I hadn't intended to do that.

Fate had a wicked sense of humor because now I was the one running after him and capturing his hand. "If the world were different, I think I would feel the same way."

He paused but kept his back to me.

My gut said I didn't have long to salvage our friendship. I was on borrowed time, and I needed to use every second wisely. "You need to understand. Angels don't feel strong emotions. I never truly felt anything very strongly except for what I believed was right and wrong. That's one reason I became friends with you all and gave you my loyalty. Sterlyn's arrival was destiny, I believe, and she changed the core of this group funda-mentally."

Killian's body went slack, and he turned to me. "I agree with that last part."

I'd known he would. Our opinions were closely aligned. I'd found that only with him and Sterlyn. "She is the glue that put this group together and prepared us for Ronnie, Cyrus, and Annie." She'd even changed me for the better and had rekindled Mother's hope. "And because of that, you became an important person to me. One of the *most* important ones." I paused and inhaled slowly. The next part would be hard to get out, but I needed him to understand. "And if I could *choose* the right person, it *would* be you. However, if Levi is the other half of my preordained mates—"

He smiled sadly and sighed. "I know. But Rosemary, he *is* our enemy."

Boy, didn't I know it. "Why would fate do that?" The question had been tickling the back of my mind.

Angels were taught to follow fate and her divine plan—that was the basis of the Divine Doctrine the Shadow City Council followed. Any time we ques-tioned it, we were essentially questioning our existence, and angels didn't like feeling unsure. To survive the test of time, we had to be confident and sure of our purpose.

"I don't know," Killian said, and placed a hand on my arm. "But no matter what, I'll be there next to you. You won't *ever* be alone."

My eyes stung, and my vision blurred. My heart

expanded so much, it hurt to breathe. Something dripped from my eye and rolled down my cheek.

"Hey, what's wrong?" he asked softly. "Did I upset you?"

I shook my head. I didn't trust myself to speak. The other times my emotions had intensified to this extreme, I'd been around Levi, so the onslaught had taken me by surprise.

Taking a shaky breath, I steeled myself. I had to learn to navigate the storms when they raged inside. "No, what you said was perfect. I just don't know how to control them."

His brows furrowed. "Control what?"

I wiped the tear from my cheek. "These strong emotions. I've never had something impact me like this before."

He snorted. "You can't control emotions. All you can do is make sure you don't do or say something you'll regret. Even then, you'll mess up. It's part of being human."

"But I'm *not* human." If I didn't get a handle on myself, the other angels would think I was unworthy. Mostly, I didn't care what they thought; otherwise, I wouldn't be hanging around with this group. But these emotions...they were different. They would make me an outcast...a weakling. Rational thought was superior and one of the many things that made angels the strongest type of supernatural.

Killian placed his hands on my shoulders. "You have two legs, two arms, a heart, a family, and friends. If that doesn't humanize you, maybe it's a gift that you're starting to feel things. Besides, you're stuck with us, whether you act like the angel we've always known or this more complex version of you. You're still you, and anyone who doesn't understand that is a tool."

I had no clue what a tool was, but I understood his meaning. I'd never needed reassurance before, but his words eased something within me—something that had been growing and festering and taking on a life of its own.

A few more tears fell down my cheeks, and before I knew it, Killian had pulled me into his arms. My chest convulsed. "Are we okay?" I asked.

I buried my head in his shirt, breathing in his musky sandalwood smell.

"Of course we are. You're so damn important, and nothing will ever change that." He kissed the top of my head. "You're right. What we have is special, and I would never risk changing that. And if Levi does anything to hurt you, he'll answer to me."

A weight lifted off my shoulders just as something shifted inside me and the *yank* took hold.

The front door opened, and I stumbled out of Killian's grasp.

Levi stood in the doorway, his mocha eyes almost black.

Was he trying to escape now, of all times? Terror replaced my sense of peace.

I didn't want him to go, and that stemmed from more than just wanting answers. "Get back inside, Levi."

The silver wolves sprang into action, racing to the front of the house.

"Oh, I bet you'd like that," he bit out as his neck corded, "so you and the *mutt* can finish what we started upstairs." His nostrils flared as he glared at Killian. "Are you so desperate for her that you don't care if she still tastes like me?"

"You son of a bitch," Killian growled, and marched toward him.

I needed to de-escalate the situation, and fast. "That's not what was happening."

Before I had a chance to calm Levi, Ronnie and Alex appeared behind him. Alex reached for Levi's neck, but he ducked and snarled, "I'm not trying to escape. I just want to break that stupid mutt in half for touching her."

He was acting like a jealous lunatic, but I'd had a similar reaction when he'd simply called Kira a *nickname*. Even though Killian and I hadn't done anything wrong, Levi felt threatened. He didn't know I'd just turned down any sort of chance Killian had with me.

The front door to the house beside us opened, and Cyrus, Annie, and Sierra rushed out. All three of them were still in their pajamas. Clearly, we'd woken them.

Ronnie shadowed in front of Levi, increasing the tenseness of the situation.

I needed to get to Levi to calm him down.

Tires squealed not too far from us, and the familiar hum of Sterlyn and Griffin's Navigator drew closer.

The silver wolves reached the door at the same time as I did, and we surrounded Levi.

The hurt in his eyes cut into my soul.

"Nothing happened out here," I explained as the Navigator stopped abruptly at the curb.

Sometimes, the pack link was more of a pain than a benefit, especially now, when I couldn't explain to Sterlyn and the others what was going on.

"Is he trying to escape?" Cyrus rasped as the three of them came up behind me.

"He's not," Killian said, standing beside Cyrus. "Rosemary, get back. He's not thinking rationally."

Levi bared his teeth as the Navigator doors opened. We had him surrounded, but when someone knew their time was limited, desperation took hold.

Before I could tell Killian to give me space, Levi's gaze settled on him. And he lunged.

CHAPTER TWENTY-TWO

I BLOCKED KILLIAN. Not because the wolf shifter couldn't defend himself, but rather because Levi wouldn't be as likely to hurt me...or I didn't think he would.

Bracing myself for impact, I stood with my feet shoulder-width apart and my knees bent. Levi slammed into me, almost knocking me over, but I held my ground. I shoved him in the chest, pushing him through the door.

Griffin and Cyrus ran past me, entering the house as Levi flew backward. He knocked into Alex, and the vampire stumbled back. Alex hissed and wrapped his arms around Levi's throat.

Alex commanded, "Calm down, or I'll make you."

"Bite me," Levi snarked, and leaned forward, attempting to throw Alex over his body.

However, Alex gracefully flipped over the demon's head and landed on his feet just as Griffin and Cyrus grabbed Levi's arms.

Footsteps pounded into the house; Sterlyn, Killian, Kira, Annie, and Sierra had joined us inside.

"What's happening?" Griffin growled.

Levi bucked against his captors, trying to get his arm free to attack Killian. "I'm going to teach him a lesson," Levi growled as his focus centered on Killian.

"We weren't doing anything!" I wanted to punch him. Maybe that would knock some sense into him, but it could also escalate the situation. "If you'd just listen—"

"That's not what it looked like from the bedroom window." Levi sneered and turned his rage-filled eyes on me. "You two looked awfully loving out there."

"Oh, my gods," Sierra murmured. "This is just like a rom—"

"If you finish that sentence, I swear to the Divine I will kick your ass." I focused on her, making sure she felt the truth of my words. I didn't have patience for her mouth.

She lifted her hands. "Just saying."

"You know what? It's fine," Levi said coldly. "It's clear where we stand."

His words were a punch in the gut, but I wasn't sure how to respond. Even if we were preordained, we were *enemies*. Any future would be riddled with controversy, and how selfish would I be to put my parents in an even more precarious situation? Add on the fact that I couldn't trust Levi, and that left us with nothing but heartbreak.

Killian's jaw twitched. "You're being a douchebag and not even trying to listen to her."

"I told you he wouldn't try to leave," Kira said from

the doorway as she crossed her arms. "He's a good guy. He saved me from those shifters."

"See, at least *Red* is on my side," Levi said, smirking at me. His breathing had evened out, though anger still lined his face.

He was trying to hurt me, and the worst part was that it was working. Pain radiated in my chest, but I ignored it. That would only encourage him to continue acting like this.

Alex sighed. "For two people old enough to know better, you're both acting like pubescent teenagers."

He was right. I wasn't sure how old Levi was, but I shouldn't have been acting like this.

Levi shrugged and exhaled. "I'm fine. She made her feelings clear. You can let me go. I'll *behave* and be a good little captive."

Cyrus and Griffin glanced at each other, and then Cyrus nodded marginally. They released their grasp on him but stayed close.

I wanted to talk with him alone, but that wouldn't resolve anything. It would probably make the entire situation worse.

Remembering Killian's advice, I attempted to focus on the task at hand. Levi's tantrum couldn't be our focus when we had so many other things in play. Even though it hurt, I centered myself, trying to become pragmatic Rosemary once more.

I turned to Kira. "What did you learn about the attack?"

"Thanks to Levi—" Kira started, and I already

wanted to hurt her. The sensation was so strong that my foot took an involuntary step toward her, but Levi's cocky smirk brought me back to the present. Oblivious, she shut the front door and continued "—I could identify all of them, since Grady and I went to school with them."

"Wait. If you went to school with them, and they didn't try to hide their faces, that could only mean..." Ronnie's face turned a shade paler.

She didn't need to finish. We all knew where she was heading.

They'd intended to injure her to the point where she wouldn't be able to remember them, or more likely, they'd planned to kill her.

"They were going to make sure she couldn't stay leader of the fox shifters and police force." Annie visibly winced. "What is *up* with all the assholes in Shadow City?"

At one point, that would've offended me, but every day, the city seemed to grow more corrupt, mainly under Azbogah's leadership. Five hundred years ago, Azbogah had been bad, but he hadn't had as much of a following because long ago, he'd killed one of our own. People had feared him but hadn't respected him. They'd viewed him as a killer and the person who could judge their fate. That was as far as his influence had gone. But over the centuries, he'd changed people's minds about him through crafty planning and manipulation.

A memory tried to flit through my head, and a sour taste filled my mouth. Something was plaguing me, but I couldn't remember what. I had a sinking feeling it was important.

"It hasn't always been like that." Alex took a seat on the couch farthest from the door. "Seventy-five years ago, things started to change when people began discussing opening up the city. Between Sterlyn's arrival and the actual opening, there's been a huge shift in attitudes, and things have been spiraling."

That was one way of putting it.

Levi stepped toward the other couch, and Cyrus and Griffin tensed. He arched an eyebrow at the two shifters. "I'm just going to sit, if that's okay with you." His tone was condescending, like he hoped to cause friction.

"We shall allow it." Annie bowed her head slightly and rolled her hand.

That was odd, even for her. She didn't normally act theatrically. I watched as the corner of Levi's lips turned upward. Cyrus shook his head and stepped back.

She'd defused the situation, and I was at a loss for how.

Taking a seat on the end of the couch opposite Alex, Levi patted the seat next to him.

If he thought I'd throw my hurt and anger to the wind and calmly sit with him, he'd soon learn differently. I was a strong woman even if I was smitten, and I wouldn't just let things go when he'd purposely tried to hurt me.

"Come on, Red." Levi patted the seat cushion again. "You're the only ally I have. I need you beside me."

My stomach hardened, and I'd only ever felt like this when I had intense physical pain, but clearly, strong emotions could give the same results. Worse, I was certain he was doing this to hurt me.

Killian stood next to me, so close that his arm brushed mine. It was a small gesture but one I understood after he'd sworn to always stand beside me.

No matter what.

That was more than Levi was willing to do.

My head screamed *I told you so*, and my heart fractured more. The only blessing was that my head took more control again.

Learning that Levi could be vindictive was a good thing. I should've *known*. He was a demon, and I'd lost sight of that.

This was my wake-up call.

Kira walked past me without hesitation and took the spot next to him. Jealousy burned through my chest, but I kept it at bay.

"Hey—" Ronnie started, but I glanced at her and shook my head.

The way I was feeling, I could easily shed a tear, and I would not give Levi the satisfaction. If he knew his action had had the desired response, he would continue, and I wasn't sure I could handle much more. The best thing we could do was focus on the discussion at hand.

"We're sure Grady and Azbogah were behind the attacks?" I'd never struggled to keep my tone level before, but unfortunately, there was a first time for everything.

Sterlyn's purple-silver eyes glowed faintly as she looked at me. A slight frown marred her face.

With my luck, that was Killian linking with her, spilling his guts about Levi and me. I should've realized everyone here would learn about it sooner rather than later.

"Not definitively." Sterlyn made her way to the center of the room.

With her focus off me, some of the tension released from my body. She was good at knowing when to push and when to give someone space.

Griffin plopped down beside Kira, sitting close to the cushion's edge. He blew a raspberry and shook his head. "We've got someone quietly looking into Grady, but my gut says it was him."

"They'll be expecting a guard to look into it," Ronnie said as she sat next to Alex. "Even if someone does it quietly, they'll know."

Smiling proudly, Kira said, "That's why we have guards looking into it, but also one of my friends on the desk side. She keeps her head down and stays away from most people, and they tend to overlook her."

Tugging on one ear, Sierra squished her eyebrows together. "I'm not sure how that even helps. You need someone aggressive to discover the truth."

Killian chuckled. "That's not true. Sometimes, the quiet and invisible ones know the most."

"She wouldn't understand that concept." Annie scoffed. "Sierra is more of a *grab someone by their balls* type of person."

Sierra stomped her foot and moved closer to me as she glared at Annie. "I only did that one time, and *he* deserved it. If he hadn't cheated on me, his balls would still be intact."

"Balls?" I immediately regretted the question. I hadn't wanted to derail the conversation—we needed to stay on point so *Red* could leave.

Annie smiled adoringly at me. "Her innocence is sweet at times."

Cyrus took his mate's hand and led her to the open seat on the other couch next to Ronnie.

"You know, testicles," Sierra said, and gestured to Killian's crotch. "The round things that hang behind the joystick."

"Why don't you just say testicles and penis?" Modern vernacular dumbfounded me. Why call things by terms *other* than their actual names?

Placing his arm around Ronnie, Alex replied, "It's not innocence. It just reveals her age."

The vampire was going to die. It was nice having someone as a target for my rage. I'd ensure that his end slow and painful. Even though I usually didn't enjoy violence, I could make an exception—for him.

I opened my mouth, but Sierra cut me off.

"Wait. How old *are* you?" Sierra's eyes widened like a kid on Christmas morning.

Levi scratched his head and glanced at the group. "And this group has defeated demon wolves and demons with this attention span? I'm shocked."

"Hey!" Sierra placed her hands on her hips and stared Levi down. "No one was talking to you."

Rubbing his temples, Alex closed his eyes. "I've

learned that this sort of...*derailment* is common, but when it matters, we pull together to take down adversaries with an efficiency I've never seen before. However, Sierra tends to create chaos all around her. Apparently, most here find it endearing."

"Oh, Alex." Sierra lifted her arms. "I knew I was growing on you."

Levi's mocha eyes focused on me as he mouthed, *You're welcome.*

My traitorous stomach fluttered. He'd purposely made himself a target to distract Sierra.

A low hiss came from Alex. "Don't push it, Sierra. I said *most* here find it endearing. I wasn't including myself in that category."

"Don't include me, either," Cyrus murmured, and leaned over Annie.

I wanted to interject, *Me, neither*, but I didn't want to deal with her wrath; she could easily get back on the topic of my age. I had to choose my battles. Sierra could focus on Cyrus and Alex. Despite Cyrus being two hundred and eighty years younger than Alex, he acted more similarly to Alex and me than to the shifters his age. He'd grown up in a hard environment where he'd been ruthlessly trained for battle from early childhood and hadn't had nurturing family relationships like the rest of us.

Sierra scoffed. "I can't help it that you two have *no* sense of humor. I'd go as far as to say—"

"I think what Killian was trying to say was that when a person is quiet and overlooked, they overhear things," I interrupted. If we continued to let her go down this path, there was no telling which direction she'd go in next. Someone needed to get her back in line, and that someone might as well be me.

"Oh." She glanced at the ceiling and tilted her head. "That's actually smart."

"Now they're completing each other's sentences," Levi jeered. "It *must* be *love*."

I clenched my hands, again digging my nails into my palms. The way he switched attitudes was hard to keep up with and making me dizzy. He must have a split personality.

"They've always done that." Griffin shrugged. "It's not a big deal."

Levi's head jerked back, and he winced.

Sometimes, I wished this group would leave things well enough alone, but Griffin hadn't meant to cause more problems.

"Anyway..." Sterlyn sighed, glancing at her mate. Her eyes glowed faintly.

I had a feeling that she was telling Griffin about Levi and me, and I hoped to the gods I was wrong.

She scanned the group. "We've got guards looking into it while Kira's friend does some digging on her end."

"But if her friend's a wolf, that could still draw suspicion." Annie rubbed her hands together. "Right?"

"That's the best part. She's a jaguar." Kira smiled. "The jaguars opposed the wolf representatives as much as the foxes did after Sterlyn and Griffin backed me as the leader. My friend and I have gotten close because we're the only women in a male-dominated field. But we've been careful not to draw attention to her to preserve her anonymity."

That was a very good thing. Kira had always been cunning, even for a fox. She could find allies in the oddest places and hear things no one else could. Now that she was on our side, I admired that quality. Though I might not like how Levi was acting toward her, that wasn't her fault.

Maybe that was why she and Levi got along. They understood each other.

"Speaking of which, the three of us need to get back to the city." Sterlyn gestured to Griffin and Kira. "We don't want anyone to notice our absence."

"Red, can I talk to you for a moment?" Levi asked, and jumped to his feet. "Alone?" He glanced at me, then back at her.

The scoundrel was hitting me where it hurt. I wanted to jump, scream, and yell, but I couldn't do that. I had to be better than that. If I could win battles, I could overcome *this*.

"Uh, sure." Kira climbed to her feet and looked at Sterlyn. "Can we have a second?"

Sterlyn nodded. "Stay where we can see you."

"Fine." Levi rolled his eyes. "Let's go to the dining room to at least have the illusion of privacy."

The urge to pull Kira's hair overwhelmed me, and I couldn't believe my natural reactions had fallen to a new low. Pulling hair was a mortal tactic, not one of a trained warrior.

As the two of them walked by me, everything inside me screamed to follow them, but I gritted my teeth, refusing to budge.

This time, my anger wasn't channeled toward her. It was all for Levi, as it should be. First, I'd punch him, and then maybe I'd take a stab at Sierra's method. If he didn't have testicles, he couldn't reproduce. I'd be doing the world a service.

A hand grabbed me, pulling me back, and I spun around, ready to attack.

CHAPTER TWENTY-THREE

I HATED BEING MANHANDLED, so I raised a fist.

"Whoa, hold it, Cujo." Killian released me and lifted his hands to protect his face. "I want to help you, not piss you off."

"Cujo?" The random word had distracted me for a second. Something else I didn't understand.

"It's a movie reference..." He trailed off and gently touched my arm. "It doesn't matter. Come on, let's get some fresh air."

"But..." I didn't want to leave. I wanted to march into the kitchen and demand that Levi stop playing games. I couldn't get past him trying to hurt me, and what made it worse was that his tactic was *working*. I always snubbed the girls who acted like this. I'd sworn I would never let *anyone*, let alone a *man*, treat me this way.

And here I was, allowing a *demon* to do exactly that.

It burned.

"Come on." Killian's fingers dug a little into my skin. "Before you do something you'll regret."

Referencing our earlier conversation was effective. I was letting my emotions guide me again. I finally understood why toddlers threw tantrums.

Feelings were hard.

My gaze landed on Sierra. I wondered how she could constantly embarrass herself and still show up like everything was ordinary. Maybe you became desensitized to embarrassing things the more you did them. I didn't want to find out. I was still a warrior, and warriors didn't succumb to temptation.

Sierra caught me focusing on her, and she crossed her arms. "What? I didn't do anything." Her irises lightened to silver as she smirked. "That was your *lover*, not me."

Obviously, she'd learned nothing from her smart mouth. I lunged at her, but Killian countered and stepped in front of me, blocking my path. He placed his hands on my shoulders and spoke low. "Rosemary, you know how she is. Let it go."

"Whoa. I was just kidding," Sierra whimpered and wrapped her arms around herself. "Uh...I'm sorry." She stumbled toward Sterlyn and murmured, "She might actually attack me."

"Sierra and I will go watch from the stairwell and make sure Levi doesn't do anything stupid." Ronnie rolled her eyes and dragged Sierra toward the hallway.

The longer Levi was back there with *Red*, the angrier I became. Killian was right. The best thing I could do was get some distance. I couldn't allow Levi to influence me into acting irrationally. He was a wild card and a risk to my friends and our city as a whole.

After all, he'd managed to sneak into Shadow City.

Needing no further encouragement, I headed to the front door.

When I was halfway out, Alex murmured, "What is their problem? One minute, Levi was losing it, and now Rosemary. Could—"

I didn't want to hear any more, so I focused on the sounds outside. I'd be asking the same questions if I were them, so it wasn't fair to lash out. I'd already done it to Sierra.

Oh, gods. I'd have to apologize to her. She'd gloat and make me angry again, but that was a problem for another time. Right now, I was barely keeping myself together.

The door opened again, and a musky freesia scent wafted toward me.

Sterlyn.

"Are you okay?" she asked.

I'd already bared my soul once today with Killian, and I wasn't sure I had it in me to go through it all again. "You know the answer to that. I'm sure Killian shared everything with you."

"He did," Sterlyn said, coming to stand next to me. "I thought you might want to talk about it from your perspective."

"No!" I grimaced. I'd hoped to play it cooler, but alas, I wasn't handling anything the way I wanted to of late.

She snorted. "I know that sentiment all too well."

"Then why did you ask?" If I thought she didn't want to discuss something, I never would've brought it up.

"Because I didn't want to *not* ask if you wanted me to." She bumped her shoulder into mine. "I should've known better. You aren't like Sierra, who wants someone to show they care."

I wasn't sure that was true. It would be nice if Levi weren't being an imbecile. Not sure how to respond, I changed the subject. "What about the artifacts?" I'd forgotten to ask, and that was an important piece of the drama. "Are any missing?"

"Not sure yet." Sterlyn let the other topic go. "They're doing an inventory, starting in the garage. It'll take time for them to work through the whole building."

There was no telling how many relics were inside that place. The warehouse was large, and many not-so-sacred items were stored there along with truly valuable pieces. The more precious cargo was heavily guarded and located inside the building beyond the warehouse, closer to the guards. The witches placed stronger spells there. "Shouldn't they check the main warehouse first?"

"They are, but the problem is the inventory list is hard to get." Sterlyn chewed on her bottom lip. "The rarest relics were already there when the city closed, and they're struggling to find a list of them. I...I don't know how we'll account for that."

Azbogah was a son of a demon. He had to be. He'd orchestrated this whole situation, and I was afraid it would bite my family in the buttocks. I wasn't sure what his endgame was. "I bet Azbogah has that list locked up."

Mother had told me that when the gates closed, Azbogah had been somewhat in charge of Shadow City. However, when the other supernatural races banded together to take down the angel dictatorship that was becoming prevalent, they managed to strong-arm the angels to step down because the collective group working together was stronger than the angels alone. The change was for each supernatural race to have an equal say in any decisions made for the entire city, and thus, a council was created with twelve representatives, three of each race. Since Azbogah had been in power before the angels had to stand down, the dark angel had influence over what artifacts were kept in the warehouse.

The council had vowed that no one beyond the leader of the police force should have access to the list of artifacts within the building, not even Azbogah. Hindsight was clear, whereas in this moment, turmoil and unrest affected almost everyone's mind. I knew my mother *still* grappled with how she could have allowed her brother to die.

The former angel of justice had failed to help her brother, and the self-proclaimed angel of judgment had sentenced him to death. It had affected Mother deeply, despite angels' usual lack of emotion, because *she* hadn't followed through on the gift the Divine had given her.

"That's what we said." Sterlyn closed her eyes. "The silver wolves leaving Shadow City was the wrong call. Maybe if we'd stayed, none of this would've happened."

As strong as Sterlyn was, she also took on the wrongs of others, especially when it came to her pack. "The alpha of the silver wolves listened to Ophaniel and made the best decision he could at the time." Rational Rosemary was coming back, and I embraced her. "You can't blame yourself—it's pointless. It won't change our situation, and you'll be wasting energy and our time when we need to be strategizing."

"I wondered if the Rosemary I used to know was still in there." She winked and nodded. "You're right. We need to figure things out and get ahead of Azbogah for once. I hate that even after we finally take care of a threat, we're still behind."

I'd been around for far longer than her, and I still hadn't gotten ahead, either, so I understood the sentiment. Things had always gone Azbogah's way until recently. He was scrambling to regain the upper hand he'd had not long ago.

The front door opened, but I refused to turn around. I didn't want to seem desperate.

"Let's hit the road," Griffin said.

My body relaxed marginally, and I turned to find Kira stepping out of the house. Her golden complexion was a tad paler as she stuffed her hands into her pockets, and the usual sparkle was missing from her eyes. Her shoulders slumped as if the weight of the world was on them.

Worse, my heart sped up at her look of dejection. Obviously, her and Levi's conversation hadn't gone well.

I was officially the type of person I'd never wanted to become.

This ended now.

Levi didn't get to change me into a worse version of myself. I refused to allow it.

"Is something wrong, Kira?" Sterlyn asked, picking up on the same thing as I had.

A forced smile spread across her face, and the tension around her eyes relaxed. "Yeah, sorry. Just a lot going on. I do need to get back, though. I'm getting pinged."

Killian and Alex appeared in the doorway, and Alex leaned against the frame. "What's the plan from here on out?" he asked.

"We figure out who organized the shifter attacks and uncover what, if anything, is missing from the artifact building." Sterlyn pushed her shoulders back, looking every bit the leader she was. "You all make sure Levi doesn't escape and try to get more information from him. If Hell is buzzing, that means they're up to something. We need to know what it is."

We'd had Levi all this time, and he hadn't shared much. I was done being nice. If he wouldn't talk, I'd remove his tongue. The longer Hell had to organize, the worse off we'd be up here. We needed as much time to prepare to fight them as they had to plan against us.

"And beating him is off the table still?" Killian smirked, his eyes darkening. "Because sometimes, it *can* be effective."

As usual, he and I were on the same page.

"He's a *good* guy," Kira said loudly.

Griffin arched a brow. "Just because he saved you doesn't mean he's *good*. He could've saved you for a reason. Have you thought about that?"

"I'm good at reading people," Kira said defiantly, lifting her chin. "Maybe if you stopped treating him like he's unworthy, he might share more information with you."

My newfound control started spiraling. I took a deep breath, forcing myself to pause and think through what I was about to say.

Barely.

"Then I guess we'll have to agree to disagree." I kept my voice level, which was way harder than it should have been. "Because he hasn't done anything to prove his loyalty."

"He *saved* me," Kira parroted, as if we weren't all aware of that fact.

"*After* he sneaked into Shadow City," Sterlyn said softly. "I get that you feel as if you owe him, but he shouldn't have been there."

That was the entire point. He'd done nothing to prove he was trustworthy, even though part of me was desperate to trust him. And there was a reason he'd slipped into the city. We had to determine what it was.

My phone rang, and I was glad for the interruption. My mother's name flashed on the caller ID. I'd been dreading this conversation, but I couldn't delay it any longer. Mother was worried, and we were under scrutiny.

"We'll come back in a few days to provide an update," Griffin said as he removed his keys from his pocket. "We need to be careful discussing things within the city, so it's safer to talk here."

Great. That meant Kira would be coming back.

Maybe Levi would have spilled his guts by then, and we'd have already cut him loose. I'd hate to have to deal with another private conversation between them.

My phone rang a third time. "Okay, let me know if you need anything. I have to take this."

I walked toward the tree line in the direction of the river, happy to get away from the drama though still keeping an eye on the house. I sucked in a breath and answered, "Hello."

"Thank the gods. I was starting to worry you were in trouble." Mother's voice sounded more human than mine did. There were times when she felt more than I did, which I'd always found odd.

My mind raced for something to say. "I apologize. I was talking to Sterlyn's group, and it took a while for me to answer."

"Sterlyn. Oh, at the condo."

She was trying to determine where I was without asking. She should have realized I was on to her tactics. I wasn't a little angel any longer. "I'm in Shadow Terrace."

"Shadow *Terrace*?" Surprise leaked through her tone.

Most of the time, when I wasn't in Shadow City, I was in Shadow Ridge. We rarely came to Shadow Terrace unless there was an issue. The exception had been for Ronnie and Alex's wedding. "Yes, and it's best if you don't ask anything more."

Mother sighed. "You and your friends are good at finding trouble."

It wasn't worth denying. "It normally resolves long-lasting issues that have either been ignored or we couldn't address before."

She cleared her throat. "We need you here. Azbogah is on a crusade against me and gaining more followers. I need you and Pahaliah to stand beside me."

"I *do* stand beside you, and by staying where I am, I am following through on that promise." I was trying to do the right thing. "I want to be there with you, but it's better if I'm not. Trust me."

"Are you safe?" The clacking of high heels echoed on her end, and I guessed she was at the capitol building. "And do you promise to tell me if you're in danger or find what you're looking for?"

She must have been stressed if she was at work this early. Most of the council members came in later in the day. "I'm safe, and I will tell you everything as soon as I can."

We'd had several of these conversations over the past year, and she understood I was on the path of justice, so she gave me immense leeway.

"That's all I ask." Voices that sounded like Azbogah and Erin filtered through on her end. "I've got to go, but I'll call you later."

She hung up, and I stayed there, taking a moment to myself. I stared back at the house. From here, one wouldn't know there was so much drama occurring inside. The sun had risen high in the cloudless blue sky, eliminating some of the chill in the fall air. The redbuds' leaves were a mixture of yellows, reds, and oranges, and added to the picturesque view of the town. Chad and Theo were still in wolf form a few feet deep inside the tree line, so if a human passed them, they wouldn't notice the wolves' presence.

I exhaled...and found a little peace within.

I wanted to stay out here longer, but that would only raise more questions from everyone and draw more snarky commentary from Sierra.

Forcing my legs to move, I marched to the front door and stepped inside before I could change my mind.

The television was on. Cyrus, Annie, and Sierra were on the couch farthest from me, with Killian, Alex, and Ronnie on the closer one. Levi leaned against the wall across from Killian, his eyes on the door.

"You're just in time!" Sierra beamed as she mashed buttons on the remote. "We're looking for a movie to watch."

"This early in the morning?" That was usually a late afternoon or evening thing. I didn't have the patience for it now.

Sierra lifted the remote. "We don't have anything better to do unless Levi is willing to talk."

Levi didn't say anything, his mocha eyes locked on me. He took a few steps toward me, and the buzzing between us kicked into gear without him even touching me. He scratched the back of his head. "Hey, can we talk for a second?"

Oh, *now* he wanted to talk. "Do you want to go into

the dining room?" That was where he had taken *Red*, after all.

"Yeah, that'll work." He shrugged like it wasn't a big deal.

And that was when things became clear. It was time to draw a line.

CHAPTER TWENTY-FOUR

NOT WANTING him to reach the dining room first, I stalked by the closest couch, and Killian took my hand.

Levi growled low, but I ignored him. We were irrational when it came to each other, and one of us had to at least *try* to stay calm. I was determined that it would be me.

Following my lead, Killian leaned toward me and asked, "Are you sure this is a good idea?"

No, I wasn't. It was probably a horrible idea, but Levi and I were stuck together in this house for the foreseeable future. It could be hours, days, or even months. There was no telling how long he'd drag this out, and we weren't cold-blooded killers. He wasn't actively threatening us... that we could tell. And killing him in cold blood would put us on the same level as our enemies. We *had* to be better than that.

So to prevent myself from lying, I said the only acceptable thing: "It's inevitable."

Levi and I had to find an amicable way to exist with each other—one where we weren't either fighting or kissing. There had to be an in-between.

Jaw twitching, Levi stood beside me, glaring at Killian's hand. Oh, so he could call Kira a nickname and sit next to her, but he lost it when a friend of mine reacted with concern? Well, he could go back to Hell.

"We won't be long," I assured Killian with a tight smile. It felt foreign on my face, but it was an expression that resonated well with the others.

Killian flicked a glance at Levi and wrinkled his nose.

"Please." Sierra sat directly across from Killian on the other couch and rolled her eyes. "We all know Rosemary can kick his ass, and if she needs us, she'll only be, like, twenty feet away. She'll be fine."

Disgruntled, Levi cleared his throat. "I wouldn't be so confident. I do have excellent fighting skills."

"Talk is cheap." Annie chuckled, her irises sparkling as she knocked into Sierra. "All we've seen you be is sneaky and mouthy."

Ronnie snapped her fingers. "Much like Sierra. He could very well be the male version of her."

"Hey!" Sierra leaned back in her seat. "I am *not* sneaky. I do and say everything to your face. I don't do the 'sneaking out and getting into trouble' thing."

"Really?" Killian's eyebrows shot up. "That's what you're going with? I remember when—"

"That was *before* my twenties." Sierra gestured for him to stop. "None of that counts."

"Didn't you *just* turn twenty?" Cyrus glanced over his mate at Sierra.

Alex rubbed his temples, a common gesture when it came to him tolerating Sierra. "You're encouraging her."

I couldn't have said it better myself. Sierra thrived on being the center of attention because she had so many siblings. She had to be loud and outgoing to get attention when surrounded by her brothers. I'd never met any of them. Even though Sierra was close to her family, they weren't trained to fight with the pack and worked various jobs in town.

"Sometimes, it's hard to keep up with your conversations," Levi complained as he edged between Killian and me. "It's like you can't stay on point, which is that I want to talk to you...alone."

Bitterness bubbled inside me. That was the same way he'd asked Kira to talk, and I hated that he put her on the same level as me.

I clung to the sourness churning inside me. I'd need it to stay calm around him.

Killian leaned forward as if he might stand, and all that would accomplish would be making this situation tenser.

I took a few steps toward the hallway. "Let's get this over with."

"Wow, that sounds *so* pleasant," Levi deadpanned.

I didn't bother to respond, instead channeling my frustration into walking more quickly than necessary. He followed as I went into the dining room and turned. I would stare my adversary in the face as always.

His espresso hair was a little longer now and messy, adding to his attractiveness. Unlike all the guys in the other room, Levi didn't try to look perfect. He wasn't flashy, and I liked that. "Should I stand where *Red* did so we can recreate the scene?"

I flushed. There went my composure. After all my resolve, the first thing out of my mouth informed him just how much that had bothered me. It was the complete opposite of what I'd been going for, yet here we were.

He smirked. "It's not very pleasant when someone you have feelings for pays attention to someone else."

"Is that why you did it?" I needed the answer. It wasn't about me needing to confirm it had merely been a ruse but whether he had purposely meant to hurt me.

He shrugged. "Would you blame me if it were? You did go outside to fondle your little plaything."

So he had. The knowledge both hurt and made me stronger. I would never be with someone who manipulated me. Not that I would be with him anyway, but even if the stars had aligned, this would have been a dealbreaker. "I didn't go out there with Killian to upset you. He's become one of my closest friends, and he followed me to check on me because you were acting like a scoundrel."

"Closest friends? Is that what you angels call them?" He crossed his arms and glared.

"Killian and I are *just* friends. You're asking about what angels call lovers." Angels didn't get caught up in what we called each other. We shared fleeting moments to cure boredom. "Sometimes, we don't label it anything."

Levi scoffed. "And you say demons are bad."

"That is *not* the same thing." His audacity to compare a consensual sexual encounter to the terror and pain demons inflicted was nonsensical. "Just like me talking to a friend and telling him he and I will never be a thing wasn't me trying to hurt you."

He froze. "*That's* what you talked about?"

"Not that it's any of your business." I shouldn't have shared that, but I needed him to realize he'd made a fool of himself. And Kira. And me.

"Of *course* it's my business! Anything related to you concerns me because I ca—"

"It doesn't matter." I'd had to stop him there. I couldn't listen to anything else that would mess with my head. We'd been dancing around some invisible line in the sand, and we hadn't considered the damage that could do.

At least, I hadn't. Maybe he had, and that was part of the method to his madness, but Killian was a friend, and I cared—no, *cared* no longer described these emotions. I truly *loved* my friends and family, and though part of my heart was perhaps meant to belong to Levi—even though that sounded insane—I couldn't put his drama and turmoil before them. They'd earned my loyalty, whereas he was trying to rip me to shreds.

What kind of connection was that?

The only answer I had was a toxic relationship, and I was way too old to start something like that. It would've been more acceptable to fall for it as a young angel.

"I'm still not enthused that it happened, but I can get

past it." He winked, as if his flirty demeanor would change the direction of this conversation.

Not today, demon.

"To be frank, I don't care if you can get past it or not. You deliberately tried to hurt me." *And succeeded*, but I left that part unsaid. I bet he already knew. "And it's a *good* thing because we could never work out. We're sworn enemies."

He shrugged as his face smoothed. "I guess what they say about you in Hell is true."

"Me?" My legs went weak, but I managed to stay upright. I didn't want to be the topic of gossip, especially not in Hell.

"You. Angels." He sneered. "Same thing. You're all pompous know-it-alls."

He was lashing out, and though his words stung me, I remained resolved. His vengefulness proved my point. "What did you want to say to me?" I wasn't sure how much longer I could stand here without the wall surrounding my heart crumbling again or my anger and hurt getting the best of me. I needed to apply my warrior training to this situation—get in and out with as little damage as possible.

"Nothing." His irises darkened, and he fisted his hands. "Absolutely nothing."

I had no desire to deal with childish actions. If he wanted to behave like a child, he'd have to find another audience. Maybe *Red* would be up for the challenge. "Okay, then I guess we're done here."

"More than done." He spun on his heel and marched back to the others.

Unfortunately, a large piece of my heart left with him.

THE NEXT COUPLE of days went by slowly even by my standards. Usually, days passed quickly when I wasn't at risk of dying, so for the last two days to have crept by at a snail's pace spoke volumes about my mental health.

After our confrontation, I'd gone back outside. Annie and Ronnie had come to talk with me instead of Killian. Now Cyrus was the one sleeping on the couch in Levi's room while I stayed in the other house with Annie and Sierra.

I felt ashamed that I'd had to remove myself from the situation, but I reminded myself that I was doing it so I didn't make a stupid decision...like kiss Levi, sleep with Levi, lick—whoa. I would stop right there. Making the switch had obviously been the right decision.

The urge to be with him grew stronger at night, maybe because I didn't have a revolving door of people checking on me and distracting me. I was in a room, alone, with only my thoughts for company.

I slept in the same bedroom in this house as the one next door, but with two main differences: Levi was missing, and I got to sleep in the bed. But I couldn't get past wishing I was over there with him.

I'd become pathetic.

Annie, Sierra, and I were watching a World War II documentary. I was a little surprised that Sierra had put it on for me instead of demanding we watch one of her stupid movies. This was one of the rare moments that made her annoying attributes easier to handle.

Out of the corner of my eye, I noticed that Sierra had tensed. She was easy to read. "Is the demon up to something?" I could be there in seconds.

"Nothing major. Killian just linked and said he was on his way over." Sierra paused the show. "He won't tell me why, so I'm guessing it has something to do with Levi."

Sierra was sitting on the couch further from the door next to Annie, while I'd taken the couch across from them. I had my wings spread out, trying to relax.

All the relaxation went out the window.

The front door opened, and I glanced over my shoulder to see Killian walking in. It was around ten at night, and he was in his flannel pajama bottoms and a black T-shirt. When his eyes focused on me, I knew what this was about.

"No." I climbed to my feet, standing firm despite my heart yelling at me to go to Levi. "I don't know what he's up to, but *no*."

"I fully support that decision." Killian rubbed his hands together. "But you two have something weird going on, and I didn't want to *not* tell you and have you find out and get upset with me. He said he feels bad about how things went down, and he'd like a minute with you."

My lungs froze, and my brain became fuzzy. It was as

if my heart were trying to override my brain by making it weak so I'd run to him. Every bone in my body wanted to see him, emphasizing that I *couldn't*. "No. It wouldn't turn out well."

"Rosemary," Sierra whined, "he wants to talk to you. How do you know it won't go well?"

I laughed, and the sound came from deep within. "Uh...past experience. That's how I *know*." Every time I thought we were making headway, something got in the way. All we were doing was torturing each other with something that could never be.

"But—" Sierra started.

Annie patted her arm and sighed. "Sierra, this isn't your decision. It's Rosemary's, and it's clear she's made up her mind. You need to respect that." Her honey-brown eyes darkened as she looked at me with sympathy.

She and Cyrus had been in a similar situation not long ago, but with a major difference. We'd thought she was a demon, but she'd turned out to be a wolf shifter, just like him. They could be together even if they were demon wolf and silver wolf. They were both *good* people who'd been broken but found their way to each other.

Levi was *clearly* a demon, and I was definitely an angel. We had nothing in common other than this forbidden connection.

"Are you sure?" Killian asked tenderly.

This was the final decision. I hated that he would make me say no again, but he wanted to make sure I'd thought it through. Old Rosemary, he would've never doubted, but this turbulent one? Well...there was no telling what she'd do. "I won't see him. There's nothing left to say." Sharp pain shot through my heart as it shattered more.

But the decision was made.

Killian stepped toward me.

My eyes burned, and if he hugged me, I wasn't sure what would happen. I stood, needing space. "Look, I'm tired. It's been a long day." One of the longest I'd experienced in my life.

"Wait. All we did was lie around here." Sierra crossed her arms. "Sit down so we can finish this show. I'll leave you alone about him."

"An idle mind is no one's friend." The words had left me, but I wasn't sure where they'd come from. I'd heard them somewhere. The tickling sensation from before nudged the back of my mind.

Then pain and confusion crushed me. I had to get away.

"Go on to bed." Annie mashed her lips together. "And if you need me, all you have to do is call."

"But—" Killian began.

"Night." I didn't have time for his sympathy. I had a feeling it would be my undoing.

I spun on my heel and marched up the stairs.

"Leave her alone," Annie murmured.

Killian sounded broken as he said, "She's hurting. I need to help her."

"You can't." Annie sighed. "This is something she has to figure out on her own, and she wants space to process it."

I was upstairs in the room when Sierra chuckled sadly. "I always wanted a more human Rosemary, but I didn't realize that meant she'd be in constant pain."

Constant pain.

That was an accurate description, except for those few moments I'd had with Levi...like the kiss. He dominated my thoughts and emotions, and we were sworn enemies, destined never to be together.

I shut the door and didn't have the energy to move. Instead, I pressed my head to the back of the door as tears spilled down my cheeks.

Tears.

The fact that I knew what they were now made my chest throb. I'd *never* experienced pain like this. It hurt to breathe. Without Levi, I was constantly struggling. He must have known, and that was why he'd asked to see me.

Was it another big manipulation?

My chest contracted, and I made a weird gasping noise. It hurt even when I wasn't even breathing. How did anyone survive this? My world was caving in, and I was just a bystander.

Like I was insignificant.

My body shook as the pain and turmoil within tried to escape, but there was no outlet. What I wouldn't give to change our circumstances. Whether it was both of us being human or never meeting at all, any alternative had to be better than *this*.

I crawled across the floor and dragged myself onto the bed with shaky arms.

It'd be so easy to run next door and be with him, but

that wouldn't accomplish anything. I had to stay strong, even if it killed me.

I buried my head in the pillow and cried myself to sleep.

THE FOLLOWING EVENING, Annie had gone next door to spend time with her mate, and I was in my room, desperately avoiding Sierra. Surprisingly, she'd been good at distracting me for the past few days, but that had ended when Killian had asked me to see Levi. She was all over me to reconsider, and I didn't have the energy.

Just forcing myself to say no last night had taken everything out of me. I needed to recharge, both physically and emotionally.

I stood at the window, watching the darkening cobblestone road. The sun was setting, and I'd stayed up here for most of the day, only going downstairs to grab something to eat, which had again ended with Sierra hounding me about the demon.

The one thing I'd determined during my "separation" from Levi was that he must truly have feelings for me. I wasn't sure if they were as strong as mine—I didn't see how they could be—but his irrational actions proved he felt *something* as well. His actions had actually caused more problems between him and the group, and if he was trying to trick us, he needed us to trust him.

An engine purred close by, and I recognized the Navigator. Sterlyn and Griffin were on their way, and if my luck continued, Kira would be with them. We'd been waiting to hear from them, and I'd have to go next door to get the news firsthand.

My stomach fluttered.

Determined not to be left out, I opened the door and headed downstairs.

I found Sierra on the couch closer to the door, facing me. Of course, she was flipping through the channels, looking for something ridiculous to watch.

She turned off the television and tossed the remote onto the couch beside her. "I figured you'd be coming down."

My neck stiffened, causing my head to hurt. "Why didn't you tell me they were on their way?"

"Because you snubbed me." She shrugged and grinned. "I figured I'd let you figure it out on your own."

Even emotional Rosemary didn't understand Sierra's logic at times. She was over the top with everyone, and I didn't want to deal with her, not when I needed all of my restraint to not jump—er—attack Levi.

"Is...uh..." I'd never had an issue asking if Kira was with them before, but I couldn't form the words. I didn't want to know the answer.

"Yes, Kira is with them." Sierra sighed, and some animosity flitted away. "That was the real reason I didn't want to tell you sooner. You would've—"

This was not helping. "Let's go." I marched past her, hitting the door as Griffin pulled up in front of the house. I glanced at the backyard and noticed that Darrell and Chad were on watch.

"Hey!" Sierra called behind me as she hurried to catch up, slamming the door. "Don't leave me behind. I was being a *friend*."

She was, I'd give her that, but she wanted to talk about something I did *not* want to address. Going next door was bad enough. I needed to handle the situation directly.

Sterlyn and Griffin got out of the car, and Sterlyn bit her lip. "Is everything okay?"

As soon as Sierra opened her mouth, I spoke first. "We're eager for an update."

Sierra cocked her head, informing me that Annie, Ronnie, and the others had been filling her in on everything. I shouldn't have been surprised, but I'd hoped that we had enough on our plate without adding my drama to it.

I waited for the back door to open, but it didn't. When I finally scanned the back, looking for bright red hair, I realized no one was there. "I thought Kira was coming."

Griffin snorted. "She will be, but she said she'd be along in a few minutes. She needed to handle something first."

Sierra pursed her lips. "When did she get a vehicle?"

That was a good question. She usually came with Griffin.

"She got one when she officially took over as head of the foxes. She hasn't driven much, but we wanted to get out here and fill you guys in while we wait on her." Griffin walked past me to the front door.

I took a moment to let Sterlyn and Sierra go in before me, but they looked at each other, not moving.

Fine. I'd go in first. I didn't want to deal with any more awkwardness.

I stepped inside to find Levi on the couch closer to the door with Cyrus and Annie, and Killian, Alex, and Ronnie on the other. Of course Levi was sitting on the outside, right where I'd have to walk by.

The air buzzed between us, and my legs moved forward even when I tried to plant my feet. Levi turned in his seat, his mocha eyes meeting mine as he felt the same pull. I'd swear there were sparks in the air between us.

Sierra and Sterlyn walked in behind me, not seeming to sense a hint of the *yank* between Levi and me. It was almost unworldly, and there was nothing I could do. His breathing turned into panting as he leaned toward me. The world faded away like we were the only two in the room.

It had been a terrible decision to come here. I should've let Annie and Sierra fill me in on the details. I wasn't sure I could walk out the door again, but the longer I stayed here, the harder it'd be.

I turned to head back to the door, but Levi stepped in front of me.

CHAPTER TWENTY-FIVE

MY HEART RACED. Levi *cared* enough to stop me. That, or my pulse had risen because I was furious that he was preventing me from leaving. Either explanation was plausible, but realistically, it was a combination of the two that made me sway dizzily.

This split personality thing was becoming a pain in my ass and leading me to use today's common vernacular. Maybe the university classes and hanging out with this group had influenced me more than I'd realized, and Levi had officially forced the final evolution.

"I'm sorry for..." Levi murmured as he lowered his head while maintaining eye contact. He raised his hands like he wasn't sure what to apologize for and begged, "Please don't leave."

Did he think that would fix everything that had happened since he'd shown up? Or was he apologizing for something specific? I couldn't tell, but my lungs worked a little more easily just from being next to him.

Something inside me *wanted* to let him off the hook. But I needed to see a change for myself, not just niceties, and I couldn't allow him to turn me into someone else. "Words are easy."

The past three days had given me ample time to reflect on everything. Sorting through my feelings for Levi had hurt worse than any stab wound, but it was something I'd needed to do. I'd felt lost and disoriented, but these emotions, though painful, were making me a better person.

"I *know* words are easy, but that's all I *have*." His hand cupped his mouth. "I'm stuck in here, and I haven't had a chance to *show* you anything before you're trying to walk right back out that door."

"If I don't leave, I'm not sure I'll be able to later," I whispered so softly that only he could hear me.

"Rosemary?" Killian said, bringing me back to the present.

The connection swirled between Levi and me, the emotions overwhelming and strong. But there was more at stake than our feelings for each other. The world didn't revolve around us, even if we did each other.

"Yeah?" I rasped, then cleared my throat, needing to pretend I was okay. I forced myself to turn to the couches and immediately regretted it.

All eight of them were looking at us.

Sierra stood next to Ronnie, her eyes glistening and a hand pressed to her chest. She sniffed and sat on the armrest, placing her head on Ronnie's shoulder, then whispered, "This is even better than watching it on television."

"Dear gods," Alex grumbled, and leaned away from Annie. Then he cringed when he realized how close he'd gotten to Killian beside him. "Not everything is like a *damn* movie." He glanced at Killian. "Can you alpha-will her to stay on course? We have issues to discuss."

"Hey!" Sierra sat upright and huffed. "You didn't get on *them* for the distraction they caused."

My cheeks warmed. I'd never been one to cause a scene, and I wanted to hide my face.

"Let's focus on facts." Sterlyn strode into the center of the room, commanding our attention.

Exhaling, I moved toward Sterlyn, acutely aware of Levi staying close to me.

"Why don't you sit back down on the couch and get away from the door," Griffin said, and it wasn't a question. He was telling Levi what to do in a more diplomatic way.

"Like I have a choice," Levi muttered.

He took the opportunity to brush his arm against mine as he walked by, and the buzzing intensified to an alarming level like a lightning bolt to my core. The mix was both painful and euphoric, like I suspected a drug would feel, and I was already yearning for my next fix.

I forced my foot to take a step back. If I didn't put distance between us, I would wind up in his lap, and Sierra would never let me forget it.

When he sat on the couch, I pulled in my wings and pressed my back against the wall across from him, by the television. "What's the update?" Somehow, I kept my voice level.

Sterlyn got straight to the point. "We've jailed the four shifters who attacked Yelahiah and Kira."

I'd always loved her blunt nature. She was one of the few people outside the angel race who spoke directly, and somehow, mortals didn't get upset with her. However, she did it with compassion, helping the recipient of the news feel safe. Angels tended to just say the truth, not worrying about the delivery. Facts were facts, and there was no point in anyone getting upset or hurt. I'd thought the same thing until recently.

Griffin put his hands into the pockets of his khakis. "They're being presented to the council in the next hour, so Ronnie and Alex need to head back into the city for the meeting."

I almost didn't conceal my groan, but I caught it at the last second. If Alex and Ronnie were heading into Shadow City, I'd be stuck even longer in this house with Levi.

Lovely.

Fate had to be laughing at my expense. I wondered what I'd done wrong for her to do this to me.

Before now, I'd have rolled my eyes at that kind of dramatics. Fate didn't care about individuals, but rather the entire world. If something difficult was happening to me, it wasn't because of an injustice I'd served. It was required to bring the world into balance, according to the Divine.

But now I understood how it could feel personal.

Alex frowned. "Why didn't Gwen call us?"

"She *did*." Killian fidgeted in his seat uncomfortably. "I yelled for you, but you two were...busy."

Something burned in my chest, and I rubbed it to ease the discomfort. I wished I could find someone to be *busy* with. Maybe that would get Levi off my mind for a few minutes.

The lump in my throat told me otherwise.

There was no getting over him. I'd have to learn to survive without him. Which was ridiculous! I'd only known him for a week. How could I become that invested in someone in such little time, especially someone I could *never* have?

I wanted to vomit at the thought of being with someone else.

Ronnie's cheeks reddened. "Uh...I don't even know where my phone is."

Rolling his eyes, Levi said, "In the kitchen, where you left your food and blood before you two ran upstairs, giggling."

Again, I had a feeling we were thinking similarly.

"Giggling?" Sierra asked, and lifted her eyebrows as she eyeballed Alex.

Alex pinched the bridge of his nose. "Now's not the time."

"Oh...so later, then?" She grinned wickedly.

"Why does there even need to be a council meeting?" Cyrus leaned forward, putting his elbows on his knees. "If they attacked Yelahiah and Kira, it should be an easy case."

"One would *think*," Griffin growled. "But that's not how things work there."

Leaning against her mate, Annie shook her head. "It's insane how things are done in the city. They have a meeting just to have a meeting."

And sometimes, they met to discuss what to meet on next. Azbogah loved bureaucracy and had spent time teaching humans his ways before we'd locked ourselves inside. "I can't go back," I said, "especially with Ronnie leaving."

"Notice she didn't say Alex." Sierra waggled her eyebrows.

She was goading Alex hard tonight. Maybe I shouldn't have left her alone downstairs so much. She seemed to be getting all her sass out of her system at once.

"Leave him alone." Ronnie sighed. "You know it's because he couldn't see Levi if he shadowed out. It has nothing to do with him not being strong and sexy."

A car engine sounded, alerting us that someone was heading this way. My stomach hardened when I realized who it was.

Kira. Or as she was known by Levi—*Red*.

I inhaled deeply to keep my irrational thoughts at bay. Kira hadn't done anything to deserve my dislike, so it wasn't fair to feel this way about her. Levi was the problem, not Kira.

This was like all the shows where the wife blamed the mistress for her husband's affair. Women were the worst about blaming each other, and living as long as I had, I'd learned that it was due to how females were raised. I refused to be part of that cycle. I wouldn't resent someone who was coming here to give us information on something that could affect my mother and my people.

A loud thumping noise crescendoed in my ear, and I realized Kira had a flat tire.

Sterlyn glanced out the window as the thumping grew closer. When a light blue sedan lurched to a halt behind Griffin and Sterlyn's Navigator, she said, "That's Kira."

Needing to prove to myself that I wasn't petty, I went to the door. Levi tensed, and his reaction irritated the hell out of me. Did he think I would refuse to let her inside?

I'd remedy that expectation now.

I opened the door to find Kira with her hands on the wheel. She had her eyes closed, and I could see her chest moving slowly, filling with air.

She was either upset or uncomfortable. She hadn't been here since the day Levi and I had had our falling out. Foolishly, I knew that because I'd stalked everyone who had come around the house. I'd have liked to pretend it was just for security, but it was more than that. I'd wondered if she would come to see him, and she hadn't...until now. But that wasn't true. She wasn't here to see him, but rather to give the group an update.

Opening myself to my surroundings, I tried to sense something odd that would make her react in such a manner, but I sensed nothing out of the ordinary. The silver wolf sentries were settled in the woods. The nocturnal animals were beginning to scurry into the velvety darkness. The river rushed nearby, and faint voices came from the town, which was busier than normal due to the season. There wasn't any negative energy hinting that a demon was close, which still jarred me with Levi not even twenty-five yards away.

I strolled out of the house toward the car.

That action pulled Kira from her thoughts. She dropped her hands and turned off the engine, then quickly climbed out, smiling at me. "Hey. I got a flat on the way here."

I tilted my head, examining her. She resembled the Kira to whom I'd become accustomed, but something was obviously weighing on her heavily. "We could hear. Are you—"

"It's just been a *stressful* few days." She shivered slightly as she breezed past me. "Is everyone inside?"

She didn't want to talk, and I could respect that. I didn't, either, but this was about being a good person, even when it was hard. "Yes, but..."

Kira paused and faced me. Her smile finally reached her eyes, turning them light emerald. "Seriously, I'm okay. Just had to do some things I hate having to do. You know?"

I understood that all too well. I nodded, and my shoulders relaxed. Lately, we'd all had to do things we didn't want to do and sometimes weren't even proud of. She was dealing with her father and cousin working against her, and people she'd assumed were friendly had attacked her. If that wasn't a burden to bear, I wasn't sure what else could be.

My skin itched. I hadn't been the nicest to her when

she'd been struggling, so focused had I been on my jealousy.

Maybe I wasn't as good of a person as I liked to think.

The two of us entered the house, and Levi frowned at us. He lifted his chin, but the action was jerky.

Why would he need to give the illusion of confidence when he'd been cocky the entire time before?

"Okay, I don't have long." Kira walked over to Sterlyn. She focused on Levi for a second and jerked her head once, too quickly to be considered a nod.

Some of the tension melted from his body.

I frowned. What could they be communicating about that they didn't want the rest of us to know?

The odd saying Ronnie had quoted earlier flitted into my head: *You catch more flies with honey than vinegar.*

Dear gods, I finally understood the mortal colloquialism. I would have to be careful around other supernaturals, especially angels.

"I have one substantial update, other than our having tracked down the four idiots." Kira rubbed her arm. "We finally located an inventory list of *all* artifacts housed in the warehouse."

Alex's mouth dropped. "Where?"

Kira snorted. "It magically appeared in a guard's desk drawer at the building. Erin encouraged us to look through all the documents in the warehouse one more time."

Of course it would be Erin. Azbogah wouldn't risk having his name attached; he'd sent the witch who was trying to prove her value.

"Wait...*magically* appeared?" Sierra's eyes widened. "Like just—"

"Nothing that dramatic." Kira mashed her lips together. "I do love your style, but no, it wasn't there, and then we looked again, and it was."

"The list was planted," Ronnie spat. "This *has* to tie back to what we found in the woods when the Ezra situation went down."

That was the day Annie had located bones in the woods. They'd been placed and spelled to allow a coven of witches to spy on the area. If the sets of bones on the roof of Thirsty's were from Erin's coven, that would mean that the Shadow City witches had cloaked themselves and left the city without a trace to set them up. They could easily sneak something into a desk. An unlocking spell on the desk might be difficult, but that coven had been around for centuries, even before Shadow City had been built. My gut said they were responsible.

Annie placed a hand on her belly. "Are you working through the inventory list now?"

My chest constricted. I'd always desired to have a child, but I'd never met an angel with whom I was willing to conceive. At least, as part of this group, I could experience watching a child grow and learn. That had to count for something.

Kira dropped her hands. "As we speak, but it's a huge list. It'll take a week or more, especially since I'm allowing only certain people access."

"To the best of your ability." Griffin's jaw twitched.

"Guys, I hate to interrupt, but if we need to get back to Shadow City, we better get moving." Ronnie stood and glanced around the room. "You know Azbogah will get there early to start something or get something locked into place."

"If I ever find myself alone with the man, I may very well *kill* him." Cyrus's nostrils flared. "He was most likely behind all of our misfortunes."

Ironically, Azbogah was the one who'd said that each race should handle their issues from within unless it affected all the races equally, but he was the one trying to sabotage everyone while having other supernaturals do his dirty work. "If you did that, you'd have his followers wanting retribution," I said. "There wouldn't be a win."

Levi smirked. "And here I thought angels were *perfect*."

He was pushing my buttons. "We aren't perfect, but we do what we *think is best* for the world. He hasn't fallen, so he must truly believe there is something right-eous in his madness." That was what scared me.

"My wife is right. We should get going." Alex climbed to his feet and took Ronnie's hand.

Sterlyn took a few steps toward the door. "Kira, you need to come, too. They'll need you to officially identify your attackers."

"Uh, I have a flat tire," she replied. "Can I ride with you and come back later to get my car? If the king and queen are going, they'll need to take their car, so they can bring me back if you and Griffin get stuck in Shadow City for a while."

"Sounds good." Sterlyn headed to the door.

"Leave the keys."

We all turned to Levi, who shrugged. "Someone"—he glared at Killian—"can change your tire for you while you're gone."

"Yeah, thanks." Kira tossed Killian the keys. "The trunk is pretty much bare except for a bag back there. If you don't mind changing the tire and you need to use the car for anything, it's mostly free."

She was acting as if we might go on a road trip. I *guessed* if we left, we might need to pack supplies in case we couldn't get back soon.

Ronnie hugged Annie. "If something weird happens, call. Even if you think we're still in the meeting. We'll be back right after."

Ronnie hesitated when she reached me, then pulled me into a hug. My throat burned at the gesture. She murmured into my ear, "Talk to him. I know it seems impossible, but feelings like these don't come around often, and he's been kicking himself for days. It tore him up when you refused to see him last night. I've been trying to leave you alone because I remember the feelings, but at least make peace with him. You may regret it if you don't."

Her words washed over me. She was right. If he left tomorrow, I'd kick myself for ending things on such horrible terms. A relationship between us wasn't possible, but I didn't want to live the rest of my existence with regret, especially since I might never die.

She pulled back and smiled sadly. "See you soon."

As the others left, Sierra took Alex's place in the center of the couch next to Killian and patted the vacant seat open next to her.

Levi bit his lip as his gaze landed on me. "Um...Rosey?"

"Stop." My body wanted to race over to him, but I had to be strong. My breathing increased, but I pushed the pain aside. Talking to him alone would be torture, but I couldn't leave, not with Annie and Cyrus being the only ones who could see him in shadow form. I wouldn't abandon my pregnant friend and her mate.

"But—" he started.

Annie glanced between us and chewed on her bottom lip. "You should talk."

Both she and Ronnie were right, but I wasn't sure I was strong enough. "Fine, but if we bicker..."

He lifted his hands in surrender. "I won't waste a breath begging you to stay."

Whether the conversation went well or poorly, the outcome would be the same. Maybe I could get some closure before our time ran out. Eventually, he'd either escape, or we'd have to let him go. "Let's go." I headed into the dining room, hoping I wasn't making a horrible mistake.

CHAPTER TWENTY-SIX

WE ENTERED the dining room in silence.

Neither of us bothered turning the lights on as our supernatural vision kicked in. I could see every line etched into his face, which showed signs of guilt, worry, and determination.

I walked to the window at the other end of the table while he remained at the entrance to the room.

"I've been an ass." He sighed. "And I hate it because it's the last thing I *ever* want to be to you."

My lungs froze. He'd gone straight to flattery, and my resolve was already crumbling. "Yes, you have. You purposely tried to hurt me, but—"

"That *should* be expected since I'm a *demon*, right?" he asked coldly. "Because we're all the same."

"Well..." His words from days ago circled through my mind. I *was* being biased. I closed my eyes, embarrassed it had taken me until now to understand what he'd been trying to say. Even though he was a demon, nothing negative floated off him. His essence felt similar to Alex's before he'd met Ronnie. At the time, Alex hadn't decided whether to be good or bad—it was as if he'd been existing in some sort of purgatory.

Levi chuckled humorlessly. "Please continue. Don't hold back for me."

I'd apologized before, albeit rarely, but I had never felt shame, so in a way, this was my first time. "I'm sorry, too."

He exhaled and took a tentative step toward me. "That was unexpected."

"If we're going to try to be"—I wasn't sure which word to use in this situation, as nothing seemed adequate —"friends..." I winced, but that was the best I could come up with. We couldn't be more than that, and dancing around our issues as if we could be more wouldn't do us any good. "Then I need to be accountable, too, and you're right, I've judged you without considering your essence and the fact that you haven't tried to hurt us."

"Are you going to add *yet*?" Levi lifted one brow in challenge.

He was almost daring me to contradict what I'd said, but I wouldn't. I *was* wrong, but that didn't mean we shouldn't be suspicious of him. "I don't know yet."

His forehead creased as he scratched his chin. "You've lost me."

I reverted to my roots: blunt Rosemary. This time, I'd speak with more compassion. Everyone deserved that until they proved themselves unworthy. "Your essence— it's not evil like the essence of other demons, but it's not pure, either. You haven't decided which side you're on. However, I didn't take the time to notice that, and I saw you as evil because that's what I expected to see. So...I'm not sure if I should say, 'You haven't tried to hurt us *yet*,' or not. You might never try to hurt us, but there is still a chance you *could*."

"That's...fair." His head jerked back. "But it isn't right or wrong like you make it out to be."

My chest tightened. "I didn't say it was easy. Those types of decisions never are. However, once you decide your path, things will become easier for you. I just hope you take the right one."

"And which one is that?" He arched his brow again.

Part of me didn't want to tell the truth anymore. All it could do was lead us down a road we shouldn't travel. But lying wasn't an option. "The one where maybe we could stay in each other's lives and not be set on killing each other."

He chuckled, the sound deep and sexy. "We haven't killed each other yet."

"There have been some close encounters." The edges of my lips tipped upward without permission, then stopped. "Like when you hurt me."

"You keep saying that, but when did I do that?" Levi searched the room like he could find answers there.

My blood heated, and I took a calming breath to remain level-headed. We were trying to have a peaceful conversation, and we couldn't do that if I let my emotions take control. "Calling Kira 'Red' when you knew it bothered me, asking her to sit next to you on the couch, then asking to speak to her alone."

Grimacing, he placed his hands behind his back. "I didn't mean to hurt you. Maybe *rile* you up, but not actually inflict pain."

"How did you feel when you saw Killian talking to me outside? And that wasn't me asking him to sit next to me and giving him a nickname." He had to put things into perspective like I was. All this time, I'd seen only one side of the story. I almost missed the simplicity, because seeing both sides threatened to rip me in two.

Levi's eyes tightened, and his lip curled. "Kira didn't have her *arms around* me."

We were treading back toward an argument, and I refused to humor him. "I didn't do that to hurt you. Killian hugged me because I was upset." He opened his mouth to retort, but I lifted a finger. "We're about to argue again. It's too easy to fall into that with you."

Rubbing his hands against his jeans, he nodded. "It's the connection between us. Every time I fight it, it's like I'm coming unhinged."

That was a perfect description.

"Maybe instead of fighting it—" he began.

"I'm not ready for that." If he'd finished that sentence, I might have lost all sanity and not realized how bad of an idea it was. I waited, unsure how to proceed.

"What do you mean? You feel the same connection I do. I see it in the way you look at me, and I feel it in the energy that sparks between us. I swear, fate made you mine just like she brought my parents together." He closed the distance between us until we stood inches from each other.

"If she did, would we be tormenting each other like this?" Sterlyn and the others made their relationships look so effortless. They brought out the best in each other, not the worst.

"Okay." He lifted his chin and stared into my eyes. "Easy solution."

The room spun as I waited for what he would say.

"I'll *prove* to you that I'm serious." A dark glint sparked in his gaze. "How about we start over as friends?"

My heart shrank as disappointment surged through me. I wanted to kick myself. I shouldn't have *wanted* him to say anything else. Being friends was the best solution for us, and even then, it could cause hiccups. "We can *try*, but we both have to stay rational. Killian is my friend, and"—I took a shaky breath to steady myself for my next words—"Red is yours." Somehow, I managed not to emphasize Kira's nickname.

He smirked. "Oh, it won't be a problem."

Nausea roiled in my stomach. Had he gotten over our connection within minutes and moved on to contemplating a relationship with Kira? My brain said that would be for the best, but my heart constricted until I was sure it would burst.

He winked as his fingers brushed my cheeks. "Because I will prove to you that we should be *together*."

Electricity surged between us, and my body flooded with warmth. I'd never craved someone's touch as much as his, and it petrified me. "We can't." Those words somehow left my lips despite my body responding in the opposite manner.

"These last few days, I've never felt so alone and depressed. You were *all* I thought about, and at night, I even dreamed about our kiss." He dropped his hand, but the electricity still charged between us. He vowed, "I'll prove I can treat you the way you deserve. Then we can find a way to be together. You'll see."

My mouth dried, and I couldn't quash the hope rising in my chest. I wanted him to prove me wrong and that we could be together.

I just didn't think he could.

By the halfway point of the romantic comedy, I was at my limit. Levi and I had informed everyone that we were putting our differences aside to get along. Annie and Cyrus had glanced at each other with unreadable expressions, and Sierra had beamed as if that were the news she'd wanted to hear.

Killian had sat stoically, glaring at Levi the entire time. I'd felt the iciness coming off my close friend.

I'd thought Sierra would support our decision to be friends. She'd seemed approving, but she obviously had ulterior motives, since she'd put on a stupid movie about a boy and a girl from different sides of the world. Their families were also enemies, but they were determined that their love would conquer all. Every time they kissed or did anything romantic, Sierra would eyeball me, then Levi.

Between that and watching two people pretend to struggle with what Levi and I were grappling with, I was about to explode. The movie was insulting, not motivating. Those people didn't feel the connection Levi and I did. It was impossible.

I sat next to Annie, across from Levi, and every few minutes, I felt his gaze on me. Each time, my heart quickened, and I tried to calm down.

We'd been at odds with each other since our first encounter. I had to keep reminding myself that being together romantically, even for a fling, was a horrible idea. The truth was, I *knew* that if we slept together, even casually, I'd never recover. However, no one else needed to be aware of that.

Needing a glass of water, I stood just as Annie bolted up from Cyrus's shoulder. Everyone in the room froze, their gazes on the demon wolf. She leaned forward, grabbing her chest.

"Babe? What's wrong?" Cyrus asked out loud, mainly for our benefit. "Is it the baby?"

I'd never healed a pregnant woman before, but there was a first time for everything. I'd do whatever was needed to ensure both Annie and the baby were fine.

Tapping into my center, I raised my hands, lighting up the room.

"The baby's fine," she rasped. "The *tug* inside me suddenly got stronger like that day in the forest last week. I think demons are nearby."

A faint negative energy swirled past me, confirming what she'd said.

"Stronger? You mean it never went away?" Killian asked as he jumped to his feet.

She placed a hand on her chest. "It's always kind of there, but Cyrus and I decided not to look into it until we'd settled things with Levi. But something big is happening."

Of course it was. Sterlyn, Griffin, Ronnie, and Alex were in Shadow City, and something would happen while they were away. My focus went to Levi, who'd gone a few shades paler. He wasn't happy about this news, either.

"The rumblings in Hell say they know about your group, and with an angel and silver wolves involved, it wouldn't be hard to figure out where you are." Levi rubbed his temples. "They've probably been stalking the area."

"But we're on the vampire side of the river." Sierra turned off the television. "Wouldn't they expect us to be in Shadow Ridge or the city? Why would they come here? Are they planning to attack the city?"

"No," Levi said a little too confidently. "They aren't equipped for that."

But if they knew they weren't equipped, that proved that taking over Shadow City had been on their minds. However, if even one of the princes of Hell walked through the portal, all the angels would feel it. That was how inherently evil they were.

Annie shook her head. "The silver wolves just moved back to this area."

"But the demons don't know that," I said. Some of the pieces were finally coming together, and I didn't like the picture. "They left Shadow City before the silver wolves were created, when it was intended to be a safe haven shortly after the angels came to Earth. However, the truce wasn't made until a huge war was brewing between the demons and angels, which was shortly after the first silver wolf was born."

"Meaning that when they saw you"—Killian pointed at me—"and the silver wolves, they assumed you were all from the city, so a demon or two could've staked out the area to form a plan."

Cyrus groaned. "And then noticed the silver wolves and followed them here."

I stared at Levi. "They're coming for you." But why? He'd said he couldn't go back to Hell because his father would be beaten up. What could Levi do for them that was so important that they were ready to start a war for him?

"They won't attack here," Levi assured us. "They don't want to start the war y—" He cut himself off.

We all knew what he'd been about to say: *yet*. This was the most information we'd received from him, and I wished he'd been more forthcoming from the very beginning. "If they won't attack in the two towns, then that has to mean they're waiting for an opportunity to take someone or something important to us," I said. "They'll likely strike when the guards from Shadow Ridge are coming to relieve the ones watching the house. There are only two ways into Shadow Terrace—through Shadow City, which isn't an option, or over the bridge off the main road." Even though the territory switched from Ridge to Terrace, the connection point was right on the edge via a public street. Attacking there would be less risky than coming farther into one of the towns.

Sierra shrugged. "If the guard shift doesn't happen and everyone stays on their side, nothing will happen. We've been doing that, anyway."

The poor girl needed a lesson in strategy. They'd find a way to get us out of here. "The best thing we can do is head them off and hopefully surprise them." I glanced at Levi. "Right?"

"True. That day in the woods, those demons left to track you down. They didn't expect you to show up the way you did, but they'll be on guard this time. If they're coming for me, they should be close to where you fought the other demons." Levi stood and turned to the door. "Let's get moving so we can strike when they least expect it."

We might be starting over, but I *still* didn't trust him. "You aren't going anywhere."

"What?" His mouth dropped. "But the demons—"

"Are coming for *you*." If he thought we were just going to hand him over, maybe I wasn't the only biased one. "You're staying here."

"With Annie and me." Cyrus blew out his cheeks. "Because we can both see you."

"Killian and Sierra should stay here, too. They can

connect with the Shadow Ridge pack if something strange happens close by." Under normal circumstances, I'd want Killian with me, but it was too risky with him not being able to see the demons.

Eyes hardening, Killian growled, "I should go with you."

"I need you here to keep an eye on things." I didn't want to insult Sierra openly, so I hoped Killian understood that I didn't trust her strategic instincts.

"Is it strange that I'd feel better if he went?" Levi smirked. "You could sacrifice him to one of the demons. He would never know, and that would keep you safe."

The five of us glared at him.

"What?" He shrugged. "It was just a *suggestion*."

We didn't have time for this. My wings exploded from my back as I marched to the front door. "Not one a *friend* would make."

"Darrell will go with you, and we've linked with Sterlyn," Cyrus called after me. "They're in the middle of identifying the four attackers. After that, they'll come back."

If they left without finishing the identification process, Azbogah would wreak havoc. But the proceedings shouldn't take too long.

"Hey," Levi said as he snagged my hand, turning me toward him. He cupped my face and laid his forehead against mine.

The gesture was so tender that a lump formed in my throat.

"Be safe," he murmured, and kissed me softly.

My lips tingled, and I froze. I'd expected him to be ornery, not sweet, and the sentiment threw me off balance. "You, too."

Before I could change my mind and stay, I raced from the house, heading toward the fight.

Darrell waited for me outside in human form. The biggest challenge with demons was beheading them when you had shifters in wolf form fighting on your side. Darrell being in human form would slow us down a bit, but it was a risk we had to take. He could still move quickly if he tapped into his animal.

We took off toward the woods, and I waited until we'd reached the tree line to take flight. I flew slowly over him, and we pushed forward, ready to face our enemy.

WE MET up with ten more silver wolves a few miles south of Sterlyn's old pack neighborhood. Eight shifters were in their wolf form, and three, including Darrell, remained in human form. That gave us four fighters who could behead demons and eight who could fight more strongly in animal form. Each shifter in human form had a knife.

As we neared the old neighborhood, the sounds of the raccoons, flying squirrels, and owls disappeared. The forest was silent, a dead giveaway that trouble was near.

The slightly over quarter moon rose in the sky, and I wished it were a full moon so the silver wolves would have been stronger.

Negative energy floated toward me, indicating we were close to our endgame.

I dropped lower and flew between Theo and Darrell, the signal for when I sensed the demons were nearby.

Our group slowed, and we used the trees for cover, waiting for the enemy to arrive. The energy grew heavier and heavier, coating my skin, as they moved in our direction.

When the first demon floated over the cypresses and redbuds, my heart picked up its pace. With each one that appeared, more adrenaline coursed through me. So far, there were fifteen, but they continued to come.

As more and more came into view in their shadow form, the air sawed at my lungs. Soon, the air above the tree was so thick with shadow forms that it looked like one huge low-hanging rain cloud. By my count, there were fifty demons.

We were severely outnumbered, and there was no getting out of this now. They'd see us as soon as we moved.

CHAPTER TWENTY-SEVEN

WE NEEDED MORE FIGHTERS, but our options were limited. Killian and his pack had the largest numbers by far, but they couldn't *see* the demons. If the regular wolves tried to fight the demons in their shadow form, it would put us in a worse spot because we'd be distracted while trying to protect Killian's pack.

We needed all sixteen silver wolves and anyone else who could see the demons. We couldn't risk Annie, but we could desperately use Cyrus, Ronnie, and Sterlyn.

Darrell stood close to me, and I glanced at him. His midnight-brown hair hung in his blood-orange eyes as he squatted behind a huge cypress. He was shorter than most of the other silver wolves, but he had wisdom and power that made him stronger. He was one of the older silver wolves—if I had to guess, early fifties. In the shifter world, strength usually correlated with height, but he was an exception to the rule. I'd learned that determination put the impossible within grasp, and Darrell was the epitome of hard work. That was how he could outperform his larger peers.

His attention cut to me, then to Theo on my other side.

Following his gaze, I turned my head toward Theo and found his mint green eyes faintly glowing, contrasting with his shaggy dark brown hair. He and Darrell must have been communicating via their pack link.

Theo was one of the taller silver wolves, coming in close to Killian's height of six foot four inches, and slightly more muscular. Theo enjoyed showing off his strength, usually by wearing a shirt one or two sizes too small. He was older than Sterlyn and Cyrus, but not by much. From what I remembered, he was in his late twenties, as was his mate, Rudie.

Not wanting to risk speaking too loudly, I leaned toward Darrell. The demons were buzzing around each other, the faint murmurs crescendoing as if they were preparing for something. "What are you planning?"

"Nothing yet," he whispered back. "We're talking to Cyrus and Sterlyn. Sterlyn's group is leaving Shadow City and heading straight here. Cyrus and Chad are on their way as well. Martha isn't happy about being left behind again, since we need everyone we can spare, but our mates can't see the demons. We want to leave two silver wolves in Shadow Ridge with our families and Killian's pack in case they attack there."

Even though we could have used those two, he was right. If a demon or two split off to head to Shadow Ridge and there were no silver wolves on hand, the pack could be decimated because they had no way to defend themselves. With two silver wolves there, they had backup *and* could alert the pack here of what was going on.

Suddenly, my blood ran cold as I spotted the flaw in the plan. "Wait. They're leaving Annie alone with Levi?"

Darrell kept his gaze on the demons, but he flinched, telling me *everything*.

"They're bringing him here, aren't they?" My chilled blood warmed fractionally. We were in a horrible situation and could use his help, and if he turned against us, our situation wouldn't be much worse. There wasn't a huge difference between fifty and fifty-one.

But I wasn't worried about him betraying us.

I hoped trusting him so completely wasn't a mistake. He'd earned the benefit of the doubt.

The demons separated as if they had settled their plan and floated our way.

We couldn't wait until the others reached us to engage. We would have to do the best we could with the twelve of us. That meant we each would have to take on four demons, with two of us fighting five.

If I were the demons, I'd focus on the strongest opponents and eliminate them first. We would need a distraction so that Darrell and Theo didn't become overwhelmed immediately.

As for me, I'd manage...or die trying.

"Why are there so many?" Darrell's jaw twitched. "Last time, there wasn't even half this number."

He was comparing the demons' numbers to the silver

wolves. "Demons have been around for millennia," I said. "I'd bet they have thousands on their side, and this isn't even a fraction of their numbers. The first group of demons we fought was probably scoping out the area. This group is more trained for battle." At least, that was what we angels would do.

The angels who fell to become demons comprised more than seventy-five percent of our numbers, and the angelic race was still trying to recover its population. We hadn't made much headway since our reproductive cycles were so slow.

The demons inched closer to us. We needed a plan before it was too late. "I'll go straight at them and get them to chase me. The rest of you, pick them off one at a time."

"No," Darrell rasped as his head snapped toward me. "That's a suicide mission."

"What do you propose?" Our options were limited, and I could move as rapidly as the demons could.

He pursed his lips. "Uh..."

We were running out of time. "It's our best shot. Be ready." I placed a finger to my lips, informing him to be quiet. The demons were upon us, and even our murmurs could be heard.

A muscle in his jaw twitched again. He thought I was being reckless, but I *knew* my abilities. I'd fought enough demons to know how they operated, so I was confident I could pull this off as long as they didn't catch on too quickly. Whether I wanted to admit it, demons were former angels and had an aptitude for strategy. My hope was that they didn't figure out our strategy before we killed some of them.

Not wanting to receive any other disapproving looks, I flew skyward.

As soon as I broke through the top of the trees, the demons had their sights on me.

"There she is! *He* must be close by," the one in front yelled, and lifted a small blade at me. "It must be our lucky day. We don't even have to deal with the silver wolves."

Our suspicions had been correct. They'd planned to wait for the change of guards to capture some silver wolves to negotiate Levi's release. What was so special about Levi that the princes of Hell were desperate to bring him back? The only thing I could conclude was that he was among the few who could walk the Earth without alerting Shadow City, and he still cared enough about someone that they could manipulate him into doing whatever they desired.

There was no way they would get a hold of Levi. I couldn't allow him or his father to suffer further, and we couldn't allow Hell to gain the upper hand.

I should have pretended to be scared, but I didn't have it in me to humor the demons by letting them think they had any influence over me. It would make them overconfident, but it would also give them that sick high they craved.

I refused to do that.

Instead, I lifted my chin, wanting them to know I

didn't fear them. Even if I died today, I'd go down the warrior's way, showing no pain or fear.

"Do you think that sharp little thing scares me?" I asked.

The demon chuckled. The only signs of his mirth were his red eyes glowing brighter and the actual sound. Other than that, he looked like a giant blob. He rasped, "My penis isn't little or sharp."

Why in the heavens would he inform me of *that*? That was completely random and uncalled for. For a moment, I was speechless, but I couldn't let him distract me with witty commentary. "Sure, it isn't. Enjoy it while you can because soon, you're going to die."

"Oh, the big bad *girl* angel is throwing out threats." Another demon floated to the front, hovering next to the guy who'd informed me about his genitalia. "Here she is, outnumbered and talking shit. Angels clearly aren't as smart as they like to believe."

They were trying to rile me up and make me irrational. These were the demons I'd learned about—pure evil.

I fluttered my wings, rising higher into the air. "And you're just like the *demons* that have been described to me, all talk and little action."

"Fun's over. Let's get her so we can get Leviathan." Genitalia Demon lifted an arm over his head and gestured his weapon at me.

This was the moment I'd been planning for. I stayed put as the demons charged at me. All fifty came at once, each one trying to get an edge on the other.

Each desperate to hurt me.

Saliva filled my mouth, and I forced myself to swallow my disgust.

Refusing to glance down to give the demons any warning of my plan, I focused on my peripheral vision. The wolves in wolf form were hunkered in the woods, spread out five to ten feet among the trees, along with Darrell, Theo, and another silver wolf named Walden still in human form. Walden's curly hickory-brown hair looked wilder than normal, and even from this far away, I could see the quickening of his breath.

The silver wolves knew we were in a precarious spot and were ready to fight.

I noted where each wolf was before refocusing on the demons in front of me. I could fly across the edge of the tree line first so the wolves there could pick off one or two demons before the rest noticed. I'd need to fly a hundred yards away so they could remain partially hidden.

The demons needed to focus solely on me at first.

When they were within five feet, I spun and flew toward the ground.

A few laughed behind me, enjoying the thrill of the chase.

The chill of the night air felt great against my hot skin as I leveled off moments before I would have hit the dirt. I needed to let them get close enough that they got careless, thinking they had me in their grasp.

I took a left, wanting to lead them close to Darrell. The three wolves still in human form had clustered together, since they were slower than the shifters in wolf form. I needed a few demons beheaded right away to give the rest pause and make them believe that there were more of us here than there really were.

The demons' negative energy slammed into my back, coating my skin with a sludge-like sensation. They were so close, I could smell their overly sulfuric scent, and I barely held back a gag.

Levi didn't smell anything like them. These souls were corrupt. The realization eased some of my worries— for them to be that evil and still be able to come to Earth without alerting the rest of the angels meant they were weaker demons.

I flapped my wings hard as the demons gained on me. I cut loose, using every ounce of speed I had. Darrell was a few feet away, crouched and ready. Another silver wolf stood next to him, having used the distraction I'd created to reach his beta's side.

Thank the gods for that.

As I cut through the trees beside them, the wolf inched forward. He was waiting at the end of the tree line. If the wolves attacked the front, all the demons would see. The demons farther away from us were the weakest, but reducing their numbers would still eliminate some of the threat.

The wind blew my hair behind my shoulders as I wove through the trees. I was hoping a few demons would miss a turn, but so far, that hadn't happened.

Taking a slight turn to fly past more wolves, the demon in front of me yelled, "Stop! It's a trick. I smell wolves."

I'd hoped we'd get away with this a little longer. These demons were smarter than I'd expected.

The demons paused, and there was no reason to wait. We needed to attack hard. "Now!" I yelled.

Snarls echoed as the wolves lunged straight for the horde of demons that were in easy striking distance close to the grass.

Not wasting a second, Genitalia Demon charged at me. I had to give him credit for not mouthing off. In the past six months, I'd learned that many evildoers liked to say pointless things to prove they were manly. Genitalia Demon might be more trained than I'd originally thought.

Six others raced behind him. As expected, they were focused on taking out the strongest threat, and again, they'd determined it was me without considering the rest of the pack.

I flipped my feathers, ready for battle. I would behead them as quickly as possible and help the others.

When Genitalia Demon got within ten feet of me, he threw his small blade. As the weapon spun toward me, adrenaline rushed through my body.

His shadow form had hidden half of the weapon. It had a handle in the center with blades on both sides, making it bigger than I'd realized.

Flapping my wings hard, I pushed myself to one side in a desperate attempt to dodge the blade. The weapon whizzed past me, way too close to my ear. If I hadn't moved when I did, it would've lodged in my head.

He'd expected me to fly upward, not to the side.

Some of the tension eased in my chest. The demons must not have realized that every angel was required to go through rigorous training. We'd increased our training regime significantly after the city had closed itself off.

Why had we done that if we'd expected to stay in Shadow City forever?

The answer was clear: Azbogah hadn't.

An issue to address later.

The blade lodged in the tree, and the demon moved to retrieve it. He foolishly believed he'd injured me.

As I prepared to attack him, five more demons rushed me. Three came at my front, while the other two circled behind me. If I allowed them to surround me, I'd be in trouble.

Two reached for my arms, and I dodged the one on the right as I kicked the one on the left in the side, causing him to float back several yards.

Before I could straighten, a demon fisted my hair and jerked my head back as the demon I'd dodged before punched me in the gut.

They'd surrounded me. Out of the corner of my eye, I saw Genitalia Demon retrieve his weapon. This would get worse if I didn't do something.

Just as the one I'd dodged reached for my neck, I snapped back, headbutting the demon behind me. I flapped my wings, elevating myself slightly, and kicked the demon I'd dodged in the head.

The demon's grasp on my hair went slack, and I reached over my head, digging my fingers into...something. I couldn't see from this angle if it was his head or shoulder. But his guttural grunt told me I was doing some damage.

The other three charged me again as Genitalia Demon hurried toward us.

I had to kill these five before Genitalia Demon reached me. I spun around, moving my wings as my weapons. Targeting the one on my left first, I lurched, and the tip of my wing sliced through his neck. His eyes widened as his head fell from his body and splatted on the ground.

As I moved to attack the other one, the demon in front of me pulled out a dagger.

I had two choices: behead the demon as planned and get stabbed in the heart, or move to the side and allow myself to be surrounded.

Neither choice was ideal, and either could result in the same thing—my death.

CHAPTER TWENTY-EIGHT

WITH ONLY ONE TRUE OPTION, I moved to the side just as the demon breezed by me. If I'd delayed another millisecond, I would've been dead, or my arm would've been injured.

At least now I had a chance to determine a way out of this mess.

Genitalia Demon and the other four circled me, stalking their prey, wanting to scare me. They reminded me of the humanity-stripped vampires I'd fought a few months ago. They wanted me to become their prey so they could enjoy the attack that much more.

Demons had created vampires out of boredom. The story was that a group of humans had learned about the supernatural world and had been desperate to become immortal. So the demons offered them a gift, knowing that all magic came at a cost. The cost of being a vampire was the bloodlust, which, when surrendered to, made them lose their humanity and become more demon-like, though they still weren't true descendants.

Instead of cowering, I fluffed my wings. If death was inevitable, I refused to go down without a fight. I'd kill as many of them as I could until my last breath.

"I'll admit, I'm impressed. You are a far superior fighter than I expected," Genitalia Demon cooed as he waved his strange-bladed weapon in front of him. "Because of that, I'm willing to give you a choice: fall and join us or die."

He was attempting to recruit me. I hadn't expected that, and laughter bubbled deep in my chest. Out of all the scenarios, I hadn't even considered this possibility, as there was no question of my allegiance. "I serve justice on behalf of the Divine."

"Justice?" the demon to the right asked. "That's laughable, but oh, of course your kind could *never* be villains."

That wasn't true. I viewed Azbogah as one, though he somehow hadn't fallen. He wreaked havoc for his own personal gain, but he likely believed he was helping our race rather than fragmenting it. However, I wouldn't be sharing that information with *demons*. They'd find a way to exploit it and divide the angels further.

I had to be confident and decisive. I didn't want them to think they'd influenced me whatsoever. "If you want to kill me, get on with it and try."

Tilting his shadow head, Genitalia Demon chuckled. "Okay. Either way is a win for me." He lunged, not wasting a second.

He hadn't caught me by surprise like he wanted because he'd already proven that he was a trained fighter. He didn't talk too much, and he was efficient with his weapon, so I'd expected his assault.

I jerked back, dodging the blade. He hadn't expected me to move, so he hadn't factored in a countermovement.

Flapping my wings, I swung my body sideways. The other four demons were just as stunned, but they recovered within seconds. The demon who had been behind me was now to my right, and I moved so the tip of my wing sliced through his neck.

Blue blood splattered on my pale orange shirt and slicked my wings. The first demon I'd killed hadn't gotten much on me, but the wind was blowing against me, spraying the blood toward me. The drying blood would make it more challenging to fight, making my feathers stick together, but it was a necessity to survive.

I turned to the demon who'd been between the one I'd killed and Genitalia Demon, hoping to eliminate him before they recovered, but the remaining four moved closer, tightening the circle, blocking me in. No matter which way I turned, one of them was directly behind me.

Snarls sounded from the wolves, informing me that most of them were still fighting. The stench of blood wasn't heavy, and I hoped that meant they weren't injured.

Lifting my hands in front of me, I hovered, ready for their attack. They were taking their time, playing with their victim.

Victim.

Something I *refused* to be.

My best line of defense was to fly skyward, but they would anticipate that, so I needed to fake them out. I flapped my wings, rising quickly toward the top of the trees, and the shadows rushed after me. They were on my heels, and their negative energy coated me, making it hard to breathe.

I wove through the trees, waiting for the moment to implement my plan. They were giving me room to evade, suggesting they had a bigger plan. If I didn't execute *my* plan exactly right, this would all be over, and I'd be dead.

No pressure.

One of them grabbed my ankle, and I knew the time had arrived. This was the only chance I'd have to get out of this situation.

The air sawed through my lungs as I flew toward a tree. The demon dug his fingers into my ankle and yanked me toward him, but I'd expected that, and my wings countered the tug. I needed to ram him into a tree and change direction.

The demon was stronger than I realized, and he slowed my ascent, allowing the other three to catch up to me.

Genitalia Demon hovered in front of me, his weapon raised, blocking the way to the tree I'd planned to use to knock out the demon with a hold on me.

"There's no way out of this." He floated toward me, his eyes bright with anticipation. "But that was a good try."

I wouldn't give up that easily.

As he swung the blade down, I flew backward. Pressure sliced into my side as I lifted my feet, using the demon latched on to me as a shield.

Stabbing pain shot through my body as my brain registered the injury. My legs shook from holding the demon's weight. Genitalia Demon's eyes widened as he realized my intent, but it was too late. His blade cut into the demon's back, and he released his hold on my ankle. Though the demon didn't die, the injury would slow him for a while.

Warm liquid soaked my shirt, and I turned right as the demon swung his dagger at me again.

Another shadow barreled toward us, and my limbs grew heavy.

I was going to die.

My chest fluttered as determination fueled me. I'd take at least one more of these abominations with me.

I dropped several feet, and Genitalia Demon and the demon with the dagger aimed for the spot I'd been milliseconds before. I placed a hand on my side, the warm liquid seeping between my fingers. Breathing hurt, but I refused to show them I was in pain.

"How the hell is that possible?" Dagger Demon growled. "When she jerked back, I stabbed her."

"It doesn't matter. We'll get her now," Genitalia Demon said. "Let's end this."

The three remaining demons charged at me again while the newcomer gained ground.

Taking slow breaths, I tried to focus through the

intense pain. I'd had worse wounds, so this wasn't anything I couldn't handle.

The third demon pulled out a sharp, hooked weapon. My brain raced, and I remembered from my weapons class that it was called a sickle.

It was problematic that these demons could keep their weapons hidden until they needed them.

No longer surrounded, I flew away from them. I was moving more slowly with the injury, and they'd catch up, but at least it gave me a second to think.

I glanced at the silver wolves. The one closest to me had crimson blood coating his fur. There was no question it was his and not the blue blood of the four demons he was fighting.

My chest went numb. I couldn't believe this was what had become of us. For the first time in my life, I understood what defeat felt like, though there was no other way we could've handled this.

No. I refused to spiral. I needed to focus on killing as many of them as I could before I perished. My side hurt, and my head was woozy, but I would persevere for as long as I could.

The three nearly had me in reach, and the fourth demon had almost caught up to them. I had to make a decision. My guess was that the dagger was thick enough that my feathers could hold it off like bullets, but I wasn't sure about the sickle or the two-bladed weapon.

Ignoring the sharp, throbbing pain, I moved my wings, blocking the dagger aimed for my injured side.

The sickle ripped into my shoulder, and I gritted my teeth, swallowing a whimper.

Genitalia Demon laughed as he moved his weapon to the side. He planned to behead me as if I were a demon. The insinuation was clear: he wanted me to feel unworthy...like I viewed them.

"It's only fitting for you to die the same way," he rasped as the new demon materialized behind him.

But before he could move his weapon, the new demon grabbed his hand, and mocha-brown eyes focused on me.

Levi.

"Don't you *dare* hurt her," Levi said, confirming it was him.

Why were his eyes not red?

Immediately, I knew. He hadn't decided which side he was on and hadn't turned truly evil.

My heart warmed, but then the demon yanked his sickle from my arm. More pain flared in my body.

"Well, lookee there." Genitalia Demon smirked. "Who would've thought hurting an *angel* would get Levi here? Clearly, we arrived in the nick of time."

Levi flashed beside me and punched the other demon in the face. "I won't allow you to kill her." A growl emanated from deep within him. "Rosemary, go. They won't kill me."

I wasn't sure about that, but my blood loss was getting to my head. The world spun, but he was outnumbered just like me. "No."

The demon with the dagger snorted. "At least she knows our loyalty isn't to him—"

This was when they decided to get mouthy? While I was leaking blood and hurting throughout my left side and right shoulder? Knowing I might pass out at any time, I sprang into action.

With every ounce of strength I had left, I flew past Levi. The agony in my side increased with every flap of my wings. My head fogged over as I pushed through the pain and used my wings to behead Dagger Demon.

"What the—" Sickle Demon grunted with surprise.

Levi rushed toward me, and before Dagger Demon's body dropped more than an inch, he had swiped the weapon from the dead demon's hand.

With my injuries, they hadn't expected me to attack like that. I wanted to cry out, my side feeling as if it were ripping in two, but I wouldn't allow them the pleasure.

I inhaled shakily as my eyes burned.

Using Sickle Demon's and Genitalia Demon's surprise to our advantage, Levi swung his newly acquired dagger and sliced through Sickle Demon's head. As he pushed the dagger through, Levi snarled, "That's what you get for *hurting* her."

Even in my injured state, his words made my heart skip a beat.

"And then there was one," Genitalia Demon said hatefully. "And I *will* kill you."

"Yeah, right." Levi chuckled cockily, sounding like the man I'd come to know. "You and what army?" He must have turned his head because those mocha eyes focused on me. "Get help." He turned around just as Genitalia Demon swung his blade. At the last second, Levi raised the dagger to protect himself from the blow.

I didn't want to leave him like this, especially if he wasn't trained for battle. The day we found him, he'd been hiding and had come out only when I'd chased the demon who had gotten away. I'd always assumed he was a poor fighter hiding from the others.

But as I watched Levi expertly fight his adversary, my perception changed. He timed his moves and could read his enemy as well as I could.

I had to risk leaving to heal myself enough to stop the bleeding. Everything inside me screamed at me to stay, but the edges of my vision were darkening.

I didn't have much time.

My wingbeats began to slow, and my body descended of its own accord. If I didn't get to the ground soon, I'd fall and have no way of protecting myself.

With every bit of energy I had, I forced my wings to move quickly enough to prevent a crash.

Cyrus and Chad howled as they arrived on the scene. I glanced at them and saw one silver wolf lying eerily still.

They'd lost another of their own, and I'd failed to protect them once again.

Midway down from the height of the trees, I tugged at the magic inside me. I couldn't wait any longer, or I wouldn't be able to access it. Even as I pulled, it didn't want to respond.

My hands glowed, and I placed one on my side and

the other on my shoulder. My magic funneled inside me, and the pain ebbed. When my feet touched solid ground, my body crumpled, unable to stand from the pain and energy I'd exerted.

Soon, the trickle of blood stopped, and I released the core of my magic. I didn't want to waste too much on myself, since I had an inkling I'd need it to heal others if we pulled off a win.

With the pain eliminated, I was already feeling stronger.

I slowly climbed to my feet and surveyed the area. The silver wolves were engaged in battle, but a second wolf lay still, thick crimson blood covering his chest and a large, gaping slit in the middle where his heart was located.

We were being slaughtered.

Wheezing, I tried to swallow the lump forming in the back of my throat. This must have been how Mother had felt that day when Ophaniel and some of the silver wolves had died. History was repeating itself.

No time to dwell. These people were my extended family, and I had to help them.

Not wanting to risk flying, I crept toward the nearest battle. My skin and some of my muscle had healed, but deep aches made it harder than normal to move.

Even the wind blowing through my wings made my muscles tense and scream. I'd never noticed how hard and heavy my wings were until now.

Another shadow figure appeared overhead, and when the emerald-green eyes found mine, my vision blurred.

Ronnie had a demon blade of her own and was a natural fighter. Her presence made the situation seem less dire, and her presence meant Sterlyn wasn't far behind.

I rushed toward a silver wolf with three demons attacking him. He had cuts across his fur, but he was holding his own. However, his moves were becoming more sluggish, and the demons were striking as a team.

As I moved steadily toward him, refusing to limp, my heart sank. Every silver wolf was in the same situation. The demons were playing with them, dragging out their agony before finishing them off.

Adrenaline pumped through my veins, dulling the pain. I'd planned to be careful with my injury, but what was the point if we were on the brink of extinction?

When I neared the closest silver wolf, one of the demons turned my way, its red eyes bright in the darkness.

Though I couldn't make out its features, I could feel the increase of negativity swirling around me. He was anticipating making an *angel* suffer.

Demons hated angels as much as we disliked them.

I spread my wings, and I couldn't hold back the sigh. The pain intensified as the torn muscles strained, but that didn't matter. I'd be dead in minutes—I'd find a reprieve from the pain then.

He floated toward me as his buddies slashed at the wolf. The wolf whimpered but didn't give up the fight. He had to be feeling the same fate as me, but the silver wolves were part angel, and we didn't go down as cowards.

Of course, the demon had a weapon, and the image of a grim reaper flashed in my mind. He had a scythe and looked like the embodiment of every reaper figure in history.

The demon surged toward me and swung his weapon.

Grinding my teeth, I forced my right wing to move, blocking the onslaught. However, the muscles in my back groaned, and the dull throbbing sharpened. The pain stole my breath, and I forced my lungs to move so my head wouldn't become cloudy.

A piercing whistle sounded around us, and the demons engaged in battle froze.

After a second, the whistle sounded again, and groans filled the area as Sterlyn, Griffin, and Alex ran into the clearing. Sterlyn and Griffin were in human form, Sterlyn brandishing her knife, while Griffin and Alex each had a dagger. I wanted to yell at them to leave, but that would only make more demons focus on them.

Several demons floated skyward, leaving the wolves alive.

My skin overheated, and I stared blearily at the demons. I didn't understand why they were leaving. This had to be a trick.

"Rosemary!" Levi screamed, and I jerked toward his voice. His mocha eyes were wide, even in shadow form. "Watch out!"

My attention turned back to Scythe Demon. He chuckled evilly as he swung his weapon at the wound in my left side.

I tried to move my wings, but they didn't budge. There was no way I'd block the blow. Stumbling back, I tried to get out of range, but the demon floated my way and threw the weapon at me.

Time slowed as I regretted not being with Levi. I'd been so stubborn, and because of my shortsightedness, I would miss out on the kind of love that only those blessed by fate could find. It was sad that it had taken this for me to acknowledge the gift of being one half of a preordained mate. The final moments of life truly did bring clarity.

The only comforting thought was that at least we'd had some time together.

By joining with Sterlyn and our allies, I'd found friendships that had never been possible within my own kind.

Unable to get out of the way, I chose to go down with my head held high. But just as the blade should've sunk into my flesh, a shadow flashed in front of me, blocking the blow. I gasped...and inhaled the all too familiar scent of sweet peony.

"Levi!" I screamed as his body crumpled, the scythe protruding from his chest.

CHAPTER TWENTY-NINE

THIS WAS WORSE than when I'd thought I was the one who would die. I couldn't believe Levi had taken the hit for me.

Forcing myself to think strategically, I checked our surroundings. Every demon was leaving without trying to finish us off. None of this made sense, but right now, I wouldn't overanalyze it.

Dropping to my knees beside Levi, I ran my hands over his shadow form and turned him over. Because he hadn't lost his humanity, I wasn't sure if he had to be beheaded to die. Could a wound to the heart kill him the same way it could kill the rest of us?

"I..." His voice broke as his eyes cracked open. "I just need you to know..."

He was saying goodbye, and I didn't want any declarations to be forced because of the moment.

"Don't you *dare* die on me." I grabbed the scythe's handle and almost cried with relief when it didn't burn. I hadn't been sure if this was a demonic weapon, but since my skin wasn't being fried, it couldn't be. I yanked the weapon out of his chest as tears streamed down my face.

Levi tried to lift his head. "I'm sorry for being such a jackass and that it took so long for me to realize what you are to me. It's just that it was so strange, and there's so much working against us, but I wasted time and didn't get to say what—"

"Save your energy." I tapped into my core, refusing to give it an opportunity to not respond. I yanked on the magic, and my hands lit up the surrounding area. I placed them where the blood was dripping from his chest.

"What are you—?"

Instead of responding, I pushed the magic inside him.

Heat surged into him, my magic mixing with his. Though his magic was icy cold, the opposite temperatures collided and blended with each other. It reminded me of when a cold breeze caressed my hot skin, refreshing me.

Keeping a constant flow pouring inside him, I listened to his heartbeat and breathing. The sounds were still shallow. My throat closed. Maybe my magic couldn't heal him.

Desperate, I pushed more magic into him. I *couldn't* lose him, not now. Not when I'd just found him. My breathing rushed as I continued to pour myself inside him.

His heartbeat strengthened, and a little weight lifted off my shoulders. Maybe, since he was a strong demon, I had to use more magic on him. I dug deeper despite my magic being at least half empty.

I had to make sure he recovered.

"Rosemary," he said. "You healed me."

Wanting to make sure, I kept pushing more magic inside him.

A shadow hand touched my arm. "Rosey."

He'd used my nickname.

That was enough to snap me out of my nightmare. Now that I was paying attention, I could sense that his heart was fine. I tapered my magic off, letting it flow back inside me, needing to conserve it in case the silver wolves needed my help. "Are...are you sure?" Despite knowing what I'd felt, I needed his reassurance.

"I didn't know you could do that. I mean, I saw you place your hands on another wolf shifter that day, but I thought it was because you were mourning his death." His voice sounded normal, and his body flickered back into its human form.

Removing my hands from his chest, I noticed that his black shirt had a large gash where the scythe had stabbed him, but I could see the smooth, unblemished skin underneath.

I threw my arms around him, vowing never to let him go.

"Hey, I'm okay." He hugged me tightly and took a deep breath. "God, I love your rose scent. I love—"

"Stop." My body warmed as I jerked back and placed a finger over his lips. "Not here. Not now."

Hurt flashed in his eyes, darkening them. "How foolish—"

"I want you to finish what you're saying when we get back to the house. Not here with our injured friends surrounding us." I bit my lip, my heart so full I thought it would burst. "I want us to do this the right way. Once we say those words, there's no taking them back."

A huge smile spread across his face as he nodded. "I'm in."

I kissed his cheek gently, wanting him to know I meant what I'd said, and stood.

Things were worse than I'd realized. Acid inched up my throat as I counted two dead silver wolves. I'd failed them.

Another two were severely injured, and Sterlyn and Griffin knelt beside them. The other wolves were bloody but standing.

Sterlyn's shoulders sagged when she noticed me. "Rosemary, thank the gods you're okay." Her lavender-silver eyes darkened with despair. "I hate to ask, but we could really use your help."

Without a second thought, I rushed toward her. On the way, I noticed that Cyrus was pretty cut up, but he, Chad, Darrell, and Theo were watching the perimeter in case the demons returned. Our best plan was to heal these two enough to get the hell out of here so we could regroup.

In fairness, we could probably all go back to stay in Shadow Ridge. Levi had proven his loyalty to us, even against his own kind. My heart ached for having ever doubted him, but there was nothing I could do to change that now, no matter how much I wanted to.

The two wolves were badly injured, so there was only one option, even if it took twice as much energy. I knelt between them and touched their chests, not bothering to see where the wounds were located. I pushed my magic inside them, this time meeting a similar magic to mine.

Their wolves retracted, allowing my magic to flow through them freely. My magic was running low, so I couldn't heal them completely...just enough so they would survive.

As my body sagged, strong arms circled my waist. The electricity of the touch informed me whose it was. No longer wanting to fight our connection, I didn't resist Levi's touch and surrendered myself to his help.

The silver wolves' heartbeats became stronger, and I funneled more magic inside them. I had to ensure I wasn't just slowing their deaths but preventing them completely.

"You can stop," Levi rasped. "Their breathing is strong and steady."

My ears had picked up on the same thing, but I wanted to push a little harder. If the demons came back, we would need everyone at our disposal.

Musky freesia filled my nose as Sterlyn came to my other side. "He's right. We can take it from here."

That was good, because my eyes couldn't stay open. Thankfully, Levi held on to me. If he hadn't, I'd have fallen.

I woke up to Levi's wonderful smell surrounding me as he lowered me onto something soft. My eyes fluttered open, and the room I'd been staying in came into view. However, the sheets didn't smell like me, but rather like Levi.

"Go back to sleep. The others are burying the dead. The demons are gone, and if they return, Annie will inform us." Levi slipped into the bed beside me. "I hope you don't mind, but I brought you to my room. I can't stay away from you tonight."

"Of course," I murmured.

I didn't want to be away from him, either.

Not anymore.

Everything between us had changed.

My side twinged as I rolled toward him, but the ache was gone. That was odd, but I didn't want to focus on that. I just wanted to get closer to him.

He pulled me against his chest delicately and whispered, "Easy. Don't hurt yourself."

"It doesn't ache anymore. I must have healed myself more than I realized." I wanted to reassure him so he wouldn't loosen his hold on me. I was desperate to stay close to him.

I lifted my head and grimaced when I noted the ripped, red blood-soaked part of his shirt where the scythe had hit. We were both bloody and lying in bed, but I didn't care.

Because I was with him.

"What's wrong?" he asked, his mocha eyes darkening. "Are you hurting?"

"No. Wh—" My breath whooshed out of me as the realization settled in. "I was looking at the blood on your shirt. Are *you* okay?"

"More than okay." He smiled tenderly. "I wish we could freeze this moment and that nothing ever had to change."

He thought I might become ornery with him again. My stomach fluttered. "Actions speak louder, I know, but this *won't* change. This isn't an aberration in me from being in battle or almost losing you. All that did was open my eyes, and I swear to you, no matter what, I'm in this *forever*."

His eyes tightened as he said, "You can't make that promise. Things have already been set into motion that could change your mind and make you believe things about me again..." He trailed off as he stared at my face.

"You fought the demons with us and *saved* my life by risking your own. How could I ever think anything unsavory of you again?" He had a right to doubt my loyalty. Like I'd told him, words were easy, but I was determined to prove my belief in him.

He brushed my cheek with his fingertips. "Just know that most demons do need to be beheaded. That's always the safest bet. But the ones who..." He stopped and pursed his lips.

"Who are undecided?" I offered. That was how I'd described him not even six hours ago.

"All the ones who haven't gone evil, well...they can be

killed through their heart." He inhaled deeply. "Not all of us are still trying to choose. There are some who *are* good."

I had no reason to doubt him. "I take it those are the ones without red eyes. Like you and Ronnie?"

"That's one way to tell," he said gently as he rested his forehead against mine.

His sweet breath hit my face, and the urge to taste him overwhelmed me. I pressed my lips to his, reveling in the feel of his firm mouth and his unique flavor on my tongue.

He pulled away slightly. "You need your rest. You're healing."

"You're healing, too." I placed my hand on his chest, enjoying the shock that sparked between us. Each moment we were together, the connection between us solidified. The energy around us was palpable.

"I'm alive because of you," he said tenderly as he placed his hand on top of mine. "And this is the happiest moment I've *ever* experienced."

My body warmed as desire flowed through me. My magic was still depleted, but the nap had given me some energy, and my soul was desperate to connect with Levi. "I...I *need* you, but only if you meant what you said."

He took a ragged breath. "Rosemary, I *want* to make love to you. You have *no idea*. Believe me. But you were hurt and lost a lot of blood. I don't want to rush you or pressure you into making a decision you'll regret."

Make love. I'd heard it called that before, but it had never made sense...until now.

"My heart is yours, if you want it." My pulse hammered with my declaration. I'd never been so vulnerable in my entire life, and he could ruin me. "We're preordained to be together. Why fight what fate has put into motion? When we were apart those two days, it hurt to breathe. I wanted to run to you and mend the void that had settled deep inside me. No more. I know I want you. There's no doubt, and I'm sorry I judged you so horribly."

Though the air between us had been magnetic before, my declaration amped up the electricity surrounding us exponentially. Something inside me was *desperate* for him in a way I'd never experienced before. I didn't just *need* him; I *required* him. "I know that I love you," I said.

His head tilted back, and his eyes widened. Then something *surged* between us. He rasped urgently, "We should clean up first."

My brain hazed. "I probably do stink. I'll be right back."

I climbed to my feet as he stood and grabbed two shirts and a pair of pajama bottoms. He threw them over his shoulder and turned to me, then picked me up. He had no intention of letting me bathe alone. The quick motion made me dizzy, but he had us across the hall into the guest bathroom within seconds.

He gently placed my feet on the red oak tile with my back against the white sink. He put the clothes on the edge of the marble counter, then went to the tub and turned on the water.

Watching him take care of me made my heart feel so

full that I thought it might burst. I was about to grab some towels from the cabinet under the sink when he placed his hands on my sides, keeping me upright. His eyes lightened as he pleaded, "Let me take care of you."

My stomach tightened. If it had been anyone else, those words would've irritated me, but I wanted *him* to. I wasn't sure how to process that.

He leaned over beside me and withdrew two towels, which he placed on the end of the counter closer to the shower. Steam drifted into the room, indicating that the water was hot.

As he turned back to me, he took the edges of my shirt and asked, "Are you sure?"

Unable to speak, I nodded. I'd never been so sure of anything.

His face scrunched as if he were in pain. "Rosemary, I need you to know that what I feel for you is real. I'm completely in love with you, and you mean more to me than anything in this world. I'll do anything in my power to not hurt you if I can."

I hated that I'd made him feel like this. I'd insulted him so much that he was scared to complete our bond. "If you don't want to, I understand. I treated you *horribly*." I could own up to my mistakes.

"That's not it." He cupped my face and gazed into my eyes. "I'm just saying I'll have to make some decisions that might hurt you or that you won't like. I can't leave my father behind."

Did he think I wouldn't want him to save his own family? "Of course there will be. And I will do things that you won't like, either." It was inevitable. We were two different people even if we shared a soul. We'd grown up under different circumstances and in completely different worlds. "But as long as we're willing to make it work, there's no reason we can't be together. It'll be hard, but Levi, I'm done fighting this."

"We haven't shared everything with each other." Levi bit his lip. "And I want to, but we just don't have time."

I'd humor him. "Hi, Levi. I'm Rosemary. I'm slightly over one thousand years old, and my favorite color is orange."

A wicked glint filled his face. "Wow. Over one thousand. I didn't realize I was into older women."

My face burned, but he was a grown, strong demon, so he couldn't be under five hundred. "Oh, and you're how old?"

"Nine hundred and ninety-eight." He booped my nose. "So, shy of a millennium, unlike *some* old woman in this room."

"If that's the case..." I'd never teased someone like this before, and it almost felt like the high I got when soaring through the sky. "I'll leave you to get *yourself* clean."

He chuckled sexily and flashed in front of me. "Not a chance." Then his mouth was on mine.

I quivered, unable to hide it. His touch, taste, and smell drove me wild. When he slipped his tongue into my mouth, I sucked on it.

A deep groan emanated from his chest as he took the edges of my shirt again. More steady now, I was able to pull my wings into my back, making it easier for him to remove the shirt.

"You are stronger," he rasped as he gently tugged it over my head. "Thank the gods." His hands snaked around my back and unfastened my bra. He slipped a strap off each shoulder and took a step back, scanning me from head to toe. "Even crusted in blood, you're so damn sexy."

I grabbed his shirt and used the hole the scythe had created to rip it from his body. It was ruined, anyway.

He wasn't so bad himself.

His six-pack of abs was on display, and all the things my tongue could do to him flitted through my mind.

I stepped closer to him, unfastening his pants. I had priorities, and finally seeing his penis was at the top of the list. I pushed down his jeans and boxers, making my intentions known.

"A woman who knows what she wants," he chuckled. "I like it."

My eyes drank him in. He was even harder and bigger than I'd imagined. My breathing and desire increased just by staring at him.

"Damn it, Rosemary," he groaned. "You're making it difficult to go slowly."

Good. I wanted to torment him my way.

His fingers slipped into my waistband, and I stepped out of my jeans and panties. His mouth fused to mine, and I couldn't get enough.

"Gods, you're gorgeous," he murmured as his hands caressed my breasts, making me need him more.

Taking the lead, I slowly walked him back to the tub, and we climbed inside. The hot water immediately eased some of the tension in my back. However, I knew of one particular way I wanted to relieve the rest of my stress, and that was with Levi between my legs.

My hands rubbed down his body, enjoying every muscle my fingertips grazed as the two of us went under the spray. As we kissed, the water mixed with his spearmint taste, adding fuel to the fire coursing through me. Ready to complete our bond, I eagerly stroked him.

He pulled away, gritting his teeth. "It'll be over before it begins if you keep that up."

"Then why wait?" I climbed his body and wrapped my legs around his waist, ready for him to fill me.

Again, his hands firmly grabbed my waist, putting my feet back on the ground. "Gods, I never thought I'd be the one to say this, but let's take a moment to enjoy each other."

I didn't understand. "But this *is* enjoyment." Having him inside me was the only thing I wanted at this moment. I didn't understand why he was being so difficult.

His eyes sparkled as he reached over and squirted shampoo on his hand. He stepped out of the spray and motioned for me to follow.

Confused, I obliged. I didn't understand why I needed to get out of the water to watch him soap up his hair.

He twirled his finger, indicating for me to turn around.

I was willing to do whatever he wanted to get to my release, so I spun around. After him nearly dying for me, I could at least give him some privacy to wash himself.

His fingers dug into my scalp, massaging my head. I startled, not sure what to do, but he continued to lather my hair. And he didn't stop there.

My eyes burned with unshed tears as he washed me all over. I'd never experienced such tenderness. When he was finished, my body was more relaxed than I'd ever known.

He guided me under the spray as his hands swept over my body to remove the soap. Allowing my tears to mix with the water, I rinsed the blood and grime from my body. When I faced him again, there was something animalistic in his eyes. He growled, but this time, it was my turn to give him the sweet and unusual punishment.

"Let's switch spots," I said, and grabbed some shampoo of my own.

As I cleaned him, he watched me, unblinking. As soon as I was done, he stepped under the water spray and pulled me against him.

His mouth lowered to my breast as I climbed his body once more. As his tongue flicked my nipple, I threw my head back and arched against him. He paused for a second. "You need to make sure, because once we—"

I lowered myself onto him. As he filled me, something inside me opened further. His mouth worked on my nipple as our bodies moved together. I didn't even need rough handling to get the friction building inside me.

He placed my back against the wall and pumped into me. The water washed over us as we connected in a way I'd never felt before.

I moaned as pleasure built up inside me. Needing to taste him, I grabbed his face and brought it to mine.

Our tongues and bodies moved in rhythm. I'd never been so in sync with someone, and I knew I'd never get enough of being with him, tasting him, having him. He had become everything in one moment.

Something *snapped* inside me, and part of me flowed into him and him into me. A warmth formed in my heart as his emotions swarmed me, and if I'd ever doubted his sincerity, I couldn't any longer. He loved me as much as I loved him, and I finally felt whole.

An orgasm ripped through us, the sensations intermingling. Euphoria surged between us, and I felt as if I'd never come down from this high.

It scares me how much I love you. My existence up until now hadn't made me feel alive. It took him to turn me into a better person.

He placed his forehead against mine as his breathing calmed. "I know. How I feel about you scares me, too."

My body stilled. "What?"

"You said it scares you how much you love me." He smiled crookedly. "And I feel the same way."

"I didn't say it out loud." Could angels mind link with their preordained others like wolves could with their fated mates and vampires with their soulmates?

His brow furrowed. *She has to be imagining it. Maybe the orgasm did something to her head.*

"My head is *just* fine." He was going to have those kinds of thoughts after having sex with me? Maybe I should smack him around next time, because I would not punish myself by holding out on him.

"You heard that?" His jaw dropped, and he tilted his head. "Actually, Father said he could do it with Mother. I didn't remember that until now."

A door opened downstairs, breaking the moment. One of the hardships of supernatural hearing.

Even though my friends would support my relationship with Levi, I didn't want them to learn about it by finding us in the shower. *Let's go check on things.*

I'll wait for you in the bedroom. Take a minute with your friends. His face turned a tad pale.

We'd all had a stressful night, and I didn't blame him for wanting to go straight to bed. "Okay, I'll be right back."

We quickly turned the shower off, dried, and dressed. The group remained downstairs, so Levi was able to go into our room without anyone questioning us about why we'd been in the bathroom together.

Down in the living room, Sterlyn, Griffin, Killian, Cyrus, and Annie were absent. "You just missed the others," Ronnie said from her spot on the couch next to Alex. She had her head on his shoulder as she yawned. "They're meeting the pack at Shadow Ridge. They're burying the two silver wolves in Killian's pack graveyard, since we don't want to get too close to the portal."

"Did I heal those two injured wolves enough?" I'd passed out before I could confirm it myself.

Alex nodded. "You did more than enough. They were able to get up and walk."

Sierra sat on the sofa close to the door. "You had the three of us worried. It was hard on us, seeing Levi carry you in like that."

It was hard for me to have to carry you like that, Levi interjected through our newly formed connection.

"Believe me, it was difficult for me to be like that, but I couldn't let those two wolves die." In a way, we were lucky we'd only lost a third of our numbers. If the demons hadn't left, we might have all died. Now we had to figure out *why* they'd left. Another puzzle. But we all needed to rest before we talked strategy. Though I'd had a nap, I was still drained and eager to get back in bed with a certain brown-eyed demon.

"I know, but that doesn't mean we like seeing you that way." Sierra frowned, but then an evil grin appeared. "And"—she sniffed loudly—"I smell that congratulations are in order."

I enjoy that saucy vixen, Levi connected.

Oh, gods. However, my cheeks hurt from the smile that had spread, unbeknownst to me, across my face. "Thanks."

"You get to tell Killian, though." Sierra tapped her head. "I told him you were up and looking semi-alive, but I'm not about to touch that conversation."

Alex scoffed. "Who knew she had some common sense after all?"

"Behave," Ronnie chuckled.

"Does anyone need me for anything?" I wanted to get back to Levi, but I hated to abandon my friends.

"Killian informed me to tell you to get your ass back in bed." Sierra yawned and lay on the couch. "Go back up there and get some rest. Then sex it up with Levi and come down for breakfast in the *late* morning."

"No sexing it up where we can hear," Alex instructed as he climbed to his feet and helped Ronnie up. "My wife needs rest, and we all need to meet in the morning to discuss what happened at the council."

Some of my happiness left me. "Is Mother okay?"

"Yes, but there's a lot going on." Ronnie frowned. "But like Alex said, let's wait until everyone is together and rested. We can't accomplish anything right now."

I glanced out the window. It had to be close to three in the morning, and my mother would likely be asleep. I'd call her when I woke. "Goodnight."

"Night," Sierra said, her eyes already closed.

Ronnie, Alex, and I walked upstairs, and I made a beeline for Levi's room. I both couldn't wait and dreaded telling my mother about him. I'd have to explain the demon part when she demanded to meet him...but that was yet another thing that could wait until morning.

As I stepped into the room, I shut the door and found Levi in bed. He gave me a sad smile and opened his arms. Something akin to guilt flowed into me, adding to my own.

Great, I had him misreading my emotions.

Without hesitation, I crawled into his arms, and a sense of peace washed over me as my eyes closed. I'd never tire of being in his arms. *I love you.* Those words felt both foreign and natural.

I love you, too. He held me tightly. *And please remember this moment and hold on to it forever. Never doubt how much I care about you.*

You don't have to emphasize it. I know. My eyes closed, heavy with fatigue, and I fell into a peaceful sleep.

A WEIGHT PRESSED on my chest, so strong it woke me from my slumber. My eyes opened, and my head started pounding.

Immediately, I knew something was wrong. The buzz of Levi didn't surround me, and I flipped over to find his side of the bed cold.

I scanned the room and realized his scent was faint. He'd been gone for at least fifteen minutes. *Levi?*

I'm so sorry, but I have to leave, he connected, and his pain ebbed out of me as our link went cold.

My heart fractured. The pressure on my body expanded. The warmth of our connection was gone as if he'd vanished from...Earth.

He'd left me.

After we'd completed our bond.

Numbness spread through my body, and I pinched myself, trying to wake from this horrible dream. I wasn't sure what emotion was flowing through me, but it hurt.

We'd just mated; he couldn't have left me. I got up, thinking that it was some sort of joke. He had a weird sense of humor, like the mortals, but the warmth wasn't something he could manipulate.

The world seemed to shift, which didn't make sense. Though everything appeared upright, it didn't *feel* the same. It was as if my view had changed.

That was asinine.

The scoundrel had *left* me.

Everything inside me squeezed, making it hard to breath. Why would he do something like this? Even asking the question irritated me. Maybe he'd come here to break me and to further the demon plans in some capacity. The answer didn't matter—it still resulted in him being gone.

Something cold trickled through my bones. I couldn't shut down because of him. Maybe that was what Levi wanted, but I'd show him how strong I truly was.

ABOUT THE AUTHOR

Jen L. Grey is a *USA Today* Bestselling Author who writes Paranormal Romance, Urban Fantasy, and Fantasy genres.

Jen lives in Tennessee with her husband, two daughters, and two miniature Australian Shepherds. Before she began writing, she was an avid reader and enjoyed being involved in the indie community. Her love for books eventually led her to writing. For more information, please visit her website and sign up for her newsletter.

Check out my future projects and book signing events at my website.

www.jenlgrey.com

ALSO BY JEN L. GREY

Shadow City: Silver Wolf Trilogy

Broken Mate

Rising Darkness

Silver Moon

Shadow City: Royal Vampire Trilogy

Cursed Mate

Shadow Bitten

Demon Blood

Shadow City: Demon Wolf Trilogy

Ruined Mate

Shattered Curse

Fated Souls

Shadow City: Dark Angel Trilogy

Fallen Mate

Demon Marked

Dark Prince

The Wolf Born Trilogy

Hidden Mate

Blood Secrets

Awakened Magic

The Hidden King Trilogy

Dragon Mate

Dragon Heir

Dragon Queen

The Marked Wolf Trilogy

Moon Kissed

Chosen Wolf

Broken Curse

Wolf Moon Academy Trilogy

Shadow Mate

Blood Legacy

Rising Fate

The Royal Heir Trilogy

Wolves' Queen

Wolf Unleashed

Wolf's Claim

Bloodshed Academy Trilogy

Year One

Year Two

Year Three

The Half-Breed Prison Duology (Same World As Bloodshed Academy)

Hunted

Cursed

The Artifact Reaper Series

Reaper: The Beginning

Reaper of Earth

Reaper of Wings

Reaper of Flames

Reaper of Water

Stones of Amaria (Shared World)

Kingdom of Storms

Kingdom of Shadows

Kingdom of Ruins

Kingdom of Fire

The Pearson Prophecy

Dawning Ascent

Enlightened Ascent

Reigning Ascent

Stand Alones

Death's Angel

Rising Alpha

Made in the USA
Middletown, DE
20 November 2022

15620701R00224